SPECIAL MESSAGE TO READERS

THE ULVERSCROFT FOUNDATION
(registered UK charity number 264873)

was established in 1972 to provide funds for research, diagnosis and treatment of eye diseases. Examples of major projects funded by the Ulverscroft Foundation are:-

- The Children's Eye Unit at Moorfields Eye Hospital, London
- The Ulverscroft Children's Eye Unit at Great Ormond Street Hospital for Sick Children
- Funding research into eye diseases and treatment at the Department of Ophthalmology, University of Leicester
- The Ulverscroft Vision Research Group, Institute of Child Health
- Twin operating theatres at the Western Ophthalmic Hospital, London
- The Chair of Ophthalmology at the Royal Australian College of Ophthalmologists

You can help further the work of the Foundation by making a donation or leaving a legacy. Every contribution is gratefully received. If you would like to help support the Foundation or require further information, please contact:

THE ULVERSCROFT FOUNDATION
The Green, Bradgate Road, Anstey
Leicester LE7 7FU, England
Tel: (0116) 236 4325

website: www.foundation.ulverscroft.com

Louisa de Lange studied psychology at the University of Southampton before spending many years working in HR. But she always wanted to write, and now as well as being an author is a freelance copywriter, proofreader and editor. When she's not writing, Louisa is a keen runner, blogger and photographer. She lives in Hampshire with her son and husband. *The Dream Wife* is her first novel.

You can discover more about the author at louisadelange.com

Twitter@paperclipgirl

THE DREAM WIFE

Annie Sullivan is the dream wife. She is everything her controlling husband, David, expects her to be — supportive, respectful, mild-mannered. But underneath, she is so much more than that. Annie is a prisoner in her own home; in her own life. Her finances, her routine and her contact with the outside world are all dictated by David. Annie's only reason for holding it all together is her love for her little boy, two-year-old Johnny — their time together is what keeps her sane by day. But in bed at night, she escapes into a dream world where she is free to live the life she wants, to talk to interesting people, to visit different places. To her, it feels real. But Annie is about to do a very bad thing . . .

LOUISA DE LANGE

THE DREAM WIFE

CANCELLED

Complete and Unabridged

CHARNWOOD
Leicester

First published in Great Britain in 2018 by
Orion Books
an imprint of The Orion Publishing Group Ltd
London

First Charnwood Edition
published 2019
by arrangement with
The Orion Publishing Group Ltd
An Hachette UK Company
London

The moral right of the author has been asserted

All the characters in this book are fictitious, and any resemblance to actual persons, living or dead, is purely coincidental.

Copyright © 2018 by Louisa de Lange
All rights reserved

A catalogue record for this book is available from the British Library.

ISBN 978–1–4448–4251–7

FALKIRK COUNCIL LIBRARIES

Published by
F. A. Thorpe (Publishing)
Anstey, Leicestershire

Set by Words & Graphics Ltd.
Anstey, Leicestershire
Printed and bound in Great Britain by
T. J. International Ltd., Padstow, Cornwall

This book is printed on acid-free paper

For Chris and Ben

Prologue

I'm not surprised by how heavy the gun feels in my hand. I'm not surprised that out of nowhere I know how to unclip the safety, pull back the firing pin and gently squeeze the trigger, both hands cradling the gun for support. I aim and get a direct hit, square in the forehead. I'm not surprised about that either. I'm not surprised about the mess that appears against the wall, skull splintering open, and the chaos of blood and brain scattering across the room, stray drops freckling my face.

I am surprised about my lack of caution, my lack of hesitation. Maybe I thought something would hold me back; I might think twice or have doubts about what I was doing. What I knew would happen. But no, I don't even flinch. Not even when I can taste the steel tang in my mouth and a piece of something biological hits my shoe.

I have been lied to; the people I love have been hidden from me. My patience has run out and I am angry. I am really fucking angry.

Killing someone gets easier once you have done it before. And I know I am right to go ahead. If someone threatens the only thing you truly love, the thing you are connected to with every fibre and sinew of your being, and tries to take that away from you, what would you do? Well, the decision is easy. This is easy.

After all, this isn't real, is it.

Part One

1

If the past has taught me anything, it is that nothing good can happen at four o'clock in the morning.

If the urban myths are true, four a.m. is the hour of souls. The time when people are most likely to die in their sleep. The hour when the majority of supernatural activity occurs. The time when only the most hardened criminals are awake; when the drug dealers and petty thieves have settled down for some shut-eye, and only the real evils are still up and marching about on this earth. Nothing good can happen at four o'clock in the morning.

Yet here I am, four o'clock, and it is the best time in the world. The house is silent. From where I sit on the sofa next to the window, blanket pulled over me and curtains open, I can see out onto the pavement below. The street lights cast a strange orange glow, where the rest of the world exists in monochrome. I don't need to flick a switch to see what I am doing; the light outside provides everything I need.

A lone fox canters down the middle of the road, unperturbed in his environment. Scraggy-looking and suspicious, he noses round the wheelie bins and eyes the gates into our gardens, knowing how to get in and out without a sound. He knows the world is his, that nobody will disturb him. He trots out of my view, confident in what he is doing. I envy him.

I look down, and in the dim illumination from the street light I can see the green-brown tinge on my wrist. I rub at it with my other hand, expecting the brief motion to wipe away the bruise. It doesn't hurt now, and neither it nor its matching twin on the other arm give me any problems, but the discoloration on my skin acts as a reminder I could do without.

I listen for a moment and hear my husband's snores coming from the room next door. Even with the door closed and a wall between us I can hear him take a whistling breath in and a guttural grunt back out. I imagine him lying on his back, mouth open; exposed and vulnerable, yet still dominating the environment he inhabits.

My only companion, and the reason for my state of awake, takes a break from his drink and looks up at me, beaker of milk clutched in pudgy paws. He smiles, a grin of triumph. A stuffy nose has woken him, and for once, Mummy has caved on her night-time resolution: she has pulled him out of his cot, still warm in his sleeping bag on this freezing night, and brought him into her room, to sit here and drink milk with her. Best things in my son's life — milk, Mummy and Rabbit — all here at the same time. He sticks the beaker in his mouth and takes another gulp, Rabbit gripped in his other hand.

But I don't mind being awake. He is the best companion at this time of night. Always happy to be with me, sharing his body heat, even from within the sleeping bag. Just the two of us. Alone and quiet.

Outside, it has started to rain. The grey drizzle has evolved into a full downpour, large droplets battering the window and filling the street below. Water gathers and rushes down the gutters, cleaning away the rubbish and detritus of the day. The fox has disappeared and I am not so envious of his situation now. I sit back on the sofa and pull the blanket around me, warm in my sanctuary. Content while the world continues outside. There is nowhere I would rather be. No one I would rather be with than the person I am with now.

Sometimes, when we're driving in the car, stopped at traffic lights or in a queue, I turn round. He is sitting in his car seat, usually Rabbit keeping him company, and he grins at me, and points at something remarkable out of the window. A cow or a digger or a police car; always infinitely exciting. I make a comment and smile back, a smile different to my usual one.

The smile for my husband is tired and worn out. To my mother-in-law it's pinched and forced. This smile starts in my stomach, and takes over the whole of me, filling me up with warmth. It's automatic and spontaneous. It ends with a laugh or a giggle, or a warm, sticky hug when we're not in the car. I am happiest in his company, in his toothy grin and in the clutches of his sharp fingernails and tight grip. I feel the glow of being the most important person in his life, but at the same time it's accompanied by a dread in the pit of my stomach. A constant worry about the calamities that will never befall him but that I must protect him from every day.

Random things falling. Small pellets choking him. A stray peanut. Strangers deciding he is as exquisite as I think he is and kidnapping him. It stops my heart, imagining these fates. Even a nap that goes on longer than usual must mean he has silently suffocated. I think of the small things, the stuff I can control, the stuff that won't happen, to distract me from the big stuff that might.

This time of night we are alone, with no expectation or task to complete. I should be putting him back in his cot, as I will need to be up in a few hours, but these stolen minutes are precious. I know I will be able to get back to sleep again quickly — I go from awake to deep sleep in a matter of moments. It comes in handy nowadays.

I will be up at six, ready to make my husband his breakfast and get everything ready for his work. I know what is expected of me, what tasks I have to complete before he leaves and what must be perfect before he gets back.

First thing, the lounge. My husband goes to bed after me, so I tidy up the room from the mess he has left behind. Straighten the sofa cushions; pick up the wine glass, the whisky tumbler and the finished bottle. Put his laptop in his briefcase and leave it by the front door. Straighten the coasters on the coffee table, all in a row, lined up with the edge of the table. Symmetrical, neat. Pick up the discarded packets of crisps, brush up the ones dropped on the floor; take away all trace of his mess.

Now to the kitchen. Get his coffee ready. Empty the dishwasher, the washing-up already dried and put away before I went to bed. Wash the glasses and put them away. Hide the empty wine bottle and put the whisky back in the cupboard, label facing out. Straight: in line with the other bottles.

Get his breakfast ready. Two fried eggs, two slices of bacon, two slices of brown buttered toast. One glass of orange juice, ice cold. I pour his coffee, fresh and hot, black, no sugar, and take it up to his bedroom, placing it quietly by the side of the bed, minutes before his alarm goes off.

I wake the baby and dress him, bringing him downstairs with me, ready for breakfast. Whatever time my husband is up, we get up with him, never allowed to lie in or have an extra few minutes' sleep. He says we are a family, and families get up together. We sit and eat breakfast. Me feeding the baby and my husband eating his, shovelling it down, hunched over, one eye on his mobile. I have my breakfast later, after he has left. Weetabix and banana — I still need to lose the baby weight.

I clear away the breakfast things, I load the dishwasher, I clean up my boy and let him get down to play. All this under my husband's watchful eye as he finishes his coffee and starts making his calls for the day.

Leaving his mug on the hallway table, he slams the front door behind him with a cursory kiss on my cheek. His son looks up as he leaves but doesn't even get a second glance. He doesn't mind; his father departing signals the beginning of his proper playtime, as soft animals get thrown off the sofa, and towers are demolished across the floor.

* * *

But right now, it's time to go back to bed. My little man has finished his milk and is holding the beaker out to me, eyes already gently closing in the warmth. I pick him up and take him back to his cot, where he rolls over, settling himself to sleep.

Back in my own bed, I drift off almost instantly. I dream. I always remember my dreams. I go to worlds I otherwise never see. I meet people, interesting people I would never be allowed to talk to when I am awake. I swim in the sea, I climb mountains, I shop at expensive clothes shops; I am fascinated by the randomness my brain spews out every night. And it feels real to me; everything that happens in my dreams feels like real life. I am alive and living the life I want to live, but not here. Never here.

My alarm goes off and I jump into life. My day begins.

2

On a Monday, I do the cleaning. Top to bottom, every corner, every shelf, every floor and every ceiling. The house is a monstrosity, sprawling in all directions: five bedrooms, three bathrooms, and corridors suitable for the most ambitious of racetracks.

It takes me the whole day to clean; I take pride in my work. I use all the attachments on the vacuum; all the cleaning products I can afford from my paltry domestic allowance. I scrub on my hands and knees on the granite floors, using cloths and dusters and brushes, until my head hums with bleach and my hands are red and peeling.

Any less and my husband will notice. He points out a stray cobweb and asks what have I been doing all day. He doesn't consider childcare to take any time. It's all effortless to him, looking after small people and big houses, in comparison with what he does — looking after big money.

My little boy is a fan of naps and books and children's television that takes his attention while I work. He is used to the constant flurry of activity, of Mummy being busy.

I have never understood babies. I have never been a fan, always shying away when someone goes to offer me a cuddle. Too afraid of their wobbly heads and willingness to cry. They don't do anything, just lie motionless, and I never got the attraction of the smell. It's just powder and sour milky vomit with a lingering undertone of poo. My hormones don't race.

But with my own, it was different. They placed him on me, skin to skin, and he lay there quiet, helpless, weak. I was the same, hurting and sore. I didn't know what to do. He was still no more than a ball of cells, needing to be fed, changed and put down to nap, but something connected us, something intrinsic and innate. I would have bashed down walls, I would have fought wolves with my bare hands — anything — to keep him safe.

Hospitals have a unique smell. A combination of disinfectant, bleach and sweat, with a tinge of something else, something slightly unpleasant. On that particular fuggy night in August, the night after my baby was born, there was a distinct odour of hot under-washed and over-exerted bodies, blood and meconium.

Policy dictated the nurses send my husband home, and I shut my eyes tight as my new baby snuffled. Left alone on the ward, I listened to the faceless voices behind curtains: crying babies and their weeping mums. First night of motherhood and it was already far away from the world I knew. In the dark, I could just see his shape. Wrapped tightly in a blanket, his little head poking out, eyes screwed shut. I knew I would do anything for him, and wanted to do everything I could, but I had no idea what that even was. I was terrified. Every twitch saw me pull myself up and hover uncertainly, call button in my sweaty hand.

Eventually fluorescence turned into daylight, and chinks of sun started to edge into the room. My eyes were bleary, the bump on my head hurt and my mind was befuddled with lack of sleep. I kept glancing at the time, wondering when my husband would turn up, half of me keen to have someone else share responsibility for this new little person, and the other half nervous about how he would respond.

Two Weetabix and a small carton of milk appeared, and I ate it slowly, and drank the weak tea on my tray. My baby lay in his plastic wheeler crib next to me, fast asleep, swaddled in his blue blanket. I gingerly picked him up, cradling his head as I had been taught to do. In the light of day, I could take a better look at him. He had smudges of blood on his forehead and a red mark in the centre, with dark fluffy hair. He smacked his lips together in his baby sleep.

The curtain moved and my husband arrived. Other new fathers looked nervous, protective and scruffy, while he was dressed in a smart black suit, hair freshly washed and slicked back, not a trace of stubble, coffee in one hand and BlackBerry in the other. His gaze was fixed firmly on the screen. He looked up and started, surprised by my appearance.

* * *

David was a striking figure. He stood tall at over six foot, shoulders back, head held high, with a permanent expression somewhere between welcoming and mocking. He knew he was more intelligent than you, he knew he was more successful and had more money, and he was going to make sure you knew it too. He was a supercilious bastard, but irresistible.

A month after we first met, he took me dancing, to the newest club in town and apparently *the* place to be. I remember being excited, stomach-grinding-ready-to-puke-in-a-bucket excited, to be going out with David. I spent hours buried in my meagre wardrobe, trying on outfits in different combinations, deciding what accessories, what jewellery, anything to make sure I looked as good as I could. I took a taxi to the club, a rare expense, and as I got out and walked towards David, I felt my legs crumple a little.

He was waiting outside the club, leaning nonchalantly against the brick wall, talking on his mobile. He laughed at something, showing a clean row of bright white teeth, and ran his hands through his hair, and a little bit of me relished the anticipation of being closer to him. I could imagine what he would smell like and how that would make me feel. He would be wearing some sort of cologne, something dark and earthy, mixed in with an undertone of his last cigarette and beer. Unmistakably masculine. In charge, in control. As I said, irresistible.

As I walked closer, he saw me and smiled. 'I have to go, mate,' he said, and without a second comment closed his mobile and put it in his pocket. He held both my hands and looked me up and down. 'Nice,' he said. 'Very nice,' and pulled me closer for a kiss. He smelt and tasted like I imagined. Expensive and clean.

Later that night, when I couldn't put it off any longer, I took myself off to the ladies'. The usual queue brought me head to head with the mirror and I glanced across. In the smoke and sweat of the club, my once poker-straight hair had turned fluffy, my immaculately applied make-up was smudged, with no lipstick in sight. But I looked incredible. My cheeks had a healthy glow, my lips were full and smiling and my eyes bright. This is love, I thought at the time, this is what love does to you.

* * *

But in that hospital bed, hair plastered to my forehead, red-faced, pyjama top hastily done up one button out of line, I was quite a sight to behold. Looking hot and sweaty and sexy on a night out was one thing, but this was something else entirely, and David didn't like it.

He tried hard to put on his best good-husband face, and sat down on the bed next to me. I had the Weetabix spoon in one hand and an arm full of baby in the other, so the greeting was awkward and flinching. I can't imagine I smelt that nice.

David's gaze turned to his son, and his expression changed to something approaching pride. His chest puffed up and he looked down adoringly. 'My son and heir,' he said.

'Do you want to hold him?'

He glanced at his watch.

'Are you heading off?' I asked. Other dads were here; I could hear their soothing tones behind their own curtains, ready to share the worry.

'Soon, yes, I have a board meeting at ten. Business doesn't stop because you've had a baby, unfortunately. And anyway, Mother will be here soon to help.'

My shoulders slumped. His mother. My mother-in-law. Maggie.

* * *

A straining of electric engine and an ominous grinding rouses me from my thoughts. I turn the vacuum cleaner off and tug at the tube where I've been diligently cleaning under the wardrobe. I'm at the end of my chores, finishing off the floor in my room and looking forward to doing something with my boy. He looks up as I stop, Rabbit clutched in one hand and one of the attachments from the vacuum in the other. He has a big box of garish Duplo bricks in front of him, but the forbidden dirty pieces of the cleaner are far more attractive to a two-year-old boy.

I tug at the tube again and it slowly comes free, trailing a black cable and a large mound of dust that's been sucked up from the back. I pull the cable out of the vacuum and tug to find its source, squinting behind the wardrobe at the power socket I know is located there. The wardrobe is too big for me to move, so I yank again, and something clatters high up, a sound of plastic against wood. I stare upwards, debating how much I care to investigate, and hear another series of bangs, one after another. Peering round the door, I see my son, yellow brick in one hand and red in the other, standing at the gate at the top of the stairs. He looks at me and smiles, then chucks the two bricks: I hear the thudding and the sound of them hitting the floor at the bottom.

'Game,' he tells me, and laughs, refreshing his ammunition from the box and chucking them over the gate. One brick hits a picture frame on the way down; I pull myself to my feet at the sound of the plastic against glass.

He's bored and I can't blame him. I push the black cable back under the wardrobe, out of sight, and pack up the vacuum cleaner.

'Come on, little man,' I say. 'Let's go to the park.'

* * *

Our hospital curtain swished open and the midwife appeared. 'Right, Dad, you can look after little David, and Mum can go for a shower.'

'Johnny,' I said quickly. 'We're going to call him Johnny.'

The midwife looked confused, stealing another look at the notes.

'We agreed he would be called David,' my husband said. 'David John. Same as me, same as my father.'

'Yes, but we can hardly have two Davids in the house. I would have to start calling you Dave.' David, a stickler for formality, bristled. 'Or Dad,' I suggested.

'Johnny is fine. As long as we use his proper

name for public events.'

I nodded, no idea what these public events were.

'Anyway,' said the midwife, 'shower time.'

She whisked Johnny out of my arms and held him out to David, forcing him to part with his coffee and BlackBerry onto the nightstand. He stood rigid, with Johnny against him, unaccustomed to being told what to do.

Moving at a pace faster than a shuffle was impossible due to the gash running across my middle. Every movement towards the shower pulled at it, forcing me to take a quick intake of breath. I hunched, one arm across my stomach, and slowly moved one foot in front of the other.

But it was a wonderful shower. The water was lukewarm and came out in little more than a trickle, but there was just enough to wash away the sweat from my distorted body and the blood out of my hair. It felt fantastic to be clean and smell nice; the water ran red under me as my body attempted to clear itself out in other places too. And it was so unfamiliar. For the last nine months I had seen it grow gradually; now, suddenly, it was all changed again. The bump was still there, but now flaccid pale flesh sagged around my belly button, and a surgical dressing held me together. The cut on my forehead stung from the shampoo. My breasts were tender and rock hard; my eyes were sore from lack of sleep. Nothing was good about my body; nothing was mine any more.

I wobbled back to my bed, passing other shuffling mums, giving them a knowing nod as I went. Everyone looked as shocked as I imagined I did. From behind my curtain I could hear David talking, and the unmistakable shrill of my mother-in-law. The dulcet tones of the midwife interrupted them and I paused outside, steeling myself before I went back to my reality.

'What I mean is, when will she look normal?' David asked.

There was a pause. 'She's just had a baby; things don't simply bounce back,' said the midwife. 'Not to mention a nasty knock on the head.'

My hand went up to the large red bump on my forehead and I touched it gingerly. It stung, still tender and raw. I could feel the stubbly patch of hair where they had cut it to make way for the stitches.

'But she still looks like she's pregnant.'

'Yes, that's normal.'

'I can't go out with her looking like that.'

'The two of you have a newborn baby to look after. I doubt you'll be going far,' said the midwife. I almost laughed.

'What my son is trying to say,' said my mother-in-law, 'is she doesn't look like she used to, and he is wondering when she might be back to her former self.'

'She's an embarrassment,' David blustered.

I felt blood rush to my face, and a lump form in my throat. My hands went protectively to the flabby mess where my baby used to be. Tears prickled but I pushed them down, deep into the bottom of my mind where those feelings went, where I was accustomed to hiding them so nobody could see.

Having heard enough, I pulled the curtain open.

'Better?' said the midwife, slightly too loudly.

'Yes, much, thank you,' I replied. David quickly handed Johnny back to me as I tried to pull myself onto the bed. Things become a lot harder without stomach muscles. I noticed that in my absence the sheets had been changed, and everything was looking much less sweaty. David picked up his BlackBerry.

'I must be off, I'm late already,' he said. 'Mother will look after you, won't you, Mother?'

'Of course,' she said, her smile slow to catch up with her words.

'Actually,' the midwife said, 'you'll need to come back later. Visiting hours for non-parents are between one and three p.m.'

Maggie was ushered away, and I could hear her arguing long after she had left the ward. The midwife returned and helped me and Johnny into bed.

'Don't worry, love, we'll let you see your mum when she arrives.'

'My mum?' I said. 'No, she won't be coming. She's dead.'

The midwife looked at me for a long time. 'I'm sorry.'

'It's okay, it was a long time ago.'

She put her hand on my arm. 'I'll go get you another cup of tea,' she said. 'And maybe a chocolate biscuit. Just don't tell anyone.' She smiled.

I nodded and the curtain was pulled back around us. I looked down at Johnny, and he opened his eyes slowly and looked at me.

'It's just you and me, little man,' I said quietly. 'Just you and me.'

3

On a Tuesday I do the laundry, piles and piles of laundry. I bleach and I soak. I wash and I dry. I line up the freshly washed towels in the cupboard, all precise, all neat, all just right. I iron, great piles of shirts and polo shirts, and hang them in the wardrobe, all the right way, neatly spaced and ready for the days ahead. I check his suits for stains, send them to the dry cleaner's and collect the ones I dropped off last week. I sew on buttons and mend trouser hems that have fallen down with David's lack of attention. Everything all ready for him to get up and put on in the morning, to create the image of the powerful businessman we all know he is.

David doesn't wear T-shirts, he considers them too sloppy. He only owns one pair of jeans, preferring chinos and tailored trousers at the weekend. He tells me, 'Always be aware of the image you are presenting. Always on, always ready.' I am ready for nothing, in my tracksuit trousers and stained T-shirt.

I stop now, in the middle of my ironing, and look at myself in the mirror. A strange face stares back. A face devoid of make-up, slightly red from the steam, grey pallor and black bags under my eyes. I can still see the place on my forehead where the stitches used to be, a faint white line sneaking down past my hairline. Long mousy-brown hair, needing a cut. A fringe half grown out, scraped back from my face with a tatty black hairband. Long gone are the regular trims and colours from days of old. Scraggy eyebrows, blue eyes, reasonably long eyelashes, could do with a bit of mascara. A few freckles hanging on from the summer, tan long departed.

'Annie Sullivan,' I say to myself in the mirror, depressed at what I see. 'Look at the state of you.'

For a moment I think back to the time when I was described as cute. Petite, delicate, carefully styled hair, a bit of make-up, natural. Cute. Attractive men would smile at me in the supermarket, with my hand basket and meals for one. My colleagues would flirt with me, women would confide in me, cosying up for chats in the ladies'. Now, people would stay away, nobody would give me a second glance.

A brisk knock on the door diverts my attention. I put down the shirt I am still holding, and carefully place the iron on its end, where it lets out a great plume of steam. I am not expecting any visitors, not today, not any day for that matter. Before opening the door, I briefly glance upstairs to where Johnny lies napping. Everything is quiet; I have a few more moments of peace before he wakes and demands my attention.

A woman stands on my doorstep. At first I don't recognise her, buried in hat, scarf and a coat pulled up to her ears. Outside it is raining, big heavy droplets of sleet, and a few of the icicles rest on her grey woolly hat. She pulls it off and thrusts a pink envelope towards me.

'Helen?' I stutter. 'What are you doing here?' I

haven't seen her in years, and the surprise of seeing the mother of my best friend, now ex-best friend, instantly regresses me to my childhood.

She waves the envelope again and I take it, holding it between two fingers like a bomb that might explode. The handwriting on the envelope is heart-stoppingly familiar, large fat bubble letters forming my name.

'Becca wanted you to have it.' She scowls. 'I don't know why, after . . . Anyway, I wanted to give it to you personally. See you face to face.'

Her grey hair is shorter, her ample bosom hidden under a layer of warm coat, but I can tell by the look on her face that she hasn't changed. She is looking at me in the same way she would look at me then: when I had done something wrong, something I knew I shouldn't have, and she was disappointed in me.

'Would you like to come in?' I ask tentatively, when a hug isn't forthcoming.

'No.' She is abrupt and goes to leave, then turns back to face me. 'How could you shut her out like that? After everything she has done for you. After everything *we* have done?'

I look at the envelope again, confused. 'I haven't heard from Becca in years.'

She studies me, her blue-grey eyes taking in my flushed face, the scraggy hair, the messy T-shirt and trousers. She takes a deep breath and lets it out slowly.

'I never liked it when you lied, Annabelle,' she spat, 'but you do it so easily. I rather hoped you had changed, but obviously not.' She walks back to her car, keys in hand, then turns before she climbs in. 'If that's how you're going to be, then stay away. Becca is better off without you.' I watch as she slams the door, starts the engine and heads off down the road, out of sight.

I close the front door, and lean back against the wall, feeling a lump form in my throat. I turn the envelope over and open it, pulling out a party invitation, pink and glittery, covered in cartoon animals: an invitation to a first birthday party.

It's Becca's handwriting, those childish round bubbles of letters, filling in just my name, and the date and address. Her address has changed, and seemingly so has everything else. She's had a baby; she is a mum now, like me. I always imagined us being pregnant together, comparing notes, swapping baby names, mutual sympathy for the aches and pains. We used to spend every waking moment joined at the hip, Helen looking after me as naturally as she would an adopted child, so it seemed inevitable that we would do all of that together too. But I have missed it. Those moments have gone.

I knew Becca was mad at me, and it made sense Helen would be too — she is her mother after all — but the strength of her anger has taken me by surprise. I feel eleven again, told off by Helen for skipping school, or fourteen, receiving a look of disapproval for shoplifting a nail varnish. But that was then: I was no more than a child, silly and foolish.

This time, I am an adult. I am grown-up and responsible, and I am standing crying in my hallway. And this time, I have no idea what I have done so very wrong.

4

Wednesday, and more washing. On a Wednesday I wash and change both beds, mine and David's. It's been a while since we slept in the same place. Now it's only when he wants something, and even then I'll crawl back to my own bed when I know he's safely asleep, my job done and my husband satisfied.

I take the sheets off, put them on to wash, then into the tumble dryer and back on before David gets home. White and pristine, all ready for him to drop coffee on, dribble on the pillowcases and leave great yellow marks I have to soak to get white again.

Today, before the sheets go back on my bed, Johnny and I make a den. The back of a chair, the edge of the radiator and the top of the bed are our walls, and we climb under, lying beneath the blanket of white. It sags — it's a poor effort — but it's strangely relaxing, being cut off from the rest of the world. I lie on my back, staring up at the blank space, my mind drifting, while Johnny lines up his favourite animals — Dog, Duck, Teddy and Rabbit — and talks to them, half garbled rubbish and the odd word I recognise. I hide my face outside the den and peek round, causing him to laugh hysterically at the disappearing and reappearing Mummy. I envy the simplicity of his life and his eagerness to laugh. His joy is infectious. I tickle his ribs and he cackles, his mouth open wide, soft, perfect hands pushing me away.

After a while, we settle down on pillows captured from above, and I grab a book. I roll over and lie on my front, him sitting next to me, Rabbit clutched under one arm. We are warm and cosy, the rain peppering the window-pane, sky overcast, and I feel Johnny's eyes on me as I read. It is a book he knows; he is waiting for the final word of each line.

'Whoosh,' I say.

'They gone,' he finishes. He nods and turns the page.

'Coo-ee! Anyone home?'

Johnny looks at me, confused. I sigh.

'Dragon?' Johnny says, gesturing towards the page.

'How right you are,' I mutter.

I hear footsteps on the stairs. 'Up here, Maggie,' I shout back, closing the book slowly and shuffling out of the den. I emerge as Maggie pokes her head round the door.

'My! What's going on here?'

Maggie is wearing a light grey jumper, white blouse, collar poking over the top, and a string of neat shiny pearls. Camel-coloured . . . slacks? I'm not sure how else to describe them, with brown slip-on leather shoes. Her hair is a perfect grey helmet of rigid waves, held in place with a small silver clip behind each ear.

'Doesn't look like much laundry is getting done.'

I pull myself up and kneel in front of her before getting to my feet. Johnny still hasn't emerged from the den.

'All finished, Maggie,' I say.

'You're going to need to do them again,' she comments with a wave of her hand at the sheets. 'Cup of tea,' she says, an instruction rather than an offer.

She turns and I hear her precise footsteps as she goes downstairs, carefully placing one foot next to the other on the step before moving onto the next. Slow, measured, exact.

I crouch down at the entrance of the den. Johnny is sitting inside, the book in his lap, turning the pages one by one, looking at the pictures.

'Johnny, sweetie, we need to go downstairs and see Grandma Maggie.'

He looks at me sternly, all trace of laughter vanished. 'No,' he says succinctly and goes back to his book. I wish I could join him.

I sigh. 'We're going downstairs now.'

'No.'

'Johnny, I'm not going to tell you again.'

He looks up and assesses my face. Deciding I mean business, he puts the book down, already showing characteristics I know I will recognise when he is a stroppy teenager.

We shuffle out and the sheet collapses in a tangled heap. I throw it on my bed, knowing it probably won't get made until I'm worn out at the end of the day, all my chores done.

'Carry,' Johnny demands, holding his arms out to me, his final rebellion. I pick him up, feeling his arms go round my neck and chubby fingers grab my hair. I stop for a moment at the top of the stairs and put my nose into his neck, inhaling his scent. He smells of laundry powder, his shampoo and the bolognese from lunchtime. He smells of me and where we live, individual and unmistakable.

'You indulge that boy,' Maggie states when we get downstairs and I put Johnny back down on the floor. 'How's he going to grow up to be a man when you treat him like a child?'

'He's two, Maggie. He has plenty of time to become a man.'

She is sitting on the sofa, hands neatly folded in her lap, handbag to her side. Johnny takes one look at her and makes a dash for freedom towards his playroom.

I go into the kitchen to make her Earl Grey. The proper cup and saucer from the carefully lined rows on the shelf — a wedding present from Maggie and David Senior only a few years ago, rarely used and a pain to dust. I turn the cup gently, the handle to the right-hand side.

The kettle clicks off and I pour boiling water onto Maggie's tea bag. I stop a centimetre from the top of the cup. I cut a lemon in half and divide a slice into two, removing the pip and placing the slice neatly on the side of the saucer with a teaspoon. I pour milk into a tiny jug and put it with the cup and my own mug of builder's tea, strong and toxic, on a tray, taking it through to the living room where Maggie is still sitting immobile.

I place it all on the coffee table and pick up my mug, sitting back on the sofa, clutching it in both hands for support.

'How is my David?' Maggie asks.

* * *

David suggested I should meet his parents when we had been together two months. Two months exactly. We had been on a few dates — trips to fancy restaurants, sweaty nights out in exclusive clubs, even one night at the local cinema — but the words 'boyfriend' and 'girlfriend' had never graced our lips, and certainly nothing about meeting parents. It came out of nowhere, but I enjoyed the warm glow that he wanted to crack on with the serious stuff and involve me in his life.

In an act that marked the rest of our Sundays from then on, he brought me to Sunday lunch. I changed clothes a thousand times before he picked me up, eventually swapping my favourite wrap dress in favour of a long skirt and blouse David picked out when he arrived.

'Tie your hair back,' he said, passing me a hair band, 'and take off the lipstick, it's too red.' I picked up a tissue and wiped it off, standing in front of him, pulling my shoulders back and standing up straight.

'Ready for inspection,' I joked. 'How do I look?'

David looked me up and down. He paused. 'Beautiful,' he said, mouth pursed in a tight smile.

We arrived on the dot of twelve, David ringing the bell twice and adjusting his tie.

Maggie answered, arms outstretched. 'Darling,' she said, kissing him on both cheeks, transferring some of her soft pink lipstick onto the edge of his mouth. 'And who is this?'

'This is Annie,' David said, pushing me forward, one hand on the small of my back.

Maggie gripped my upper arms, keeping me at a distance and looking me up and down. 'Lovely thick hair, blue eyes,' she said, assessing me like a prize heifer. 'Bit short, but good frame.' She stopped for a moment. 'Lovely to meet you, Annie,' she said finally.

David smiled, a big smile I had only seen a few times before, or since.

After lunch, when we got back to my flat, we had sex on the living room floor.

* * *

'I had never seen such a bashed-up tennis racquet,' Maggie continues. 'The strings were broken and hanging loose, the frame was in pieces, even the soft binding on the handle had been pulled apart. And when I asked him what had happened . . . ' She pauses for effect.

'He said his dad had beaten him at tennis,' I finish, my voice flat. I switched off a while ago, having heard this story several times before.

Maggie gives me a hard stare, sensing my lack of enthusiasm. 'He's competitive, my David.' She picks up the cup from its saucer and takes a final delicate sip, holding it out to me when she has finished. 'He'll usually win, but woe betide anyone who takes him on and beats him.'

'Do you want another one?'

'Please.' Maggie nods, and I go back into the kitchen to flip the kettle on. 'Do you hear what I'm saying, Annie?'

'Maggie, I never compete with David, you know that.'

'I don't mean you, Annie, obviously you wouldn't win.' From the kitchen I raise my eyebrows at the overemphasis, miming 'obviously' under my breath. 'I'm talking about Johnny.'

I poke my head back round into the living room. 'What do you mean? Johnny is two.' On hearing his name, Johnny looks up from his books on the floor in the playroom, then back again, uninterested. 'He can barely run, let alone play tennis.'

Maggie sighs, tired of explaining the obvious to her simple daughter-in-law. 'He's competing for you. You need to make sure David isn't second priority behind Johnny.'

'Is that what you did, Maggie?' I say, finishing off her tea. 'Put your husband in front of your son?'

'I always put David Junior first,' Maggie says smugly, taking a sip of the scalding hot tea. 'My son should always come first.'

* * *

My mother-in-law is the sort of woman you wouldn't notice in the street. In contrast to her son, she is small and thin, with arms the thickness of pencils and hands like spider's legs, spindly and bent. Her single gold wedding band hangs loose like a hula hoop around her finger, held in place only by her twisted knuckles. Her neck pokes out of a pristinely ironed blouse like a startled chicken (for she wears blouses — she would never call it a shirt), holding up her lollipop head and coiffured grey cap. Nothing on her is ever out of place or dirty. Everything is ironed by her 'girl' (her girl is about ten years older than me) and bleached, starched and pressed to within an inch of its long and unfashionable life. She says her clothes are classics ('Classics never go out of fashion, my dear') but I doubt they were ever considered on-trend in the first place.

She has a stock of favourite stories she will recite at great length. All feature one lead and important character: her. Always engaging in daring, savvy and amazing acts designed to show her in the best possible light. Failing that, she will talk about David, her David, and what a prodigious child he was, how perfectly she brought him up, and how wonderfully he is doing today.

Despite the success of our first meeting, I have never quite fitted her image of the perfect partner for her David. I am too scruffy, too short, not pretty enough, not clever enough. Just not *enough* full stop. She realised it too late; by then we were already married, and somehow I had his father on my side.

David Senior. Now there was a man I liked. He had a gentle, laid-back air, taking scant notice of the hyped-up pretence exuded by his wife and son. He liked crosswords, and strong whisky. I made him laugh when I told him my stories from the office; stories that Maggie would screw her nose up at with upper-class distaste and David Junior would disregard as petty and unimportant. 'Wait until you have a proper job,' he said. 'Then you'll see what a real argument looks like.' Of course, I never did. And probably never will now.

David Senior died much too early from a brain aneurysm in his sleep. Just never woke up. Maggie had been lying next to a still, lifeless corpse all night and didn't know it. I wanted to joke that that was what David Senior had been doing for years, but the timing was never right.

His funeral was held a week later, a small and personal ceremony. David Senior, true to form, had made plans, put away money and organised the whole thing just after his sixtieth birthday, so his dear wife wouldn't have to worry about it, as Maggie kept telling us. 'Such a considerate man, such a wonderful husband,' she said on a loop. It was a pity she hadn't said such a thing to his face while he was alive, always remarking what a waste of space he was and how he couldn't organise his way out of a chocolate teapot, mixing her metaphors with abandon. In reality I think he knew she would overdo the whole thing, turn it into pomp and circumstance he would hate. Despite his success in the workplace, he liked the simple things and was a quiet and understated man. I could never understand what he saw in Maggie.

Maggie wore a fitted black skirt, black jacket, black court heels and a long black veil, held in place with a little round hat. An outfit startlingly similar to the one Jackie Kennedy wore at JFK's funeral. In contrast, she avoided dignity of any description, clinging to David's arm and wailing, at one point prostrate across the top of the coffin. She sobbed loudly through the service and David's eulogy, and refused to leave the graveside as the coffin was being lowered into the ground. I think she considered throwing herself into the hole along with it, but maybe didn't want to take the risk of everyone seeing an opportunity and burying her at the same time.

This may seem harsh: it was her husband's funeral after all, and a widow is entitled to cry as much as she likes. But the occasional sideways glance to those around her, and the constant clamour for David's arm made me wonder whether it wasn't just a tiny bit put on. This was her moment, she was in the spotlight, and she was damned if she wasn't going to make the most of it.

David, on the other hand, didn't shed a single tear.

Back at home after the funeral, Maggie deposited at her house with a gaggle of well-wishers and one-serving dinners in Tupperware, David shut the front door behind him. He brushed his hands off, and put them together in one loud clap.

'That's that then,' he said. 'Mother will want to see a bit more of us going forward. I hope you're okay with that.'

I nodded, surprised at his lack of emotion. He's in shock, I told myself, his dad's death will hit him later, he'll cry then.

'What's for dinner?' David said, and went into the kitchen.

5

'You can't go all in after half an hour!' David threw his head back, laughing at me.

I slowly moved my hand from my poker chips. 'Why not?'

It was after work on a Friday and we were at David's house. The takeaway pizza box lay empty on the floor, one bottle of red already discarded next to it. The flicker of the candlelight caught the contours of David's face, the light stubble on his chin, his defined cheekbones. He had already discarded his tie and jacket from work, and his white shirt was open at the neck, showing a flash of tanned chest underneath. He picked up his wine glass and topped it up from the second bottle.

'It's too obvious. Haven't you heard of a poker face? Either you're bluffing and have absolutely nothing, or you have an amazing hand and I should fold right away.' He looked at me closely. I stared back, trying not to smile, our faces no more than a few inches apart. 'I fold.' He threw his cards onto the table and put his hands behind his head. 'Am I right?'

I picked up my own cards and put them back in the pack. 'You'll never know,' I laughed, and he leant over quickly and grabbed me, pulling me to his side of the table. He kissed me and the cards fluttered to the floor, my straight flush lost forever in the melee.

* * *

It's not like that any more. Friday-night poker has changed.

I wake with a deep grind in the pit of my stomach. The clock says 5.58 a.m., two minutes before my alarm is set to go off. Blissful silence; even Johnny is still asleep. For two minutes, I lie in bed, compelling myself to get up and start the day.

For most people Friday is cause for celebration: the start of the weekend and a marker for relaxation and freedom. For me, now, it's the opposite. For me, it's an evening of entertaining domineering men, primitive idiots who consider everything rightfully theirs in a world of no responsibility or care. This is their pressure release at the end of a stressful week, where only the king of them all, the man of the house, controls the disgusting behaviour.

A proper dinner is off the menu for Fridays, so I eat with Johnny in the kitchen before David gets home. It's calm and Johnny is good company, chattering away, happily sitting in his chair. I get to eat what I fancy; today I have a jacket potato and beans and lots of cheese. Lots of lovely melted forbidden cheese.

For them, I prepare barbecue chicken wings, honey-glazed sausages, baskets of chips and ketchup and a mountain of crisps. Anything greasy, full of carbs or meat-based. I get the room set out for their arrival — plumping the sofas and shining the coffee table ready for their inconsiderate rings of condensation to mark it anew. I load the fridge with beers and roll the green felt across the dining room table, smoothing every crease to a perfect lawn. I wipe down the poker chips one by one and place them in their plastic case, white markings in a precise line. I get out the cards, count the deck, and take out an ace for David to hide if he needs it later.

They all arrive on the dot of eight, bringing markedly expensive bottles of wine that David admires and they never drink, one of the men being brave and upping the stakes with champagne.

'What are you trying to do, impress me?' David laughs and the others look nervous.

'There's a fine line,' David told me once, 'between being a show-off and making a good impression. A bottle of fine red,' he nodded, 'good impression. Bottle of champagne?' He looked at me.

'Show-off?' I suggested.

'Damn right, babe,' he said, kissing me hard on the lips. 'Nobody brings champagne unless they're celebrating something, and if they're celebrating something, they're showing off.'

'What if *you're* celebrating?' I asked.

'I'm not a girl,' David said scornfully. 'I drink whisky.'

⋆ ⋆ ⋆

The chips fly and cards get thrown down in disgust. David always does quite well, with large notes passed his way when the settling-up is done at the end.

‘I should take this up professionally,’ he laughed once to me afterwards. ‘I would clean up in Vegas.’

I refresh their beers and bring out new bowls of crisps and snacks, trying to soak up some of the alcohol. I’m largely unnoticed, which is fine. I watch one hand of cards with interest. David’s colleague is holding a king of diamonds and a nine of spades, enough to combine with the cards in the middle to create a pretty good full house. I’ve seen him before but I don’t know his name — nowadays I don’t make an effort to remember. They come and go — it’s easy to offend David and get crossed off the list, and there’s always someone new to impress and invite over. He’s overweight and sweating through his shirt, throwing his cards down at the end of the round with a groan of disappointment in response to David’s three of a kind. I wonder if David knows how many hands are folded out of a tactical plan to stay on his good side. I wonder if he cares.

Full House Man recovers from his public bad fortune with grace as David pulls the chips towards him, gloating. He nods to the table then looks up and notices me behind him with a jolt, knowing that I have seen exactly what he held in his hand.

I carry a tray of glasses back to the kitchen and place them on the counter, then jump as Mr Full House walks in behind me, pushing the door closed with his foot. I try to move out of his way, but he presses up against me, his bulbous stomach forcing me into a corner of the work surface.

He breathes fumes of beer and garlic into my face, and I feel him run a pudgy finger up the back of my leg, past the hem of my skirt. I freeze, and his finger hovers at the top of my thigh, just below the elastic of my knickers.

'He doesn't know it, but he owes me now,' he sneers. 'I wonder how he's going to pay me back.' He smiles, revealing a row of uneven yellow teeth, a piece of something black stuck next to his right incisor. 'Maybe a business deal,' he continues, 'or something else.' He moves his finger up another inch, pushing it beneath the hem of my knickers.

I reach down and grab it, bending it back far further than I intend. I feel the resistance, then a click and a grind, crunching ligaments and bone.

He pulls it away quickly, backing away from me, cradling it in his other hand. 'Little bitch,' he mutters. He opens the kitchen door and leaves with a glare; I can see the next hand in the poker game has been dealt and his cards are ready for his attention.

I stand for a moment and take a deep breath, clasping my shaking hands together. Familiar feelings return: the helplessness, the impotent rage, hatred for my own body and for the weakness of being female in a world where equality is a pipe dream. My mother's boyfriends used to look at me in the same way, like property they fancied owning, with an entitlement for anything they wanted to put their hands on.

I reach for the baby monitor set aside on the worktop. I hold it to my ear and can faintly hear the sounds of Johnny breathing, steadily in and out, oblivious to what is going on downstairs. This isn't the same, I tell myself. I am a wife now, a good wife, and my husband will protect me, unlike my mother, who never could. I smooth down my skirt, stand up straight, breathe in and refresh my tray with another round, wondering deep down if that is really true.

* * *

Once the poker is over, they retire to David's study, and I bring round the box of cigars. David's study: the smallest room in the house, the one place I'm not allowed to go, locked every morning and night with a key held only by David. It's his territory, and a riot of foul decoration.

Cream and red furry wallpaper coats the walls, fading as it gets closer to the window, balding in places where the flocking has rubbed away. A few dismal watercolour paintings of horses are scattered round the room, along with a photographic print of a plane, reminiscent of a teenage boy's bedroom. A tacky world globe table sits next to the window, and opens to reveal a drinks cabinet fully stocked with spirits older than the decor. Even Maggie describes it as an interior designer's worst nightmare and keeps on nagging to let her 'gay boy' (as she calls him) work his magic. But David says no, and locks the door to make sure neither Maggie nor I get anywhere near it. At least, that's what he says.

And so it never gets cleaned. The carpet remains musty and stained; the lack of open windows holds the cigar smoke and sweat from a thousand Friday nights. He's welcome to keep his study.

I stand in the kitchen, listening to them roar and slur, and place six tumblers in front of me on a tray. I open the whisky bottle, and take a large swig of the toxic brown liquid, wincing as I swill it round my mouth. Then, pursing my lips, I carefully spit it back into the bottle, delicately wiping my mouth clean with the back of my hand, watching my saliva mix with the expensive liquor. I smile, and pour six generous portions, taking them through to the group waiting in the study.

* * *

I was aware of the rough carpet under my naked bum and the feeling of a stray playing card stuck to my thigh. Once the heady moment of lust faded, I felt only too aware of my imperfections as I lay on my back, staring at the ceiling. David leant up on one elbow, his hair falling in his face, and ran a finger across the perspiration on my stomach.

He touched my cheek and leant in to kiss me, slowly.

'So beautiful,' he muttered, looking into my eyes, then stood, confident and resplendent in his nakedness. 'Time for a shower?' he asked, and held his hand out to me, pulling me to my feet, my legs wobbly.

As he led me to the bathroom, I smelt burning and looked over to the table. A long tendril of smoke wound its way towards the ceiling; one of the candles had extinguished itself, suffocated in the excess of its own melted wax.

* * *

After the alcohol and nicotine is distributed, I'm allowed to go to bed, while the men stay up for hours, discussing their women, their conquests, and massaging their egos. The smell from their cigars drifts up to my bedroom; I can hear their loud dirty laughter, their guffaws and chortles, each one outdoing the other to laugh at David's stories.

But it's after the door slams and the last one leaves that my body tenses and my stomach rolls. I hear David move around, hitting furniture as he heads upstairs, and I try to gauge how drunk he is. Just the right level to go to his room, or enough to make him want to come and find me? He rarely bothers with me nowadays, only when the alcohol takes over and he remembers I have another use aside from just cooking and cleaning. How much of the talk tonight has been about women, about tits and arse, to make him want to come and find mine? On those days he leers over me, breathing his stench of cigar smoke, alcohol and barbecued meat, stale sweat from the day, drunk rough hands and heavy pushing body.

'My wife,' he slurs, 'I can make love to my wife,' when making love has nothing to do with it.

Tonight, I hear him pause outside my room,

and place one meaty hand on the wall with a thud. I hold my breath, I don't move. Every cell of my body is repulsed by the thought of him flailing around on top of me, but I know it's not my decision. He sniffs loudly, and I hear Johnny murmur in his sleep, distracting him. David snorts and moves again, going down the corridor to his own room and shutting the door behind him.

I breathe out, and lie back on my pillow. I don't want this. I don't want him near me, but I miss my husband, that other David who seemed to care. That other man who used to look into my eyes, touch me gently, who gave a shit who I was as a person. I fall into an uneasy slumber, restless and worried, pillow damp from my tears. Where did he go, that man, and would he ever return?

6

Saturday morning I throw open the windows and let some clean air in, whatever the season, however cold it is. The stale odour of testosterone, cigars and dirty burps lingers for hours. I clear up the glasses, discarded plates, and cigar stubs put out in the half-eaten bowls of dip.

I vacuum first, scouring the carpet for any stray fragment of nut. I have to be careful: Johnny's nut allergy induces itchy red hives on him at the very least, and coughing or more at its worst.

The first time it happened, a year ago, we were lucky: the first responder arrived within minutes, a man in leathers on the back of a luminous green motorcycle. He took one look at Johnny, his lips turning blue, and administered an injection without hesitation. By the time the proper ambulance arrived, Johnny was looking much better, even managing to enjoy the trip to the hospital, sirens blaring. I phoned David's mobile; it rang twice then went to voicemail. I phoned his PA, asked for him to call me back immediately, it was an emergency. He didn't.

David swung home that night without a care in the world. Johnny and I had been home from the hospital about an hour, warnings about peanuts and allergies and anaphylactic shock echoing in my head. We were both exhausted, so

I put him to bed, hovering outside his bedroom door for much longer than was necessary.

'Where were you?' I hissed at David, trying to avoid waking Johnny.

'What?' David said, baffled. 'He's fine, isn't he?' he added after my explanation.

'Yes, but . . . '

'But what?' David said, going into his study. 'What's the problem?'

No problem, David. It was only the scariest moment of my entire life. When I thought my baby was going to die. When I stood powerless and panicked as he struggled to breathe, watching the oxygen drain out of him, growing limp in my arms. All caused by my own carelessness with a peanut butter sandwich. No problem at all. How ridiculous of me to want some support, how silly to want my husband there.

Ever since, I'm a woman possessed, checking the back of wrappers, and glaring at strange lunch boxes in public places. Especially since the idea of a poker night without nuts is unthinkable in David's eyes. Worse than his son dying, apparently. So I vacuum, I get down on my hands and knees, I wipe and I clean. I don't argue.

* * *

Johnny likes playing with the poker chips, so until David comes downstairs, I let him. He puts them into small even piles, then knocks them over with a chortle, placing them carefully into various buckets and the trailer of his truck. It takes a while to find them all again and put them back in order in their little box, but it's worth it to see his enjoyment. He helps me put them away, lining up the colours and markings exactly, as I fold up the green felt, count the cards and put them back with the aces on the top.

I know David won't be downstairs much before midday. After the excesses of the night before, he is left to sleep, a deep sleep. He calls it his weekly cleanse, when the sins of the week before are washed away. Sleep may have many remarkable properties, but miracle-working isn't one of them.

When he finally awakes, he sweeps downstairs, comical in his checked shirt, pink collar raised to protect his neck from the elements, trousers neatly pressed. I have already lined his shoes up by the front door, studs picked free of mud. Saturday is all about the golf, whatever the weather.

He pauses in the kitchen, where I am washing up the plates from lunch. Johnny has eaten and has run off to his playroom to have one last look at his trains before nap time starts. Nap time for Daddy has ended, and I make a coffee for him before he goes.

'You were rude to my friend last night,' David says quietly. He raises the mug and sips his coffee slowly.

'Rude? To who?' I ask casually, tea towel in hand, drying off the plastic bowls and plates and replacing them in the cupboard. I instantly feel guilty, thinking of Full House Man, and turn away from David so he can't see my glowing face.

'Jim Bakewell. He says he asked for a beer and you ignored him.'

'I'm sorry, David, I can't have heard.'

David scowls, then pulls uncomfortably at the waistband of his golf trousers, casting his eye over my dirty plate from lunch, still sitting on the side in the kitchen. He looks at me, one eyebrow raised. I pick it up quickly and put it in the dishwasher.

'And we ran out of salt and vinegar crisps; you know they're my favourite.' He slams the coffee mug down in front of me and heads towards the front door.

I nod, silent, taking solace in remembering the tendrils of backwash and spit dissipating through the whisky. The door crashes shut and the house is quiet.

'Nap time,' I call softly to Johnny. 'Time for your nap, little boy.'

* * *

This time on a Saturday is sacred. David has gone to golf, and nothing will bring him home before eighteen holes are done, not hail or floods or even snow.

Maggie is also busy, doing what she calls 'visiting my people'.

'One has to be charitable,' she told me once. 'It is good to see people less fortunate than oneself.'

'It's good of you to help,' I conceded,

surprised at her selflessness.

'Seeing these people in such awful states just helps me appreciate what I have,' she replied. 'Helps remind me what a good life I lead. Good to put my hard work into perspective.'

Selflessness is not something Maggie does well.

So I know she won't be over for a visit, and Johnny is tucked up safe and sound in his cot. When the chattering on the monitor fades, I sneak up the stairs to check on him.

There's nothing better than the sight of my sleeping child. He's wrapped up in his sleeping bag, rolled on his side, his tiny hands clutching his blue Rabbit firmly by one ear. He has pushed it up against his mouth and his eyes are shut fast, fluffy hair falling to one side. I envy his easy sleep, his innocence. I wonder what he dreams about.

Outside, it is a crisp winter's day. I have been up and dressed for hours, but enjoying the quiet, I take a cup of tea up to my bedroom, leaning against my pillow, window open, savouring the warmth under my duvet and the little piece of silence I have been granted. This is my time for escaping into other worlds through the pages of a book. From an early age, I found solace in the words of other people: new friends, boyfriends or family created by the imagination of others, a little bit of respite from my own. It was easier to lose myself there than in reality.

I haven't been able to find the time lately. Any spare time after housework is reserved for Johnny, and David demands my company when he's back from work. He says he finds my silent reading unnerving. But Saturday is different, Saturday is mine.

I pull out my latest paperback, hidden in my bedside table, and in doing so see the pink party invitation. I take it out of the drawer and turn it over in my hand. I want to go to the party, I want to see them all so much, but Helen made it clear I wasn't welcome, despite the invitation. The force of her anger shocked me and I wonder what Becca has told her about the chain of events all those years ago. I wonder how she has poisoned her mum against me.

I clear my throat and pick up my tea, forcing my mind away from the emotion that threatens to bubble to the surface. Outside, I hear the cooing of a pigeon, the brief revving of a motorcycle and the hum of cars on the main road, miles away. I can see a pale blue sky out of the window and listen to the chatter of excited children and the deeper murmurings of their fathers talking to them, spending time together after a busy working week. Normal fathers, normal lives.

I'm not sure what these are, having never had one myself. For the most part my mother was fragile, prone to having moments that would lay her up in bed for days on end. I'd make her breakfast, go to school, then come home again to cook dinner and clean up the house. She obviously did move during the day — the mess of the kitchen and bathroom confirmed it — but by the time I was home, she was back in her stinking bed.

My father, I don't remember. All I know is what Mum told me. About a man who missed his freedom and wasn't ready to have a wife and a daughter. He left and went off to another country, she said. Whatever the truth, he was never around; it was always just me and my mother. No grandparents, no cousins, no uncles or aunts.

And then Becca came along, and suddenly, there it was — a normal family. Helen didn't hesitate to take me in as a semi-permanent fixture when I was barely five, collecting me from school when my mother forgot, feeding me when there was nothing in the fridge. By the age of six, she laid a place for me at the dinner table every night, assuming I would be over. She washed my clothes, bought me new gloves when I lost mine, and doused both of us in nit shampoo when it was needed. She was the matriarch of the household, ruling over her husband, daughter and adopted stray child with brisk repeated commands, kisses on the forehead, and long hugs. What would I have been like if it hadn't been for Becca and Helen?

I am glad Johnny's life isn't like mine. He has a mummy and a daddy and everything he could ever wish for. I didn't want children — I didn't want another child to have to grow up as I had — but when David came along, I saw the life I had always looked for. Family, a home, food on the table, warmth. Security.

* * *

We met in a bar. He was there with some friends; I was there with my workmates. It was quite a posh bar — ridiculously uncomfortable chairs, very high tables, bar staff who would barely look at you unless you were beautiful, that sort of place. But for a change, I felt pretty happy to be there. I was working as a PA to the managing director, I was good at my job, had just had a pay rise, and work was going well. I had made an effort with my hair, which was still in place at the end of the day, new make-up slapped on and lipstick applied.

And there he was. I was at the bar, buying a round of cocktails, and he appeared next to me, expertly slotting into a gap between people and getting served instantly. It was clear that he received respect wherever he went, oozing entitlement and confidence. Nothing about him was an accident; there was nothing he didn't deserve. I liked his eyes. They were a soft hazel, with long black lashes and crinkles round the edges. They were crinkling then as he smiled at me.

'Do you want a drink,' he asked through the din. I instantly forgave him for having pushed in front of me.

'That's okay,' I replied. 'I'm getting some for my friends.'

'I can get theirs too,' he said.

I didn't know how to refuse. He wasn't the sort of man you said no to.

I was instantly popular with my workmates. He came over with his colleagues, all attractive single young men in posh suits. All charming and polite, with corporate credit cards they weren't afraid to flash. Cocktails turned into expensive wine, and singles turned into couples, disappearing to dark corners. Soon it was just the two of us at the table alone. He picked up the bottle of red and poured the last few drops into our glasses.

'What's next, blue eyes?' he said, knowing what was going to happen.

I opened and closed my mouth redundantly, then cleared my throat. 'My flat's just down the road,' I croaked. I was too drunk and too in lust to go home alone. I wanted to see what was under that black suit; I wanted to see what that slicked-back hair looked like tousled and messy in the morning.

'You finish that,' he said, pushing the glass over to me. 'I'm going to visit the facilities.' And he got up, leaving his phone on the table in front of me.

In the darkness of the club, it suddenly flashed with a text message, lingering on the screen.

Hey babe, it said, from someone called Sophia. I imagined her dark curls, her smooth tanned skin, her big brown eyes. *Are we getting together tonight? I miss you. Love you. Xxxx*

It sounded serious. But when David got back to the table, he looked at the phone and slipped it into his pocket without a word, holding out his hand to me. I was flattered. He had chosen me over Sophia. Over the girl who loved him, who wanted to spend time with him, who would be ten times prettier and thinner than me. I got up and took his hand without a word.

* * *

A scream from outside my bedroom window attracts my attention. Hysterical bawling is joined by a second voice, male and soothing. I get up out of my cocoon and peek from behind the curtain to the street below as the sobbing continues.

I can see the top of a blonde head — thick short hair, neatly cut and swept to the side, strong shoulders and a tanned neck. A blue sweatshirt over jeans and trainers. He is sitting on the pavement, a small blonde girl with ringlets in a pink coat sitting on his lap. Even from this distance I can see the vivid red blood on his hand, some fresh, some already drying.

I put down my cup of tea and race down the stairs. Opening the front door, I pull on a pair of boots and join them on the pavement, crouching down to their height. The little girl is still crying, great racking, frantic sobs, and he is trying to calm her down, talking gently, bending to see where the blood is coming from.

He looks up at me. 'She proper face-planted the pavement. I can't work out what she's done, and there's too much blood.' The little girl's face is covered with a mixture of blood, tears and snot as she thrashes hysterically in his lap.

'Come inside,' I say, pointing to the front door. 'We live just there. We can check it all out properly in the warm.'

He glances over, then effortlessly lifts the little girl into his arms. 'I don't know how she did it. One minute she was running along, the next — bam.'

Inside, I gesture towards the dining room table. He sits on a chair and positions the girl on his lap. She's still crying, but in tiny snuffles now, blood still oozing. Her little hands are balled into fists, hanging from the sleeve of her dad's jumper.

'Let's take a look,' I say. I scrabble around in a cupboard in the kitchen and pull out our first aid kit. It's well worn in a practical green plastic box, but enough of the little bandages and plasters are still in their original plastic. I open up a few antiseptic wipes and kneel in front of them both. The girl pulls back from me.

'It's okay, munchkin, this nice lady is going to clean you up.'

'Annie,' I say, smiling at the man. I face the girl. 'I promise I'll be gentle. Will you let me wipe your face a bit?'

She nods slowly, pushing the side of her face into her dad's jumper. I lean over and wipe her cheeks and mouth, removing the mess, the snot and the tears, trying to find the source of the blood. I gently clean around her eyes, and over her forehead where I eventually find a large gash, running down through her left eyebrow. It's still bleeding, and looks sore and angry.

'She's got quite a nasty cut there, see?'

Her dad turns her around and looks at her head, pushing her blonde curls away from the gash. 'Oh crap,' he mutters.

'I think it might need some stitches. We could call an ambulance, although it'll probably be easier for you to take her to A and E.'

'No, no, don't call anyone, I'll take her in myself,' he replies.

He stands up and pulls his daughter up with him; she clings onto his waist with her legs. His jumper where she's been resting is covered in rust-coloured blood, drops have scattered down to his jeans and it's all over her dress and coat. There's a hole in the knee of her tights and a small graze underneath.

'Your jumper, it's ruined. Would you like to borrow a change of clothes?'

'No, we're fine.'

'For your daughter? I'm sure she would fit something of Johnny's.'

'No, really.' He turns towards the front door. 'I'm sorry, we've taken up so much of your time. Thank you for your help, we won't disturb you any longer.'

He hurries out, his daughter still clinging to him. As they make their way down the road, I watch them like a wildlife expert observing a rare animal. A loving, tender, caring father. Once they have rounded the corner and are out of sight, I sigh and shut the door, climbing back up the stairs to my bedroom and the cold cup of tea, feeling the hole open up in my chest. The weight of all things missed and lost and absent.

7

The front door slams and I jump. For a moment, standing by the sink, my mind had wandered back to my first job, washing up in the local pub. The mind-numbingly boring task — a row of dirty pots and pans and cups and dishes and cutlery that didn't ever end — all made okay when the pub closed and the owner placed the crisp ten-pound note in my hand. Four hours, a crisp tenner and a few pound coins, what a feeling! It was my money, all mine, and I squirrelled it away week after week, hiding it under my bed in a Tupperware lunch box. The lunch box contained all sorts of treasures: the good stuff, the memories I tried to preserve. A perfect grey pebble from my first trip to the beach with Becca. A receipt from the coffee with that boy, name long since forgotten; a ticket stub from an underage viewing of *Reservoir Dogs*. And a bright yellow pompom.

Johnny is sitting still with his toys, big blue eyes looking at me, aware that his daddy has returned home and waiting for me to tell him what to do. He has a large green brick from his Duplo set paused in one hand, his tower incomplete in front of him. I finish the washing-up and dry my hands slowly, listening to David taking off his coat and shoes in the hallway, gauging his mood. He is humming under his breath; I struggle to place the tune.

He swings into the living room and bends down to give Johnny a pat and a ruffle of his hair. Johnny stands up and follows his dad into the kitchen, where I am waiting, unsure of this sudden change in circumstances.

'My wife!' he says, with gusto. He strides over to me and puts his hands on my waist, kissing me on the lips. I laugh, still slightly unnerved.

'Did you have a good day?' I ask.

'Fucking fantastic!' he announces. 'I only landed the most money-laden client in the whole of the northern hemisphere. Let's go out for dinner. Let's go celebrate!'

* * *

Astonishingly, Maggie is free, and available for babysitting. She arrives with a thick book and her reading glasses on a chain around her neck.

'I was only going to catch up on my novel, so I can do that here,' she says, sitting delicately on our sofa. 'Cup of Earl Grey would be lovely,' she directs at me. I'm still not dressed to go out, not a shred of make-up on, half drenched following Johnny's enthusiastic bath. I go to the kitchen and put the kettle on before racing up to get changed.

'Hurry up, slowcoach,' David shouts, having spent the last half-hour in the shower, then covering himself with a dousing of aftershave and hair gel. 'I want to go out tonight, not tomorrow.'

I take the stairs two at a time, my brain running through options for the rarity of a night out. Having a baby does horrible things to your wardrobe. Even if you return to the elusive post-baby weight, things seem to have, well, shifted. A saggy tummy exists where things used to be taut, boobs are more prone to the influence of gravity, and the bags under the eyes need just that little bit more care with the concealer. Any restaurant David is going to take me to requires tailored, refined, sophisticated. I stand in front of my wardrobe and sigh. Those things just don't fit me any more.

I finally settle on a safe option — black trousers, black top, black jacket. I straighten my hair and apply my make-up with more than the usual care. I stand back from the mirror and take in the overall effect. My shoulders slump. What the hell has happened to me? Shrunk into nothing, into a uniform of black, of please-don't-notice-me, of I'm-not-important. I poke my stomach with self-loathing, pushing it out so I look pregnant again. Oh for crying out loud. I've turned into the same meek little things I used to feel pity for and mock, with their doubts and worries and lack of confidence. Is this who I am now? I use the ounce of poise I have left to pull my shoulders back and give myself a pep talk. I am going out to a posh dinner with my husband. Stand up straight, suck the tummy in, and smile.

I walk down the stairs to where David is waiting by the front door, my coat in his hand.

'You took your time,' he says, ushering me out the door. 'And you could have made a bit more of an effort.'

* * *

The restaurant is everything I imagined. Sleek, handsome waiters move effortlessly around, balancing scalding-hot plates on their arms. The candles on the tables offer a dim romantic light, setting up isolated pools where couples whisper intimately. As we arrive, the maitre d' greets David with a broad smile.

'Mr Sullivan, how lovely to see you again. We have set up your usual table.'

David smiles broadly. 'Thank you, Gemma,' he says, following her through the restaurant. I notice his eyes dip to take in her bum in its tight skirt, and I see her through his eyes. Delicate heels, toned calves; all the bumps in the right places.

'And you must be?' Gemma asks, offering me a menu.

'This is my wife,' David says quickly.

'Oh, of course.' She turns away from me. 'Enjoy your meal.'

I look across at David. 'This is nice,' I say. 'Do you come here often?'

'Company discount,' David mutters. 'With clients and sponsors, you know, the usual.' His gaze stays on the menu in front of him. 'The steak is always good, and the lamb.'

I smile and look at the menu. An array of odd-sounding foreign words dazzles me, scattered with a few terms I recognise.

I look up and David is fiddling with his phone, his face in a frown.

I put my menu on the place mat in front of me

and look around the restaurant. It's a weekday night but I'm still surprised to see it half full, and people indulging with the relaxed attitude of a lie-in in the morning. Glasses of wine are full on every table, and small scatterings of laughter can be heard in the air.

A couple sit directly to our right, just far away enough for me to be able to watch them discreetly. He is clearly older, jowls well formed and hair delicately backing away from any semblance of youth. He is wearing a double-breasted suit with a waistcoat, neither fulfilling their role of holding his cultivated belly at bay. It sits like a domesticated pig on his lap, while he shovels in his starter and picks up a large glass of red, taking a big gulp without putting down his fork.

His companion is young, slender and pretty. Her hair is styled precisely in delicate curls around her face, her make-up expertly applied, bringing out large doe eyes and pouty red lips. Everything about her screams sex, with an undercurrent of desperation. *Please love me and take care of me*, you can hear her crying out. *I don't care about anything else, but look after me, please*. She is listening intently as he puts the world to rights, laughing in all the appropriate places; finally she reaches out and lays a slender hand on his arm. He pauses for a moment and looks at it, jaw frozen mid-chew, then he puts his slab on top of it, his wedding band glinting in the candlelight. A moment of infidelity decided and put into place in that fraction of a second.

David looks up from his phone. 'What are you having?' he asks me.

'Steak,' I reply, and he nods approvingly.

* * *

Our conversation sticks firmly to the banal. David tells me about golf, the club and who he's managed to charm. I tell him about Johnny and how well he's behaving, what he's eating and how big he's getting. I say a silent prayer he's still asleep for Maggie or I'll never hear the end of it.

'Mother says you're not focusing on Johnny's development.'

I take a deep breath. 'We do plenty of work on his development. What does she expect?'

'She says every time she comes round you're playing and messing around.'

'Children learn through play. And besides, she's rarely there; we do all sorts of things when she's not around.'

'Such as?' David puts down his fork and looks at me. That intensity, that focus. I get a taster of what the poor interns in his office must feel like when they are under his scrutiny.

'We sit at the table and do colouring. He does his jigsaws and number puzzles and he learns about letters. We read books together, we go out and he runs and kicks and jumps. We do a lot of things — all of which help his development. And yes, we play and we have fun.'

'Good.' David picks up his fork again. 'I just want to make sure we're doing right for our son.'

'We are, David,' I say, stressing the 'we' with

the slightest amount of sarcasm he doesn't detect.

He picks up a piece of steak with his fork. 'This is excellent steak,' he says with a nod. 'What do you think?'

'Yes, excellent,' I say, putting a morsel in my mouth.

David talks about his work, the fun he has tormenting his staff, and his view of the world. He's not keen on the latest government, he thinks they're too weak on people who claim benefits and they need to do something about the NHS. I nod in all the right places, occasionally asking him appropriate questions, quizzing him about his views and letting him hold forth on everything that interests him. Watching him speak, I remember our first date. This confidence, this assurance, it was everything I wanted in a man. David was so sure of his place in the world — there was never any doubt in his mind that he would achieve what he had set out to do. He was clear, he was certain. He would look after me.

* * *

We exchanged numbers, but from my previous experience with men, I knew that meant nothing. My expectations were low the night after we had met. Yes, we had gone back to mine and had messy drunken sex, awesome, frantic hands-and-mouths-everywhere sex, but I knew what men were like. I was annoyed with myself for letting it happen again, another man sneaking away in the early hours of the morning.

I was home alone enjoying a rare evening in my flat in front of the television. I had a glass of wine in my hand, to deaden the disappointment, but there was no way I was going to polish off the whole bottle, no way at all. So when my phone rang past eleven, just as I was contemplating bed, bottle drained and head woozy, I thought about ignoring it until I saw the number.

'I'm sorry I didn't call earlier,' David said, his voice alone putting a big smile on my face, 'but I've only just finished work. I would love to see you again. Do you want to get together?'

'What, now?' I said.

'No, not now, what sort of man do you think I am?' He chuckled quietly. 'At a normal hour, for a normal date.'

I was stunned into silence.

He carried on. 'Let's go for dinner, and then we can talk and I can get to know you properly.'

My mouth opened and closed a few times before I managed to get some words out. 'That would be lovely.'

I put down the phone, barely believing what I had heard. A man, an actual living, breathing, *handsome* man, wanted to take me out for dinner *so we could talk*. It was strange, odd, incredible. I took myself off to bed but couldn't sleep. My head buzzed with the possibilities.

The next day rolled around and I was dressed, ready and willing a full half-hour early. And he was late, of course, held up by work. He had come straight from the office, suit rumpled, tie and jacket discarded, sleeves rolled up and shirt open at the collar. As he leant in to kiss me hello I got a waft of the most amazing smell, remnants of aftershave, mint chewing gum and cigarettes, and was intoxicated by the feel of his stubble on my cheek. As he stared across the table at me, in the nice posh restaurant with white linen napkins and cream menus and huge great wine glasses, I felt something inside me give, even then. The little wall I had happily built had started to come down.

'And what about your parents?' David asked, after a lull in the conversation. 'Are you close?'

I laughed loudly, and he looked at me. 'Both dead,' I said. 'My mum died on my sixteenth birthday, my dad — well, actually, who knows? I don't even know who he is, I just assume he's dead. He might as well be,' I finished, a trace of anger creeping into my voice.

David reached across the table and took my hands in his. 'I'm sorry,' he said, softly.

'Don't be, it's okay, I'm fine without them.'

'My little orphan Annie, I'll look after you.'

'I don't need anyone to look after me,' I said gruffly, pulling my hands away from his.

'Everyone needs someone to look after them,' David replied, looking at me with his dark brown eyes. 'Even you, Annie.'

We talked. We talked all night, even after the food was eaten, the coffee drunk and the waiters lurked around us trying to close up for the night. We talked as we walked to the car and as we drove back to my flat — about our childhoods, growing up, our jobs, our lives. He listened; he was interested.

'It was rough,' I continued. 'Even the teachers were scared of the bullies. But Becca and I stuck together. We've been friends since we were four; I met her on my first day at school.'

Aged four, Becca was the most amazing person I had ever seen. She had long blonde hair, tied back with a bright red ribbon, a crisply ironed white shirt, and white knee socks with lace round the top. She had a mummy and a daddy, and the zips on her school bag were decorated with yellow wool pompoms.

'I made them,' she told me proudly, as I touched one with a grubby finger. 'Here,' she said, and took one off, holding it out to me. 'You have it.'

I took it, my mouth open, and held it in the palm of my hand. I gently stroked one of the bright yellow pieces of wool, looking at it as if it was the shiniest of jewels, the most dazzling thing I had ever seen, from one of the most wonderful people.

'She sounds like a good friend,' David said.

'She is.' I smiled. 'Her parents always looked after me, then took me in after my mother died.'

'At my school, the kids would go out to the gates every lunchtime to buy drugs with their dinner money,' David said. 'Anything you could imagine — pot, E's, all sorts of pills and potions — and nobody did anything about it. I remember one break time one of the bigger boys dangled this little kid out of a third-storey window by his ankles. Upside down!'

I laughed, and then put my hand over my mouth to stifle my giggles. 'How did we survive these awful schools?' I said.

'What doesn't kill you, and all that,' David replied. He stopped the car. 'Here we are.'

'Do you want to come up?' I asked, my voice hesitant.

I saw him waver. 'Let's take it slow,' he said.

I jumped away from him, my cheeks aflame.

'No, not like that,' he said. He reached over the gear-stick and took my face gently in his hand, leaning in and kissing me slowly on the lips. 'I know it's a bit late, given our first meeting,' my face went red again, 'but let's make it special. Let's get to know each other properly.'

I nodded.

'Okay?' he asked.

I nodded again, stunned, and opened the car door.

'Sleep well, my little Annie.'

Even then, I knew I was smitten. He made me feel special; that he was there for me, and only me. And that was all that mattered.

* * *

How much has changed since that first date? I look across the candlelit table to my husband. He doesn't look that different, maybe a bit less hair on the forehead, maybe a touch more grey round the temples, but men get away with that, don't they? A bit of age and they look distinguished, command a bit more respect for those extra years, those extra lines. For women it's the opposite. For every grey hair and wrinkle, you become slightly more invisible. Add a baby and attention is back on you briefly, but as cute newborn becomes noisy obnoxious toddler, the looks of understanding and cooing turn to annoyance, and cursing glances. And if you ever dare to let yourself go a bit and wear those trackie bottoms to the park, then you are obviously neglectful too. The sort of mum that feeds their toddler Coke and Wotsits at every meal.

David's suits are still perfectly pressed, his tie the right shade of blue, every hair in place and cufflink fastened. I look again at the cufflinks, and squint slightly in the low light. I thought I knew them all — presents from me or Maggie, heirlooms passed down from David Senior — but these look new, cheap even.

David stops to chew a mouthful of steak. I lean over and touch his shirt cuff.

'These are nice,' I say. 'Where did they come from?'

He looks down. 'These old things? Can't remember.' He picks up his wine glass and the purple stone reflects the light. They are too gaudy, too showy, not like David at all.

He turns back to his plate. 'What's with all the questions? Finish your dinner.'

I pick up my fork and skewer a green bean.

For dessert, a chocolate mousse so light I can barely believe it would do anything to my diet. Followed by a board of cheese and grapes and crackers. I pick at a grape, barely able to eat any more, while David pushes hand-made rustic chutney onto a water biscuit.

'You're lucky to come here for work.'

'It's never fun,' David mutters, a slab of cheddar paused halfway to his mouth. 'There's always some arsehole trying to charm you, or some arsehole you need to charm.'

'Do you enjoy your job?' I ask, cringing inside at my question, more suited to a nervous first date.

'Enjoy?' He chews for a moment. 'We're not supposed to enjoy our jobs, are we?' He looks at me. I shrug. 'I have moments I like more than others. It's certainly more fun the closer you get to the top, but then you have to work harder, and there's more pressure.' I wait, surprised by his sudden honesty. 'And people are stupid, Annie, they really are. I have seventy-five people who work for me, and on any one day I can promise that somebody will do something incredibly stupid. They try to hide it from me, making it even more stupid, but I always find out eventually and then I have to do something to stop it costing us even more money. It's all about the money at the end of the day.'

'Is it, though? Wouldn't you like to pack it all in and live a life of luxury in the South of France?'

He laughs. 'And how do we pay for that? Money! And there will still be stupid people, I guarantee you. Annie, you are so sweet and naïve, you could never understand. Dreams never come true; there is always the nightmare to keep away from.' He reaches over and strokes my cheek. 'How lucky you are that you don't need to work any more.'

Yes, lucky, I think. I am. I must be crazy to

think otherwise. Sure, I miss my job and the freedom I used to enjoy, but I have a husband who looks after me, a happy, healthy young son, a mother-in-law local enough to babysit, a roof over my head and the opportunity to go out for a meal like this one. I should be counting my blessings, not sulking about the independence I've lost. I sit back and enjoy the last of my wine as David adds a swirl to the tab.

As we leave the restaurant, I take his arm and we walk down the road in silence. It's a cold night but clear and the stars are out. As we wait for a taxi, I look up at the sky. 'What does the future hold for us, David?'

He looks up from his phone. 'Well, from the look of my emails, my future is all about firing an idiotic minion tomorrow.' He hums again as we wait, the same tune as when he got back from work. I smile up at him, trying to ignore my internal whingeing. Look at what you have, look how far you've come, I tell myself. No more takeaway pizzas in scummy bedsits where slamming doors and shouting keeps you up all night; now, it's fancy dinners and home to our big house in a nice neighbourhood.

I look back at my handsome husband, trying to take in what everyone else must see. Striking features, expensive wool coat, successful businessman. Ignore the twinge of disquiet, look at what you have. Everything you could ever want.

Hey, big spender, David hums under his breath. Spend a little time with me.

8

Once you're a parent, everybody tells you what to do. Everyone has an opinion or a helpful experience to share. It's a pity nobody tells you how to amuse a small high-energy boy on a rainy day in February.

Today the wrinkly fingers of winter are holding on as best they can, and rain batters against the windows. It's Wednesday, and upstairs all the beds are pristine and glowing. The washing machine is enjoying its well-earned rest.

It's the middle of the day, but we have the living room lights on, casting some glow on what is otherwise a thoroughly depressing day. Johnny is bored, and stands up against the back of the sofa, looking out of the window onto the street, where the rain pours down in torrents. People rush to and fro in their lunch hours, umbrellas in front of them as shields against the rain, sploshing through the puddles, their legs and arms soaked. Nobody looks at each other as they run; nobody gives Johnny's little face, pressed up against the window, the slightest second glance.

The advice first starts when you're pregnant. Immediately you are told what you can and can't eat. Where you should go, who you should tell and when.

David and I went to the antenatal classes. We drove the five minutes down the road in the black BMW to the shabby community centre and sat on grubby plastic chairs, cups of weak tea and two-finger Kit Kats in our hands. David spent the majority of the hour attached to his BlackBerry, disappearing off to answer calls. He refused to change out of his suit, looking distant and bored against the backdrop of the other dads-to-be, all worried and attentive, dressed in pink and purple striped Crew shirts or deliberately faded sweatshirts from FatFace. By the last one, he had stopped coming; the other parents gave me sympathetic looks as I stroked my bump reassuringly. At that point, I didn't care. I knew I could do it alone.

At the classes, they told us all sorts of things. That you must go to your baby the minute it starts crying or you will scar it for life. Not giving it breast milk will make it inferior both developmentally and intellectually. Having a C-section is a failure on your part and you will not bond with your baby, thus, of course, scarring it for life. Everything you did was bound up in the fear that you could damage the baby in a variety of life-limiting and detrimental ways. According to them, I do everything wrong, but still Johnny is healthy, happy and attached to me. And I to him. It's all crap, designed to get you to do what they say. Everyone has an agenda; everyone wants you to do what they want. Everyone wants to tell you what to do. To be in control.

The subject of your pregnancy is fair game for everyone, and nobody edits their thoughts. All stories of painful and protracted childbirth are relayed to you. 'You'll never sleep,' you're told.

Stories of ripping and tearing and stitches and never being able to hold pee in again. Wear it as a badge of honour, sure, well done you. But shut the fuck up.

At those classes I smiled sweetly and rubbed my belly. I knew Johnny would be different to all this shrieking and caterwauling. And I was right: I arrived in an ambulance and Johnny came out the sunroof. I can still go on a trampoline and sneeze. Everything is fine, as I knew it would be. Johnny is fine. He is better than fine, he is perfect. My perfect, beautiful boy.

* * *

And, of course, there is no greater polarising argument in the do's and don'ts of motherhood than the decision or otherwise to go back to work. Both working and stay-at-home mothers command derision from all corners, but it was an inevitable conversation for me.

'There's no point in sulking about it,' David said, over dinner. He was picking through the pasta sauce I had made, looking for bits of meat. Johnny was in bed and for once we were eating together, trying to seem like a normal couple, like people who loved each other.

'I'm not sulking, I'm just . . . ' I struggled to find the words, 'sad to see it go.'

'We agreed it was the best thing for Johnny; now move on.'

The use of the word 'we' implied I had any sort of say in the process. It was hard to disagree with the argument that the best place for a baby is home with its mother without sounding like a selfish child-hating cow.

The discussion over the past few months had taken the following form:

'We don't need the money.' Him.

'But I enjoy working, I like it.' Me.

'Do you enjoy it more than you enjoy your son? Do you like it more than Johnny?' Him, with an accompanying raise of the eyebrows. 'So that's settled then.'

Apparently so. He had even drafted my resignation letter for me. Arriving home with it neatly printed and folded in a thick white envelope. All I had to do was sign.

And so I was a housewife, struggling to come to terms with my new label.

We ate in silence for a few minutes more, David still stirring the pasta with his fork.

'Did you put any meat in this thing?'

He stood up suddenly and went to the fridge. Rummaged around then emerged with bacon. He slapped it decisively in the frying pan and turned it on. Not a word to me.

I finished my pasta, chewing silently, each mouthful tasting like cardboard. I pushed it down, not wanting to accept defeat.

David finished cooking the bacon and brought it over to his plate, mixing it into the pasta.

'Don't do that again. A man needs meat.' He didn't even look up.

'Don't speak to me like that,' I replied.

'Like what?' David said slowly, his voice cold.

'Like I'm your child that needs to be told off.'

David looked at me, hard. 'You are my wife, I

will speak to you any way I want.' He paused and took another mouthful of his dinner. 'Put meat in it next time,' he said finally.

In the silence, I thought back to my job. Nobody phoned after I sent the letter. I kept my new mobile close to me on the day my boss would have received it, expecting a phone call, at least a text in passing to say how sorry she was I wasn't coming back. But nothing, until David passed me an official-looking letter from HR confirming my leaving date. Redirected to his office, along with the rest of our post. Time moves on quickly in business and the woman who had covered my maternity leave had seemed efficient, hard-working. Childless. And I hadn't been in to visit over the past nine months: I had stayed away, not wanting to take my squawking little boy into the office, a place where children and stationery mixed like Maggie and a trip to Lidl. People were busy. I couldn't blame them. 'Quite right,' David said.

'David, I'll need money,' I said, finishing my pasta and putting my knife and fork down carefully. 'Now I'm not getting maternity pay, I'll need money to buy things for the house. Like cleaning products, food, clothes for Johnny.'

He grunted. I continued. 'Could we set up a joint account? Where all the money goes and I can use it?'

He looked at me, saying nothing, mopping his chin with his napkin. The second hand on the kitchen clock continued its journey, the fridge started buzzing. I stayed resolutely silent.

'I'll set up a transfer,' he said at last. 'I'll move

money into your account every month and you can use that for all the household stuff and Johnny. Anything additional you need, you'll need to run past me.'

'Wouldn't it just be easier — '

'No, I don't want you to have access to my money. That's my business. You'll have what I give you. And I want you to keep track of what you spend, down to the last penny. This is my money and I want to know what you spend it on.'

He threw his napkin into his plate and stood up. 'I have work to do, I'll be in my study. Someone has to keep the money coming in.'

I sat there for a moment longer, letting his words wash over me, then stood up and stacked the empty dishes next to the sink, picking up the pan he had used to cook his bacon and slowly loading the dishwasher. I had a job to do, and this was it.

* * *

Johnny turns and looks at me. 'Go out?' he asks, his voice the annoying whine only a two-year-old can master. I stop my musings about a life lost and turn to my son. He is bored, and I know anything we try to do will dissolve into a perfect myriad of bad behaviour: listless boredom, thrown toys, sulking and whingeing requests for the television.

I start to say no, then look outside again. It's not actually a cold day, just wet. How else are we going to fill the afternoon?

I rush around the house, gathering up wellie boots from the utility room, raincoats, hats. 'Come on, Johnny,' I say. 'Let's go out.'

I put him in his all-in-one wet-weather gear, instantly laughing at him dressed head to toe in blue plastic adorned with cars and trains. He has a peaked hood to protect him from the rain and his little face pokes out from the hole. His boots are similarly ridiculous, red with little blue boats on, but at least he looks impervious to the rain. He stands in our hallway smiling, his small green football tucked under his arm. My own outfit isn't quite so convincing — I own one rain jacket and a pair of wellies. But at least the jacket has a hood.

As I pull open the door, I realise the rain has got worse. It's pouring down in sheets, and a great river has now formed, running down the gutters, pulling leaves, branches and crisp packets with it as it goes.

Small boys do not care about getting wet. Johnny is instantly outside with a swish of nylon, and straight to the nearest puddle. He throws his football with force and the splash covers him with muddy water from head to toe. He shrieks with glee, and reaches down to do it again. He jumps about in it and stamps in it, squealing with delight, kicking water across the street. He puts his hands in it, he runs through it, he drops pebbles in it. The whole world is one great water theme park to a small boy.

I have been hiding in the shadow of our porch as much as possible, but Johnny stops and comes to me, holding out his hand.

'Mummy do it,' he says, and pulls me over to a puddle.

I lift a foot and plonk it down. Water flows up and out, then back again. Johnny makes another great leap into the middle, water soaking up my jeans. That's it now, there's no going back, and I whoop and leap along with him.

Just me and my boy, in the middle of the pavement, jumping and running and getting soaked.

Johnny looks up at me and smiles. 'It funny,' he says in his broken speech. 'Mummy funny.' I smile back at him, and turn my face up to the grey sky, closing my eyes.

9

At seven p.m., the front door slams. I hear David place his briefcase on the floor and move into the hallway. He pauses by the door to the office, and I hear a jangle of keys as he unlocks the door and places his briefcase inside. As the door clicks shut again, he comes into the kitchen, where I am standing behind the ironing board. I have paused, shirt in one hand and iron in the other. It lets off a burst of steam and I jump.

'One of the execs brought his son in to visit work today,' he says, 'and suddenly everyone's talking about what a wonderful father he is, and how he should make partner.' He laughs. 'It's a good job I don't need to worry about any of that shit any more.'

He takes off his jacket and hangs it over the back of a chair while I rearrange the shirt on the ironing board. I watch him: he seems slightly twitchy and restless, uncharacteristically uncertain of himself.

'Is Johnny in bed?' he asks, unexpectedly.

'He's still awake if you want to say goodnight.' I gesture towards the monitor, where the blue lights periodically flash.

To my surprise, I hear him climb the stairs. I hold the baby monitor to my ear as he goes into Johnny's room. There's a noise as the door opens, then I hear his footsteps. I imagine him leaning over the cot in the semi-darkness.

'Daddy?' I hear Johnny say, quietly. Then a few jumbled words, then 'Daddy at work.'

'Daddy's home from work,' David says. 'Daddy had lots of fun at work. What did you do today?'

Johnny mutters another jumble of syllables, and then something about Rabbit and some trains.

'That's interesting, Johnny,' David says, playing along. 'One day you're going to go to work like Daddy and make lots of money.'

I hope not, I think. I hope you turn out nothing like your daddy. I hope you become an artist or a train driver, or anything to keep you away from the ridiculous world your daddy inhabits.

I carry on listening as Johnny chatters away, but can't make anything else out. After a while I hear David say, 'Night night, Johnny,' and Johnny say, 'Night night, Daddy,' his voice pure through the crackling of the monitor. For a moment we are a perfect family: David the loving husband and father, and me the loving wife.

I put the monitor down and turn back to the ironing, finishing off the shirt and hanging it up with the rest. David comes back into the kitchen and has a look at the pot on the stove, lifting up the lid. 'Chilli,' he says. 'Nice. Have you eaten?' He comes round to my side of the ironing board and circles my waist with his arm, kissing me on the side of the cheek.

'I ate with Johnny. I wasn't sure when you would be home.' I move and flick on the kettle, glancing back nervously to where David is leaning on the counter, one hand holding the beer I've just passed him.

He smiles at me, his face crinkling in the way I could never resist when we were dating. Warm, genuine, loving. Odd.

⋆ ⋆ ⋆

Six months into my new relationship with David, I had to go away with work. I packed my little trundle case with a smile, looking forward to an all-expenses-paid trip up north.

David and I had dinner the night before I left. A quiet dinner in a simple local Italian. He had pizza, I had cannelloni. We laughed and ate and had sex at his house after. He begged me not to go; he said he would miss me.

My generic hotel room in the generic hotel chain was actually warm and welcoming. The temperature was just right. The shower was hot and powerful. The bed was firm and comfortable. Sitting on my bed watching television to pass the time, I felt a strange ache I hadn't noticed before. I picked up my phone and scrolled through photos of David and me together. Normally, away from home, I felt a sense of freedom, but this time I actually missed it, I missed David. I had something to come home to.

The trip passed in a blur. I don't remember what it was for; I don't remember what I learnt or what I had to do. I just remember that when I got home, my flat seemed sad and empty. I left my bag, still full of dirty washing, and went round to David's house, uninvited.

As soon as he opened the door, I wondered if I had made a mistake. The house was in darkness, and he seemed surprised to see me. He invited me into a room lit with candlelight; I could smell something cooking in the oven. I turned back to him.

'What's going on?'

David finished sending a message on his phone and turned to me. 'I knew you would come round. This is all for you.' He smiled. That all-encompassing smile that made me weak at the knees and stupid in the brain.

I walked into the dining room, took in the present on the table, the perfectly laid-out cutlery, glasses, red wine in the crystal decanter. Only the best.

'How did you know what time I would be here?'

'I didn't,' he said, without missing a beat. 'But I knew what time your train would get in, and I hoped you'd come over.'

His phone started to ring and he looked at the screen, his face clouding over.

'Do you need to take that?' I asked, and he glanced up at me.

'It's just work,' he said quickly, his smile switching on. He silenced the phone and shoved it into his pocket.

'Can I open this?' I asked, and he nodded. I pulled open the richly embossed box, taking off the ribbon and the tissue paper, revealing the lace and silk inside. Instantly my cheeks were aflame.

'I've never worn anything like this,' I stuttered. I looked at the tiny piece of fabric, thinking of the cheeseburger I'd had for lunch and the bars of chocolate on the train. I looked at the size. 'I'll never get into these.'

'You will,' David said. 'I love you, Annie North.'

My mouth fell open. I felt that someone was truly there for me. Someone who cared for me enough to notice when my train would arrive, and make dinner and somehow, magically, fall in love with me.

'I love you too,' I whispered, the tiny piece of lace still in my hand. I didn't have time to even try to put it on; within moments we were in the bedroom, the dinner forgotten and ignored.

I was home when I was with him. I moved in the next day.

* * *

I move round him to pour the boiling water on the rice and click it on. I go back to the ironing and shake out the last shirt, positioning it over the board. I'm only too aware of him watching me, not saying a word, drinking his beer with that same smile from years ago. I do it perfectly, not a crease remaining as I finish off the collar.

'Perfect,' he says. 'How do you do it? I think you can stay.'

'That's very kind of you,' I reply.

David takes the ironing board from me, collapsing it in one swift movement. He carries it into the utility room behind the kitchen and I hear him clipping it to the wall where it lives. I am always surprised by these little flashes of domesticity nowadays, this man who knows where the ironing board lives and when the rice is done.

'Do you fancy watching a film tonight,' he asks me as he drains it and serves himself a large dollop of the chilli from the hob. 'There's the new *Avengers,* or there might be something girlie if you like.'

'*Avengers* is fine.'

'If you look in my jacket, you might even find a little something I brought back from the office.'

I pick it off the chair and look in the pocket, pulling out a small box of expensive-looking chocolates. I go over and give David a kiss where he's sitting at the table, a fork of food halfway to his mouth.

'Now come on, stop getting all gushy. Download the film and let me eat my dinner in peace.'

As I walk through to the living room to get the film sorted, the doorbell rings. David looks up from his plate and I glance at the door. I'm not expecting anyone to visit, not at this time of night. I open it, my puzzled expression turning into a smile I can't help when I see who's on the other side.

It's the man from Saturday, a large bunch of flowers in his hand.

'I hope you don't mind me disturbing you,' he says. 'It's just I wanted to thank you for the other day. You didn't need to help us, and I have a horrible feeling I was very rude.'

'You were fine, don't worry.' I step back to invite him inside, then think better of it.

'Anyway, these are for you.' He holds out the bunch of flowers, and I take them, inhaling their sticky scent. A bouquet of tulips: a mix of the brightest red with pure white, wrapped in brown paper.

'They're lovely, thank you.' I can feel my cheeks getting hot; I'm blushing, unaccustomed to attention from handsome strangers. And he really is handsome. In all the fuss on Saturday, I didn't notice the cheekbones, the deep brown eyes, the broad shoulders, the abashed smile with the perfect white teeth. And here he is giving me flowers.

'What did the doctor say?' I ask to distract from my embarrassment.

'It was fine, it's healing nicely. It just needed a bit of superglue from the doc and a Peppa Pig plaster.' He holds out his hand. 'I'm Adam,' he adds. I shake it, awkwardly balancing round the flowers. His hand feels warm and soft to the touch.

We stand for a little longer, the cold air of the evening rushing into the hallway.

'Anyway, thank you again,' Adam says, with a little bow. 'Perhaps we'll see you around.'

I shut the door and look at the flowers. They really are beautiful. Tulips always feel like the beginning of spring to me; the relief of knowing that sunshine is just around the corner.

'Who was that?' David appears at my elbow, plucking the bunch of flowers out of my hand.

'Just a neighbour. I helped him the other day,

his daughter fell over in the street, there was blood everywhere. He was just coming over to say thank you, not a big deal.' I'm aware I'm gabbling. I need to stop talking; I need to stop sounding so guilty.

'No big deal? So why was he bringing you flowers?'

'To say thank you. His daughter had a massive cut. They came in so I could clean her up.'

'He came into the house?'

'With his daughter, not just him. I couldn't leave them in the road.'

'You invited a strange man into the house and now he brings you flowers and it's no big deal?'

David moves closer to me, his proximity forcing me backwards into the corner of the hallway. His face is barely centimetres away from mine; I can smell the chilli from his dinner on his breath.

'There's no need to be jealous, David.' I place my hands on his waist, trying to placate him. 'I'm sure he's married; he has a daughter. It's fine. He was just being nice.'

'Jealous?' David says quietly. 'Now why would I be jealous?' His voice is low and menacing, the previous good cheer sucked out of the room, replaced by a vacuum of anticipation and fear. I can feel my body tensing, my hands starting to shake.

He throws the flowers on the floor and places his hands on the wall either side of my head, leaning forward so our faces are almost touching. 'My wife lets a strange man into our house and she thinks it's fine?' He's shouting now, flecks of spit hitting my face. I close my eyes and turn away.

'Look at me!' he yells. 'No wife of mine should be hanging out, alone, with some man. Not my fucking wife in my fucking house. You will not see him again, you understand me?'

I'm still facing away, wincing at the onslaught.

'Do you understand me?' he screams, and I open my eyes to see his right hand ball into a fist, punching the wall next to my left ear with a loud bang.

I nod, little movements, quick and frenetic.

From upstairs we hear a faint cry, a small voice calling, 'Mummy, Mummy, Mummy.' David looks towards the sound, then at me. Johnny cries out again.

David moves back and I duck under his arm, rounding the corner to the stairs. I go to run up, then stumble, my legs weak and wobbly.

In Johnny's room, I crouch next to his cot and stroke his hair, whispering soft words to placate him. I want to be somewhere else, anywhere else, but how can I leave? I sit in the dark long after he's drifted off, my hands still trembling, using his gentle breathing to calm the nagging voice in my head. *It's getting worse,* it tells me. *He's getting worse.*

* * *

In the living room, David has started watching the film, a bottle of beer in his hand. I walk past him into the kitchen, forcing myself to act as naturally as I can.

I open the fridge and pull out a can of Diet Coke. I pour it into a glass, taking my time, watching the bubbles rise against the side. I silently will my body to stop racing, for the adrenaline to dissipate from my veins. There is no fight, there is no flight in times like these. As I go to put the can in the recycling, I see the flowers in the bin, the leaves ripped off, the stems broken in half, with David's leftover rice discarded on top. One of the bright red petals has missed the bin and I pick it up slowly, stroking it delicately with one finger. I place it in with the others and shut the lid.

I join David on the sofa, placing my drink next to the box of chocolates on the coffee table. The walls close in on me; the beige and cream suffocate and imprison. I sit with my husband and we silently watch the action and violence on the television, sanitised and somehow acceptable, ignoring the ferocity and aggression in our own hallway.

Anyone looking in our window now would see a woman dressed casually in jeans and a jumper, a man still wearing his suit trousers, his shirt open at the neck, slippers on. An attractive pair you would think. Maybe the wife looks a bit scruffy and tired, the husband more and more handsome as he adds on the years. They are sitting side by side on the sofa, chocolates for her, beer for him, a film with noise and CGI and adventure on the big-screen TV. The baby monitor is silent in front of them as their child sleeps peacefully upstairs. A perfect life, you might think. Except for a slight dent in the wall in the hallway and an ice pack on his hand, it all looks normal, boring even. You might envy them, wish for a piece of what they have.

Little do you know, I think. Little do you know.

The stuff dreams are made of

The first thing Annie felt was a release. Something let go and her body felt light; she was calm, her mind at peace. She took in her surroundings: she was at the park, sitting on a bench, enjoying the feeling of doing nothing. It must be Thursday, she thought. David's never around on a Thursday and Johnny and I can do what we want. The warmth of the sun on her face felt good, her breathing slowed, the tension flowed out of her body, drenching the grass between her toes. It was an unseasonably sunny day for winter, she thought, noticing her flip-flops discarded on the grass next to her, a half-drunk bottle of water, a glossy women's magazine and an apple core keeping them company. It must be a Thursday.

But if it was Thursday, where was Johnny? Somehow, Annie knew he was safe. But she couldn't remember how she had got to the park, or even why she was there. Her brain felt empty. She remembered something happening, something with David, red and white, a nice smile, and then a black hollow dread, but she couldn't grab hold of the memory. She just knew it wasn't here, where she was now.

Annie noticed the colours. Big, vivid blocks of colour, no fading or graduation. Just a large expanse of bright green for grass and sky blue for the pond. Cartoon colours. The clouds were white and perfectly fluffy, the epitome of soft cotton wool. At first she thought, how pretty, the stuff dreams are made of. And then: so that's it. I'm dreaming.

She took a closer look at the people around her and what they were doing. Walking a dog, throwing a Frisbee, lying in the sun. A young girl next to her did a perfect cartwheel and finished gracefully, hands in the air, to applause and laughter. Annie picked up the magazine by her feet, looking at the photos, something she hadn't done since Johnny was born. She let her eyes drop to the rows of text underneath and struggled to gather their meaning. The symbols swam in front of her eyes; she couldn't even start to understand what they said, an incomprehensible mess of lines and circles. Odd, she thought, and put it down again slowly.

She felt herself stand up, and move across the park. She swept along in an invisible current, feeling herself talk to people she had never met before and listen to what they were saying, walking, her arms swinging at her sides. She was a puppet controlled by her subconscious; her body did what someone else told it to. She put her flip-flops on; she took a drink from the water bottle.

What a waste, she thought. I could be doing anything and here I am walking through a park. What if I want to go somewhere else? She tried pulling her leg in another direction, and lifted it an inch off the ground. She thought about other places — a supermarket, a beach, a fairground — but nothing changed, nothing moved.

What use is knowing I'm dreaming if I can't do anything about it? Annie thought. What a waste.

Suddenly, she heard a child's voice, and her consciousness fought back.

Wake up.

10

I open my eyes. I can hear Johnny chattering in his bedroom next door to mine. I remember the dream; I can still see the colours and the park, but more distant, watching from afar. As real life takes over, the memory starts to fade slightly, turning bright colours into pastel.

It all seems very odd. I've always been someone who can fall asleep at a moment's notice — any time, anywhere — and I remember my dreams in the morning, every single one. I realised from an early age that my dreams were more interesting than most. While other people would dream about their jobs, or being naked in public, I would be flying through the air, or shagging Zac Efron. Or both. But this sudden awareness that I know I am dreaming, this is new. And I like it.

I realise next door has gone very quiet. I listen and hear a loud thud, then the slow wail of an upset small boy. I jump out of bed quickly and open the door; Johnny is sitting on the floor beside his cot, confused, still in his sleeping bag.

'What are you doing there?' I ask, scooping him into my arms and carrying him back into the warmth of my own bed. 'Did you climb out of your cot?'

He nods, Rabbit pushed up against his mouth.

'Big bed,' he says as we climb under the duvet.

I glance at the clock. I know we only have a

few moments before we need to be up for David and his breakfast, so I make the most of lying in the warmth, a small, soft body next to mine. I press my face into Johnny's fluffy hair, enjoying the hot baby smell, knowing every day he gets bigger and more adventurous. Today: climbing out of the cot; tomorrow: school, and then what? I give him a big hug. For now he's still my baby. It seems only yesterday he was born.

* * *

The first thing I remember is the siren — loud and present, in my ear, pulling me awake. Then the pain across my middle, where a huge bump monopolised my body. It squeezed and held on, causing me to scrunch up in pain, my legs to my chest, muscles tense. I opened my eyes, and a man in a green jacket looked back. I could see David sitting behind him, his hand over his mouth, his eyes worried.

'Annie, stay with me, we're nearly there,' said the man in green.

'Nearly where?' I asked, crying out as another cramp took over my body.

'At the hospital, you're in an ambulance.'

I was wheeled through corridors, white lights blazing overhead and voices talking in urgent tones.

'Female, thirty-eight weeks pregnant, fainted, period of unconsciousness, large laceration to the forehead, now in active labour.'

I was passed from white coat to white coat, and came to stop in a room, monitors and equipment all around me. A woman leant over me and flashed a light in my eyes.

'Annie, you fainted and knocked your head and we think the shock of the fall has caused you to go into premature labour,' she said. 'We're worried because the baby seems to be in distress, so we would like to take you for an emergency C-section. Do you understand?'

I nodded and winced as the movement caused a flash of pain across my skull. 'Please just make sure the baby's okay.'

'We'll do everything we can,' the doctor said. Then it went black.

* * *

'There's no way any son of mine will go to that shithole down the road!' David bellowed, marching round our kitchen.

'It gets great Ofsted reports . . . '

'Fuck Ofsted! He needs to mix with the best, he needs to be taught by the best, he needs to succeed. It's fundamental,' he shouted, crashing his fist down on the table so the breakfast bowls rattled. 'And besides, I would have thought that you, of all people, would understand me not wanting to send him to the sort of rough school that we had to endure.'

'This place is nothing like our old schools. And he's not even born yet,' I said, trying to keep it light, trying to make David laugh with the absurdity of our argument.

He ignored me. 'There's no negotiation here. He goes to the best school and that's that. And there's a three-year waiting list. We need to act now.'

'But the best school is a boarding school. I don't want to send him away.'

He waved the form in my face. 'It's not what you want, it's what's best for him!' He gestured wildly and his plate went flying, splattering his suit with ketchup. 'Now look! I can't go out like this!'

He stood up and stalked out of the room. Sighing, I heaved myself up from my chair with my arms, stomach muscles no longer functioning with a large baby pulling them apart. I picked up the form, now discarded on the table. 'Application for Boarders' it said on the top, decorated with a gold-embossed stag in the corner. 'We welcome boys for boarding from age 4 to 16.' I started to collect up the breakfast things. He would come round, I thought; he would see that no little boy wants to go away to school.

'Annie!' I heard a shout from upstairs. 'Why is my black suit still dirty?'

A loud thudding followed as David came downstairs and stood in front of me, comical in shirt, tie and boxer shorts, black socks pulled up to mid-calf. He held his black suit in his hand and thrust it in front of me accusingly.

'It's not been dry-cleaned? What the hell have you been doing except sitting on your fat arse?'

'I'll take it today.' I reached forward for it.

'Leave it, I'll do it,' David said, and pushed my chest, grabbing the suit with his other hand. I wobbled, my distended belly unbalancing me, and felt the corner of the kitchen sideboard hit me on the forehead as I went down. *Dontfallonthebump,* my body said as I fell, tilting sideways, *dontfallonthebump*.

* * *

When I awoke for the second time, I was in the hospital. My mind cleared and a kind voice said, 'Hello, Annie. Do you want to meet your son?'

Yes. Yes, I did. And there he was, placed gently on my chest. A small, spindly person, with bright red uncoordinated limbs and tiny toes and fingers. Two weeks early and he needed some chub, but he was fine. He was better than fine, he was perfect.

My stomach hurt, my head hurt, but I smiled.

'Your husband said you fainted and banged your head,' the nurse said. My hand went up to my forehead and tentatively explored. 'You've got a few stitches, but I'm sure it'll be fine.'

'Where is he?' I asked without really caring, gently touching tiny fingernails and fine black hair.

The nurse smiled. 'He's gone to get a cup of coffee; he'll be back soon. Good job he was there, otherwise who knows what would have happened.'

Yes, I thought, good job my husband was there. Good old David.

Mist

The colours were brighter. The grass was a dazzling jade and the sky was the kind of blue only seen in children's drawings.

Annie could feel the sun on her face as she sat in the park. It warmed her to just the right level — she didn't feel like her skin was burning, she wasn't sweaty or overheated. She felt the crunch of the gravel underfoot, and a gentle breeze moved her hair around her face.

Other people were in the park, but she couldn't hear them. She could feel the roughness of the wood of the bench under her fingers but knew there was no way she could get a splinter. She watched the people around her. A couple cycled past on the grey asphalt path, another group picnicking under a nearby tree. They all seemed without a care in the world, moving fluidly in their activities.

In comparison, she felt jerky and slow. She was unable to move her limbs quickly; every pull or push required a huge amount of concentration to contradict what her body wanted to do. Just crossing her legs had taken so much effort she was worn out and she sat back, enjoying the moment to rest. She ran her finger slowly over one of the rivets, taking in the rusted iron.

A gentle swirl of colour rose from the edge of every object, blurring the lines and dissipating into the air like a surreal mist. She put out her hand and ran her fingers through it, moving the colours into one other, causing the brown of the bench to merge with the green of the grass, hypnotic and tranquil.

She was strangely calm in this other-worldly environment. She knew something was missing, something usually attached to her at every waking moment, but felt reassured about his absence. She knew he was safe and she was free to enjoy this little bit of isolation.

Gradually, Annie realised the presence of someone sitting beside her. She willed her head round to face him, a robot breaking free from the remote control. He was watching her, and she wondered how long he had been there. He smiled.

'I've been there, where you are,' he said. 'It takes time, you're accessing a new part of your mind, but I promise you it gets easier. And it's worth it.'

She turned her body towards him, stiff and awkward.

'It's all new to you, you're not used to making these decisions yourself,' he continued. 'But don't push it, try to relax.'

He took long deep breaths and she copied him, instantly feeling the stiffness in her arms ease.

'Now stand up,' he said.

She looked at him doubtfully and he nodded. First, she moved her arm to the bench. Secondly, she slowly placed her feet in the right positions on the gravel. And then the final push to get up to standing. And who knew balancing could be so tricky? Something her body normally did naturally now needed her to control every correcting movement, willing each part to jump into life before she fell over.

She slumped back down on the bench, exhausted from the effort.

He smiled. 'Only do as much as you feel able, and then come back to it later.'

'How do I come back? Where do I return to?' she asked.

'Just remember this park, and this bench. I'd like to see you again.' He stood up, and she noticed his height. At least six foot, but skinny. He had long gangly limbs to match and moved them in the manner of a teenager who had grown too quickly and didn't know quite how to control them. But how could she judge? She couldn't even walk.

He was wearing jeans and Converse, a T-shirt with an obscure band name across it that she couldn't make out, and an oversized grey cardigan. She suddenly realised she had no idea what she was wearing, and her cheeks flared in anticipation of discovering herself naked. To her relief she was dressed as casually as him: jeans, trainers, T-shirt, but not clothes she had knowledge of having bought. She looked back up and caught his eye; he was smiling again, sympathetic to her confusion.

'You'll get used to the strangeness of it all,' he said. 'The more you become aware, the more you can control.'

He turned to leave and she felt a wave of

unease over-take her.

'Wait! What do I do now?'

'Wake up,' he said simply.

11

This dream stays etched in my mind when I wake up, as concrete as if I had experienced it in real life. I screw up my eyes, remembering the man's face. I instantly felt at ease round him, like he was an old friend I hadn't seen for some time, and an excitement, an anticipation. I want to see him again. Ridiculous, really, when he is only a figment of my imagination.

I hear Johnny wake in the next room and go in to get him dressed. Clean nappy on, trousers and jumper, all carefully chosen to ensure David will approve of how his son looks when he deigns to grace us with his presence. Tiny neat polo shirts and proper trousers. Little cardigans and carefully ironed shirts. Absurd. He's a baby, I tried to explain early on in Johnny's life — he chucks food on himself, he dribbles, he spills, he pukes, he poos; clothes do not stay clean all day.

'Not my child,' David said. 'Not my boy.'

I didn't know how to break it to him that his boy had rubbed baked beans into his hair the day before.

Johnny and I go downstairs, him now in his smartest outfit and me still in my pyjamas. I wonder if David will comment, but I just can't be bothered to get dressed. I still feel knackered; the dreams seem to be tiring me out rather than offering any sort of rest.

David wakes. He doesn't notice the pyjamas.

Breakfast: two fried eggs, two slices of bacon, two slices of brown buttered toast. One glass of orange juice, ice cold. Coffee. He shouts at an unfortunate underling on the phone and points to a smudge of milk left on the table, not missing a beat in his conversation. I wipe it away.

David goes to work.

* * *

Johnny hasn't had a poo for two days. He doesn't seem to mind, to be fair; he's still eating his toast and drinking his milk, but isn't so keen on dinner. I'm not surprised; if I hadn't pooed for two days, I wouldn't be too keen on dinner either.

I'm not sure what to do about the lack of poo. It's not the sort of thing you can go up to the average mother on the street and ask about. I idly wonder about asking Adam what advice he would give, but as much as I'd like to talk to him, a constipated child isn't a great friendship starter, even if I knew how to contact him.

Johnny has a big tubby tummy at the best of times, but at the moment it seems to be sticking out more than usual. Full of poo. All that poo with nowhere to go.

I like the idea of phoning David at work and asking him what he thinks I should do, but I can't imagine his response would be pleasant. It would infuriate him. I think it would be worth it just to imagine the look on his face in the middle of whatever board meeting he would be sitting in. But who am I kidding. I wouldn't dare call and he wouldn't answer the phone. Poo, or lack of, is not important to a man so regular he goes at seven o'clock every evening, before dinner. Clearing the way, he calls it.

If only his son had that regularity.

I put Johnny down for his nap and carry on with my chores. It's Tuesday, so I'm elbow deep in laundry. I pull David's shirts out of the bucket where they are soaking and throw them in the washing machine on a hot wash. I take the towels out of the tumble dryer and fold them for the cupboard, all precise, all neat, all just right. I feel twitchy. The same repetitive jobs, week after week, never-ending. My skin itches with boredom. My brain is desperate for something to keep it occupied; the mundane isn't enough any more.

I sew a misplaced button back on the waistband of David's trousers. I look at it, needle in hand, then move it one centimetre away from where it should be. Just a bit, so the trousers will still do up, but perhaps a wee bit too tightly. Enough to make David slightly uncomfortable, and to doubt that extra chocolate biscuit.

I go into Johnny's room at the end of his nap, only to be faced with a smell putrid enough to melt the paint from the walls. I carry him at arm's length to his changing mat, Johnny chatting away happily all the while, and open his sleeping bag, turning my head away. No wonder he's cheerful: he's done a poo big enough to fill up his whole nappy, along with a spectacular leak down both legs and up his back. I clean him up, wipe after wipe, silently ecstatic with the arrival of the poo but trying not to gag over the toxic smell. I change his T-shirt, put on his trousers. Then it's done and we're back downstairs, Johnny demanding bananas and a drink, eager to top up. Things are back to normal. On the poo front anyway, only with the poo.

Because today I can't wait until night-time. I can't wait to sleep, to dream, and see what I can do next.

Bright yellow cabs

Annie sat by herself, taking in the strange feeling of controlling her movements, being able to decide what to do. She was alone on her park bench, and moved her hand down to touch the wood of the seat, running her fingers across it. Taking in how the wood felt, the bumps and the texture, then to the metal of the bench, the cold, the rust. She pulled at a piece of worn paint, rolled it around in her fingers and dropped it to the ground. This time it felt more real, more concrete.

Slowly she was starting to get a better grip on how to move things around. At first, every movement of her fingers, feet, arms had felt like a huge effort, and time had passed in a flash. Every morning, back in reality, her muscles ached, and her head felt fuzzy.

She met the man again, and she had that same feeling of recognition, of him being someone she knew.

'Jack,' he said, grinning and holding out his hand. It took her about ten minutes to co-ordinate the movements to return his handshake.

He set her targets each night — at first, something small, then getting more ambitious, stretching her unfamiliar muscles.

She learnt how to run, and how to stop again without falling. She crawled, she jumped; she hopped on one foot, and then the other. He showed her how to alter what she was wearing, and swap her shoes from one foot to the other; how to change her hair colour and style, moving it from a short bob to long cascading curls.

She noticed the differences between her and the other people. Where her movements were stiff and uncomfortable, they all moved smoothly, but without any control. They seemed to be pulled — their bodies would move and their heads and eyes would follow, possessed by their own subconscious. Torso and limbs following a mind with its own agenda; zombies with no willpower or drive.

Annie was getting better. Now she could move around without any effort, and it didn't drain her once she woke up in the morning; in fact, quite the opposite. She felt energised. There was a second world out there for her to explore.

* * *

'You're doing really well,' Jack said one day after she had perfected a complicated handstand on the grass.

'Especially since I can't do these in real life,' Annie laughed, sitting down next to him on the grass to get her breath back.

'Here you can do whatever you want to do,' Jack said, crossing his legs under him. He leant back and closed his eyes, the sun on his face. She noticed long dark eyelashes, and a small scar on the edge of his chin.

'I saw it in you,' he continued, his eyes still closed. 'We are the same, you and I. We're trapped and we want to escape, we want something outside of our normal lives.'

Annie watched him, still confused about her new world.

Jack sat forward and looked at her. 'This is the way we get it. This is how we live the life we want.'

In a blink of an eye, the other people in the park disappeared. The grass, the pond, the path, all empty in a second. The wind blew and Annie could hear the leaves moving and the rustle of an abandoned crisp packet as it flew past them, but they were the only people there, sitting on an empty stage. She gasped and looked around.

'But where did they go?'

He shrugged. 'Another dream world? Or perhaps they woke up.'

'Are they real people?' Annie asked.

He smiled, and shook his head. 'You try. Just imagine it, bring them all back.'

She closed her eyes and thought of all the people in the park, faceless images going about their day. She frowned, unable to picture what they looked like or what they were doing, and opened her eyes in frustration. But they were back, moving around her as she sat on the grass.

She took it all in, slowly. 'What else can you do?'

'Anything you want. Name it.'

'New York,' Annie said. 'I've always wanted to go to New York.'

In a second, the colours of the park faded away, a watercolour draining into nothing, and in its place, darker colours started to appear. She looked down, and a wide road appeared beneath her feet. All around them buildings were growing; red brick by red brick they rose in perfect synchronicity, forming windows and doorways, glass pouring into the gaps like water. The trees began to emerge, leaves sprouting at the end of twigs, branches reaching towards the sky. The road rolled out further into the distance, a bland graze of gravel, punctuated by perfect white lines, dotting down the centre. Grey concrete, brown stone, bright yellow cabs, then the detail started to fill in — the noises and the smells, the steam rising from the manhole covers. Car engines, beeping horns, baking bread, diesel. Disjointed conversations in strange accents.

Annie sat, mouth open. 'And this is New York?'

Jack laughed. 'No — I made it!' He tapped the side of his forehead. 'I invented what you see around you, just by picturing it in my mind.' He pointed towards the Empire State Building, its sharp peak towering behind them, and the garish billboards of Times Square in front. 'So a few too many clichés maybe.'

'It's still incredible,' Annie said, twisting round on the bench, looking at the scene. She took in the pictures on the billboards, unable to make out words or headings, the letters jumbled into obscurity. A man stood behind them, naked except for a cowboy hat, gold boots and small white pants, busking with an acoustic guitar. 'What else can you do?'

'We,' Jack replied. 'Not just me, though I've

had a bit more time to practise. You have to remember you're in a dream — anything is possible.' He thought for a moment. Darkness was starting to fall, and the neon turned his face an eerie green, then bright pink. 'You try.'

Annie looked at him, then out at the busy street. She took a deep breath and screwed her eyes up tight, clenching her fists and willing a new world to appear. She thought of the first random thing that came to mind — the pyramids of Egypt — and imagined the sand, the dry heat, a few camels. Her imagination faltered; she couldn't get the images to fix in her mind.

She opened her eyes. Jack's New York wobbled briefly, making her feel sick, but stayed as it was, the naked cowboy starting on a new song with enthusiasm.

Annie looked at Jack, hoping for reassurance. 'Practise more,' he said. And disappeared.

* * *

For a moment Annie stayed in New York. Sitting on the bench, she watched the dream people come and go, a silent observer of their lives.

A man and a women, no older than their twenties, stood in front of her, facing each other in a firm embrace. The woman's arms were round his waist and his hands were tucked in the back pockets of her jeans. She was slim and pretty, her make-up and hair the worse for wear after an evening out, traces of stubble on him where a carefully shaved chin had started to make its morning rebellion. They spoke in hushed whispers, looking into each other's eyes, then he bent down and kissed her gently on the lips.

Annie wondered idly about the last time she and David had looked at each other in that way. Really taken the time to notice the other person, to be lost in the way they looked, the way they smelt and talked. Way before Johnny was born, way before that. She missed it.

She felt sad then, and sat on the bench, insignificant to everyone around her. These people didn't see her, but what was the difference between this and her waking life, where her husband went about his day and she went about hers? No more than a maid, a nanny, a cook. At what point had that all changed?

The sun was starting to come up, glimpses of gold touching the edges of the buildings. It must be morning, Annie thought. She took one last look at the surreal diorama in front of her, committing it to memory. And it was Sunday tomorrow, so she needed to be ready.

Wake up.

12

First Sunday of the month and it is lunch at Maggie's.

David looks forward to it with barely concealed zeal, eager to get to his childhood home, where he can bask in the light of everlasting maternal approval and stuff his face at the same time.

We get dressed up: David in his best smart-casual look (chinos and nice shirt, no tie), me in a dress (blue, demure, chosen by David) and Johnny in a teeny-tiny shirt and trousers. I always have to wrestle Johnny into this uniform — he knows where it will take him, and unlike David, he is not keen. He tries by all means possible to get something on his clean clothes, anything to be made to change out of them. Today, once the door is open, he attempts a daredevil dive towards the flower bed, only to be caught swiftly by my ever-ready left hand. He shouts in protest as I place him squarely back on the tarmac and levels a grumpy stare in my direction.

We stand next to David's BMW, clean clothes, hair combed and smoothed down, ready to climb in to take us the few streets to Maggie's mansion.

'Why don't we walk?' I ask. Rain has abated to a gorgeous winter's day, sunshine sparkling through the clouds and blue skies. David already has his sunglasses on.

'Get Johnny in the car,' he replies, without a second glance in my direction. He climbs into the front seat. 'What's next?' he chuckles to himself. 'Catching the bus?'

It takes longer to strap Johnny in his seat and fasten the belt than it does for us to drive there, so two minutes later, we are unloading again, Johnny staying close to me in uncharacteristic shyness. He hangs off my leg; I can feel his sharp fingernails through my tights. I bend down to his height and his hands go round my neck.

'Carry,' he demands, so I pick him up and rest him on my hip, balancing the baby bag over the other shoulder and adjusting my dress at the same time. David rings the doorbell and smoothes down his shirt. We are on time, to the dot, twelve noon. Any earlier is rude, any later unforgivable. David's attitude of being late to all social occasions doesn't apply to his mother. He is never late for his mother.

'My darlings!' Maggie says as she opens the door within seconds. I imagine she must have been hovering behind the curtains, waiting for our arrival.

We are ushered in, me in a heap of bags and small toddler, and I try to lower Johnny to the floor. He goes back to clinging to my leg. Maggie clasps me in a powdery embrace, an experience similar to hugging a spindly lavender bush, all soothing scents and sharp branches, then tunnels her full attention to David. She holds him out at arm's length, him towering over her.

'As handsome as ever,' she says.

'Correct to a fault as always, Mother,' David says, giving her a kiss on the cheek.

Despite my reluctance, I have to admit Maggie's cooking is always exquisite. I can already smell the chicken roasting in the oven, and know her potatoes will be perfectly brown and crisp, vegetables al dente, and the gravy rich and thick. In the early days of our relationship, when David Senior was still alive, I could ignore David and his mother's fawning and have a chat with his father, enjoying his blatant disregard and lack of respect for anything Maggie did or said. You always knew where you stood; there was no pretence or fakery. Now he has gone, the house has been injected with artificial sweetener. You know something has changed: on the surface it's okay, but long after you've finished, a nasty taste remains in your mouth.

Maggie clucks around David, taking his coat, practically removing his shoes from his feet, and placing a glass of wine in his hand. I kneel in front of Johnny and take off his shoes and coat, placing them neatly in the hallway beside my handbag. I open his bag and get out four small wooden trains. Johnny hangs onto them, clutching two to his chest with his forearm with the other two in each hand, terrified to let them go.

We move slowly through the house, sitting in the 'day room' on stiff cane chairs, Johnny insisting on perching on my lap. Maggie has flown off to the kitchen, but a beeping now heralds her arrival back in front of us.

'Dinner is served,' she says grandly and ushers us through.

The imposing dining room is dark wood, reminiscent of an early 1900s cruise ship. Teak panelling covers the walls from floor to midway, accompanied by dark-brown window frames and red floral wallpaper. You can almost feel the room rocking and observe the icebergs as they pass by the window.

The furniture is equally drab — dark dining chairs and a glossed table, covered with a white tablecloth and delicate white crockery with dainty pink flowers round the edge. I know it's Maggie's 'best', and to my horror I see she has laid a small side plate on Johnny's high chair. (Luckily she has allowed me the concession of providing Johnny with a suitable chair, and purchased him one from the most expensive of shops. It is polished wood and beautiful, more of a work of art than the old-style landscapes on the wall, with lots of nooks and crannies that are impossible to clean. Johnny and I would have been more than happy with the fourteen-quid one from IKEA, but for Maggie, moulded plastic was not meant to be.)

I gently extract the trains from Johnny's hands and lift him up into his chair, simultaneously fastening his plastic bib round his neck and moving the plate out of his reach.

'That's okay, Maggie,' I say quickly. 'It's probably best if he uses a plastic one.'

I reach into my bag to pull one out and David takes it from me. 'The boy has to learn, Annie,' he says, placing the crockery back in front of Johnny, who eyes it suspiciously.

'But he's only two!'

'He'll learn,' he says sternly, and that's that. Now the plastic orange plate has been removed, Maggie unfreezes from her spot and bustles into the kitchen, bringing out plates and bowls of steaming-hot food.

It does look amazing. David and Maggie chat, and Johnny eats his roast potatoes, after I quietly convince him they are chips. He eats a pea or two and tentatively chews on some chicken. I am enjoying my meal, miserably resolving to never attempt to make a roast ever again.

'So I told him, do it now, or you'll have no job to come back to,' David finishes off.

'Oh David!' Maggie exclaims. 'What did he do?'

'He did it, of course, but I fired him anyway.' David laughs, showing us the contents of his mouth, and Maggie laughs too.

'You are wicked,' she says. 'But I guess you had to show him who's boss.'

'Exactly, Mother,' says David, skewering another piece of chicken.

Johnny has stopped eating, having finished off his chips, and is looking at me with a mischievous expression. He moves his hand slowly, still fixing his gaze on mine, and I see him drop a piece of carrot on Maggie's immaculate carpet. It lands with a quiet plop amongst a few others. He smiles at me, and I shake my head, giving him a hard stare. He reaches for another piece of carrot, his gaze never leaving mine.

'Stop that!'

Johnny jumps as David thunders at him. He pauses with the carrot in his hand, weighing up the alternatives. But a two-year-old does not have a mortgage or a job to worry about, and doesn't follow orders from CEOs whether they are his daddy or not. He drops the carrot on the floor.

'How dare you,' David roars, and stands up suddenly, flinging his chair backwards. Johnny stops still, hand outstretched, eyes wide. 'You will not throw your food on the floor, you will not behave like this.'

Johnny starts to wail, his face turning red, mouth open wide, warming up into a proper scream.

'You stupid child, what are you crying about?' David shouts across the table.

'David, he's a baby.' I reach out to Johnny, about to pick him up from his high chair.

'Leave him alone,' David bellows at me, and I freeze, my arms still outstretched. 'He's a big boy now, he needs to learn good manners.'

Johnny continues to wail, lifting his arms towards me.

'Don't touch him!' David turns his attention back to his son. 'You do not throw food on the floor, you hear me? Now apologise to your grandmother.'

Johnny cries harder, becoming hysterical. He hiccups, pauses for breath, then screams again, his face red and scrunched up, his hands in tiny fists.

'He doesn't understand, David, just leave him alone.'

'Don't you tell me what to do!'

With all the rebellion a two-year-old can

muster, Johnny picks up the plate in front of him and throws it as hard as he can. It skids across the table at speed and flies off the far edge, smashing against the wall in a shower of discarded chicken and carrots. A parsnip bounces off the wall and lands squarely in the gravy boat, causing a splash of brown to spill onto the pristine tablecloth.

On seeing her best crockery shatter, Maggie joins in the wailing, high-pitched and shrill, her hands flying up to cover her face in horror.

In the silence that follows, I turn towards David with dread. His face is puce and I can see his body shaking. Never before has he been so blatantly disobeyed; never before has his authority been questioned with such defiance. Johnny is quiet, his face still red, with tears running down his cheeks. He wears the expression of someone who knows he has done badly wrong but doesn't care, and is waiting to see what will happen next. In that moment, I am proud of my little boy.

Suddenly David flies round to Johnny's side of the table, hooks his hands under Johnny's arms and pulls him out of his chair, holding him out in front of him, his legs dangling in the air. Instantly I am up, and by his side.

'David, put him down, please,' I beg as David hollers and rants, barely centimetres away from Johnny's face.

'Don't you dare do that ever again! Look what you've done!' he shouts, turning Johnny round mid-air to point him towards the shattered plate. Johnny starts crying again, great piercing screams, barely taking time to draw breath, little legs pumping in the empty air.

'David, put him down, please.' I pull on his arm, and David responds by pushing out his elbow, meeting me squarely in the bridge of my nose. I collapse back into my chair, eyes streaming and nose spouting blood, chest thudding as Johnny continues to scream hysterically.

David pushes away from the table, still carrying Johnny at arm's length. He marches out, depositing Johnny in the corridor, and closes the door on him. He walks back to the table, sits down and picks up his fork.

From behind the door, Johnny continues to scream, desperate emotional wails. The handle moves slightly, but he is too small to reach it properly. I imagine his little hands grasping at it as he tries to get back in to see his mummy, and tears roll down my cheeks and onto the napkin I am holding against my nose. I want to go to him; every inch of me wants to hold my little boy, to soothe him, to tell him everything will be okay.

I go to get up from the table.

'Don't you dare,' David says calmly, fork speared with a piece of chicken halfway to his mouth. 'You will not leave dinner before you have finished.'

I freeze, then slowly sit down and pick up my cutlery. I can still hear Johnny behind the door, the hysterical crying abating to quiet sobs. Something in David's tone stops me and makes me worry about what would happen when we got home if I disobeyed him. My stomach tightens. I am desperate to go to my baby, to hold him in my arms, give him a hug, make everything better. Tears roll down my face as I force a piece of carrot into my mouth and make myself chew, swallowing hard. My nose is blocked, so breathing is difficult; I eat with my mouth open.

I glance across to Maggie, who has got over the shock of seeing one of her prized possessions smashed to smithereens. She has calmly replaced her napkin on her lap and is carving up a green bean into three precise sections.

'You boys,' she tuts, with an indulgent giggle. 'You boys and your tempers.' And she shakes her head knowingly, as if David has stamped his foot or sworn out loud, rather than demonstrated out-of-control rage. She looks at me holding the napkin to my nose. 'I'll have to soak that for days to get the blood out,' she remarks, under her breath. She picks up the green bean on her fork and puts it in her mouth, not touching the edge of her lipstick. I watch her chew it delicately as my stomach churns, refusing to digest the remaining peas and carrots on my plate. She places her knife and fork down together at the side of her plate.

'Well, sorry about that,' she says. 'I think I rather over-did the carrots.'

'Not at all, Mother,' says David, calmly. 'Everything was perfect.'

Outside the room my two-year-old son cries. I look over to the closed door. A small blue Thomas the Tank Engine train lies on its side, abandoned.

* * *

As soon as I have forced down the requisite number of carrots, I mutter my apologies, put down my knife and fork in an orderly manner on the prized plate and look to David. As he nods wordlessly in my direction, I rush out of the room. Out in the hallway, everything is quiet. I can't see Johnny.

Bile rises to my mouth as I quickly rush from room to room, calling his name under my breath. In the day room I hear a small gulp, and stop, looking around.

I find Johnny behind the massive sofa, squished into a tiny corner. His back is to the wall and he is clutching Rabbit in one hand. In front of him are three small trains, lined up in a neat ordered row. His cheeks are red and flushed, wet with tears. He looks up as I get closer.

I edge towards him on my knees, jamming my body into the tiny space. I come to a stop in front of him, reaching over and picking him up, pulling him onto my lap. At first he resists, then he relaxes and curls up into a ball, his little arms finding a place round my middle, still clutching Rabbit.

I can hear David and Maggie talking in the dining room. Dull, calmed tones, discussing the weather or some other such banality. I put my face down to touch the top of Johnny's head, and breathe in the smell of his hair. Warm and soft, the scent of baby shampoo and warm toddler.

Johnny looks up at me. 'Where Thomas?'

I pull the little blue train out of my pocket and Johnny smiles, taking it from me and placing it in line with the other three. He taps them one by one.

'James, Gordon, Memerly, Thomas,' he says.

'Emily,' I say.

'Memerly,' he repeats, tapping the dark green one again.

I hear chairs being pulled out from the table and the clatter of plates as Maggie clears away.

'Annie?' I hear her call in her sing-song voice. 'Johnny? Come and have some pudding.'

I look down to Johnny.

'Cake?' he asks, his big blue eyes hopeful.

'I don't know, sweetie, shall we go and find out?'

I gently stand up and hold my hand out to Johnny, who takes it, stopping along the corridor to carefully put his trains back next to his bag. He hesitates slightly at the door of the dining room, but at the thought of something sugary comes inside and allows himself to be lifted back into his high chair. He smiles at Maggie as she places a large chocolate cheesecake on the table.

I look at it. 'There aren't any nuts in this, are there, Maggie?'

She stops, knife in hand, and rolls her eyes at me. 'No, Annie, no nuts.' She laughs, a little tinkle, and glances at David. 'And they said I was overprotective,' she mutters, deliberately loud enough so I can hear.

I grit my teeth as she cuts a portion for Johnny and puts it in front of him.

'Cake,' he says, nodding, smiling at Maggie.

I am amazed at how resilient toddlers can be. One adult transgression, easily forgotten with a bit of chocolate. But how long until it sticks? I think. How long until he remembers?

* * *

The rest of the meal passes without incident. I remark profusely about the wonders of the chocolate cheesecake, albeit with a smaller slice. ('Us girls need to keep our figures,' Maggie says, doling out a massive portion to David and barely a few crumbs to her and me. I imagine her finishing off the remaining three-quarters after we leave, systematically vomiting it back up later into her pristine ceramic toilet.) Johnny eats his bowlful without a word, concentrating on getting it to his mouth as quickly as possible in time for seconds. We pack up our bits and pieces and climb back into the Beamer.

'I know you think I'm mean,' David says, 'but you need to be strict with children. Show them good manners.'

I don't reply. I don't trust myself with the right response.

He pauses, leaning forward and negotiating a roundabout. 'Father was never around, as you know; he was always at work and left looking after me to Mother. Mother was firm, but very fair. I knew if I misbehaved or didn't eat my dinner it would be early to bed.' He pauses again, turning right into our drive and causing a Ford Fiesta to beep. 'Once, after a particularly bad day when I had thrown a toy at her, she took my teddy away.' He laughs. 'She snatched it out of my hands, found a pair of sewing scissors and shredded it into fur and stuffing. Right there in front of me.' He shakes his head. 'I never threw another toy. See, I can tell you that story now and there's nothing wrong with me, is there?'

I shake my head, but David hasn't waited for my answer, getting out and slamming the car door behind him. I sit with Johnny in the car for a moment, listening to the engine tick and Johnny's steady breathing.

No, David, nothing wrong at all.

Part Two

13

Oh David, just how stupid do you think I am?

I had a job once, you remember. Where I thought and did and told other people what to think and do. I looked after the managing director, the woman in charge. I was busy and got paid money that I happily wasted on clothes and alcohol and cigarettes. Was I more of a person then in your eyes? Was I more attractive? In those days you treated me like someone to spar with, someone to have fun with. Now I simply do as you say.

But how stupid do you think I am? Or perhaps, how stupid are *you*? If you expect me to take your suits to the dry cleaner's, don't leave receipts for swanky restaurants in the pockets. At first I thought it was the receipt from when the two of us went; I recognised the pretentious French name and the logo on the top. But then I realised the date was wrong: it was only last week, Wednesday night, when you were staying over at the office. I gave it back to you — 'I assume you need this to claim expenses from work?' — and you didn't even blink. Just laughed, and put it in your pocket. That's when I knew for sure. Expenses for work go in the neat little zipped plastic pouch. All ironed out and ready to be compiled by your PA every week into a tidy claim of hundreds and hundreds for your boss to sign. Instead you screwed it up and asked me what was for dinner. Steak and chips, I replied, and you grunted in approval, eyes scrolling over your BlackBerry. You turned without a word, unlocked the door to your office and went into your private man cave.

I remembered the purple cufflinks, those strange tacky things I noticed when we went out for dinner. Were they a gift from some woman or other, the same woman that goes to fancy restaurants with my husband? I wondered what else was behind that locked door.

And today, I can't resist. Johnny is having a nap, and I lurk outside, waiting for someone to catch me. I try the handle. Locked as I expected. I go up to my bedroom and grab a hairgrip, one of those little brown metal things with plastic on the ends, and bend one of the prongs up into a tiny L shape. Back downstairs, I listen again for a second, Johnny's baby monitor silent next to me in the hallway. I crouch down and look into the keyhole, heart thumping. I know what I'm doing is crossing the line, deliberately disobeying David. What do I expect to find in there? I know he's being unfaithful, I just know, so what is this going to prove?

I poke the hairgrip into the keyhole and wiggle it around a bit, turning it to and fro and trying to force the tiny prong into some release mechanism I can neither see nor imagine. I can hear the grind of metal against metal. I drop it on the floor, swear under my breath and try again. My feet go numb so I shift my legs to sit more comfortably, now at eye level to the lock. I try the handle — still nothing. I twiddle some more, then drop the hairgrip again. The tips of my fingers are getting red and sore.

I look at it on the carpet in front of me. Both of the plastic bits have come off, probably lost forever in the mechanism of the lock. A small bit of mud lies next to it, and I pick it up and flick it away, mentally noting to run the vacuum cleaner round before David gets home.

I decide a change of implement might be in order and go into the kitchen to see what I can find. I return with a skewer, a screwdriver and a variety of old keys found in a drawer with broken pieces of Johnny's toys, dead batteries and leftover screws from IKEA flat-packs. I try the keys first, desperately hoping David kept a spare, but none of them turn. I poke the skewer in, no use at all, and then look at the screwdriver. I could try and dismantle the door handle, but then I'd have to get it back together and I don't fancy my chances. What would I tell David then? There is no excuse in the world to justify taking apart a whole door.

I glare at the hairclip again. The movies always make it look so easy: a few bits of metal poked into a lock and the detectives are in and have found what they are looking for. What was I expecting, for the lock to miraculously spring open at the mere suggestion of a fashion accessory? I consider Google or YouTube but feel too tired for either. I push my fingers into my eyes and rub them until I see kaleidoscopic colours. The effort of this, of the worry and the thinking, is exhausting.

When did everything start to change? There was never an exact moment. Like a weed growing under the pavement, you could watch and never notice the difference, until one day you turn around and that little green sprout has broken right through the concrete. Maybe the signs were there and I ignored them.

At Johnny's twenty-week scan, David was grumpy. Grumpy at being forced to leave work, to sit on a plastic chair in a dirty-white corridor, the appointment running half an hour late. He fiddled with his BlackBerry, punching angry emails to his minions revelling in his absence.

When we finally went in, he softened slightly, reaching over to take my hand when the image appeared on the screen, the grainy black and white, and the rhythmic *thud thud thud* of the heartbeat. Tiny hands and feet, massive white blob of a head taking up the left-hand side. My breath caught in my throat and I looked over at David, staring astonished at the screen.

'Look at that,' he whispered, mesmerised by the gently moving image in front of him. He looked back at the sonographer. 'Is it healthy?' he asked.

'Perfectly,' she replied. 'Everything seems in order.'

David looked back and leant over to kiss me softly on the lips. 'Hear that?' he said. 'Perfect.'

I smiled back, my eyes full of tears — it was. Everything was perfect; it was all I'd imagined it to be and more. In a little over four months, my baby would be born and we would be a family. There was nothing more I wanted in the world.

'Would you like to know the gender?' the sonographer asked.

'Of course,' David replied.

'It's a little boy,' she said, and he looked at her with his mouth open.

'You won't be the only man about the house soon,' I laughed, rubbing my distended stomach clean of the sticky gel as she printed out the scan photo.

'As long as you don't forget who's the love of your life,' David said, kissing me on the cheek and helping me back on my feet.

'I think Mum's going to have her hands too full to worry much about you,' the sonographer said, handing me the photo. 'You'll be lucky if she remembers your name once that baby comes along.'

David was silent the whole way home. We pulled up in the drive, and he went straight to his study. I sighed, staring at the closed door, baffled at his sudden change in manner, then went into the kitchen, sticking the scan photo on the fridge door with a red magnet. I looked at the photo, taking in the little nose, the chin; I rested my hands on the bump and felt a slight flutter. My little boy, growing perfectly. The sonographer was right: already my love for my baby was far exceeding anything I felt for David. Back in those days, I loved David, sometimes so much I couldn't breathe, but this was different: more primal.

David emerged for dinner, sitting at the table in silence, staring at his food, then retreating back to his study when he was finished. Clearing away the leftovers, I opened the fridge, and when I closed it again, I noticed the red fridge magnet.

The scan photo had gone.

I didn't see it again.

I sit back on the hallway carpet, my back against the wall. At the time I couldn't imagine David was jealous of his own son, a child who wasn't even born, yet here we are and the triffids have taken over the neighbourhood. I didn't ask David about the scan photo at the time even though I wanted it back, desperately. Something stopped me. Maybe even then I knew something wasn't right, that David wasn't to be crossed. It's interesting what we ignore.

I look back at the locked door and wonder what I would have done if I had found whatever I was looking for. Confronted David with proof of an affair? He would have laughed in my face.

David cheating on me isn't exactly a surprise; I think deep down I always knew there was never a chance he would be faithful. A man with his ego and self-confidence would never stick with one woman for the rest of his life, especially not one like me. I am here to serve a purpose, but my role as wife does not restrict who he sleeps and has fun with. I have been waiting for this to happen; perhaps I have the excuse I need to leave. But go where exactly? My mother is dead. My friends have gone.

I sigh and pick up the hairgrip, putting it in my pocket and accepting defeat. No time for this now; the day moves forward. And best go get the vacuum before David gets home. That mud isn't going to clean itself.

Sand

Annie was bored of the park. People playing Frisbee, people walking dogs. Dogs of different sizes and breeds, big shaggy dogs, small yappy dogs. Always someone walking a bloody dog.

Sitting on her usual park bench, she took a deep breath and closed her eyes, stretching out her legs and arms, relaxing every muscle, one by one. She let her arms fall to her sides, and felt the buzz in her brain mute to a pristine white calm. It was wonderful, this new strange way of dreaming. It felt like her own private refuge, somewhere only she could go and hide.

Her mind wandered to a recent article she had seen. A white sandy beach. Green palm trees and blue skies with not even a trace of a cloud. A few deckchairs were scattered across the sand. She felt the sun on her face. She massaged the sand beneath her toes. She could hear the slow movement of the sea and feel the brush of the wind through her hair. She opened her eyes and smiled. She was definitely getting used to this — strange, but magical.

'I like your thinking.'

Dressed in only a pair of lime-green Bermuda shorts, Jack sat in the deckchair next to her, his hair wet and slicked back from his face, a trace of a tan and a scattering of freckles across his nose.

'How hard did you find this today?' he asked.

Annie thought back. 'Much easier. I just

relaxed and here I was.'

'You're getting better then,' Jack said, the sun catching his eyes and lighting them up an electric blue.

Annie sat back in her deckchair, raising her legs out of the sand and examining her feet. Her toenails were painted in a vivid red, and she noticed tan lines across the tops of her feet. She was dressed in no more than a tiny red bikini, and admired her flat tanned stomach.

'I haven't been somewhere like this in years,' she said, almost to herself.

'How come?'

'I got married and had Johnny, and then my life went to shit.'

Jack looked at her seriously. 'Is it really that bad?'

'No, no, it's not.' Annie laughed. 'Having children is a bizarre paradox. On one hand you'll happily jump in front of a bus for them, you'll do anything to keep them safe and warm and happy, and they bring so much joy and fun into your life. Johnny is just amazing; I couldn't imagine being without him. But on the other hand you do miss your old life — that freedom and independence. It's just gone.'

Jack smiled. 'Tell me about Johnny.'

'He's awesome, such a happy little man. He likes trains, and cars, and diggers, and the Gruffalo. And he's clever too, really smart . . . ' She looked at him. 'But all mothers say that, don't they? Maybe you'll meet him one day.'

'Maybe.' Jack laughed and Annie felt a flicker of recognition.

'Have we met before?' she asked.

'We are miles and miles apart, Annie,' he said quickly. He shook his head, and sat up in his deckchair. 'I have homework for you,' he said, looking out to sea. 'Next time, the next dream, I want you to try and find me. I'm not going to look for you; you'll have to find me.'

'How will I do that?'

'It's easier than you think. Just work it out, like I did.' He stood up. 'Now, enough of this pondering, let's enjoy this little piece of paradise.'

Annie nodded. 'I will. Coming for a swim?'

Jack ran confidently across the sand, diving *Baywatch*-style into the surf and swimming front crawl into the waves. Annie was more tentative, dipping her toe in to test the temperature then looking diligently at the sandy floor as she made her way in, checking for crabs or weaver fish, or anything else she wanted to avoid stepping on. But this was a dream, she reminded herself. If she wanted perfect soft sand, then that was what she'd get. She looked down and added a few colourful blue and yellow fish, delicately winding their way round her legs.

Now up to her waist, she dived forward and swam a few strokes before turning over and floating, arms out on the surface. She looked at the huge canvas of blue sky and felt the sun on her face. The waves rocked her to and fro; she felt invincible, she felt omnipotent.

And with that thought, she dived under the water, pushing out with her legs, swimming breaststroke, feeling none of her usual hesitation as she swam. She opened her eyes, everything clear and perfectly in focus. The surface loomed above her; the small blue and yellow fish had been joined by a swarm of clown fish, tiny and orange, swimming around the pinks, purples and turquoise of a coral reef. Her mind had produced a virtual Pixar movie, playing out in front of her eyes under the waves. She watched the fish for a moment, entranced, and then realised she had been down too long, she must be running out of air. But she felt no strain on her lungs, no breathlessness or stress, just an overwhelming sense of calm.

She watched for a bit longer, and then looked up, seeing Jack's legs kicking frantically a few metres above her. She pushed up to the surface, and popped up next to him.

'Where have you been?' he shouted as she took her first breath of oxygen. It tasted sweet and filled her with a sudden energy and euphoria. 'You've been gone for about ten minutes, I thought you had drowned.'

'I was fine,' Annie replied, treading water next to him. 'I was better than fine; it was amazing. I didn't need to breathe, I could just sit and take it all in. I could see you above me, and I knew I was in the sea, but the usual laws didn't apply. It was like you said, I can do anything.'

'You can't do anything, Annie, you can't take risks like that!'

'Why not? It wasn't really a risk; I could have swum to the surface at any time.'

Jack frowned and shook his head. 'What if you had drowned? What then?'

He turned and swam away from her, towards the shore. She swam after him and strode out of the waves to where he stood on the sand, hands on his hips, facing away.

'Jack!' she shouted as she got closer. 'What's the matter? I wouldn't have drowned, I would have just woken up.'

He turned to face her. 'How do you know, Annie? How do you know? This is so new, to both of us, nothing is certain. Don't take the risk, never die in a dream. What if you don't wake up?'

Annie shook her head. Even in the tropical sunshine she felt cold, a shiver running down her spine. 'But I'm okay.'

'But what if you hadn't been? What if you had died, what would happen to Johnny then?'

Annie reeled. Jack took her by the shoulders. 'You must be more careful, Annie, you're important, it's important . . . ' He stopped and shook his head. 'I'm sorry, but there's so much we don't know.'

Annie looked at him closely. The sun was drying his hair in wild waves around his face, and he looked younger to her, more vulnerable. Her previous elation had vanished, replaced by guilt for having offended her . . . what? Her friend?

'I'm sorry,' she said, quietly.

It was true, they didn't know the rules. But while Jack seemed wary, Annie felt the opposite. This was exciting, the one bit of enjoyment in her life. Something fun, something to explore

— who knows what they could achieve?

What would be the point if they didn't push it, and see just how far they could go?

14

The rock was huge. It lurked on its velvet cushion, held in place by a platinum band, two diamonds guarding it either side. I opened and closed my mouth a few times, mesmerised by the glow, then looked back to David.

He was kneeling in front of me, the Trevi Fountain behind him and about fifty tourists around us. There had been a collective gasp when he had gone down on one knee, and now all eyes were on me.

'Well,' he said, looking up with those dark brown eyes, crinkling at the edges, 'will you marry me?'

I said yes. Of course I did; what other option was there? We had been together a year, I loved him, he loved me, and I was worried about a lynching if I said no. The tourists clapped, the Americans cheered and David slid the ring onto my finger. It fitted perfectly.

Of course, I never wear it. How can I? It's annoying, it catches on everything — Johnny's clothing, my hair — and I'm terrified of losing it. And besides, it's so showy it's embarrassing. Five-carat diamond rings just don't go with your average tracksuit trousers. In the early days I called it my insurance policy, but now that's too close to the truth to be funny.

I never wanted much. While Becca talked about white dresses, tiaras, babies and big cars, I didn't have anything to add to the list. Just the basics: good food, nice house, warmth, and a husband who loved me. I'm not sure I have that last one any more.

Even now, some of my best days are the simplest.

Sure, I have my tasks to do, the cleaning, the tidying, the washing, but as long as David's shirts are ironed, I have dinner on the table when he gets home and the house looks clean and tidy, Johnny and I are good to go. This lackadaisical approach wouldn't work long-term — I can't risk piles of stray dust bunnies lining up under the sofa — but if we want to have a lazy day, we can.

The never-ending dark days of winter are behind us, the clocks have gone forward and daffodils are popping up from the ground. The sun is shining, so we take Johnny's football and walk to the park, him rushing up and down the path, little arms waving to keep his balance, a feather clutched in one hand. Me, sunglasses on, warmth of the sun on my forehead, cool breeze blowing through the trees. Sometimes it's possible to forget the rest of my worries and just exist in the pleasure of a happy boy and a happy mum.

A simple walk of a hundred metres can easily take half an hour. Johnny is interested in everything. The birds in the trees, manhole covers, parked cars, pebbles. Sticks. Trees you can hit with sticks. It must be fascinating being two.

In sight of the park, he rushes ahead, eager as

always to get to the swings, but I stop short, seeing someone already there. A man stands pushing one of the swings, a swirl of blonde hair flying backwards and forwards in front of him.

Johnny stops and looks up at me; I recognise the figure in the distance and my heart thumps just that little bit faster.

Adam smiles as we come close, turning his attention back to the swing at the last moment to give it a hearty push. I pick Johnny up and put him in the swing next to the little girl. I give it a big shove and Johnny laughs, waving his hands in the air.

'How's your daughter's forehead?' I ask, trying to look as she swings back and forth.

'Georgia,' he says. 'And it's much better, healing nicely, thank you.'

We stand in silence for a bit, both of us pushing our children. Silence, except for the quiet rustling of the wind in the trees and the excited squeaking from the swings. I push my spare hand in my pocket and look resolutely ahead.

'It's nice to have some company,' Adam says.

I glance round, unsure if he's being sarcastic. 'Sorry?'

'It's nice to see someone else, an adult, and have a conversation.' Seeing my blank expression, Adam carries on. 'I didn't realise, before Georgia, how you can go a whole day with a toddler and not have a proper chat. When you're new to the area, and work from home, it's hard to see people and make friends.'

'It can be lonely,' I say. I stop for a moment.

People, normal people, like conversation. They like to talk to each other. It is allowed, I remind myself; I am not doing anything wrong. Despite what my husband says. 'What do you do?' I ask.

'I'm an aeronautical engineer,' Adam says. 'But I work freelance, consult a little bit here and there. I have to, nowadays, to work around this little one.' He gestures towards Georgia, still grinning, whooshing to and fro. 'And it keeps the money coming in.'

I smile and nod, still not having the faintest idea about what he does for a living.

'What do you do?' he asks.

'Oh, I'm just a housewife.'

He laughs. 'There's no 'just' about it. Hardest job in the world, looking after these little monsters.'

Now that she's not crying hysterically, Georgia seems sweet — long blonde hair tied back with a pink clip, with escaping ringlets framing her delicate features. Like Johnny, she has blue eyes, and at this moment they are wide and open with the fun of the adventure. She is wearing a light-green corduroy dress, expensive-looking, clean and immaculate. A pair of blue trainers completes the outfit, effortlessly cool, even for a little girl.

'I used to have a job,' I say. 'I was a PA up in London — lots of admin, paperwork, moving meetings around.' I glance across to Adam and he's watching me, listening and attentive. 'It was a big responsibility, making sure everything ran smoothly, but I enjoyed it, I was good at it.'

'Do you miss it?' he asks.

'Not so much the job, more the people. The sense of purpose, you know?' He nods. 'It was nice to have a life I could call my own.'

I shut up suddenly, already feeling I've said too much, waffling on in front of this stranger. I try to smooth my hair down and push a few stray strands behind my ears. I go to put my fingers in my mouth, to nibble on my nails, and in the process see the state they are in. Different lengths, straggly chewed-off ends, dirt underneath them. I shove my hand back in my pocket.

I wish I had taken the time to brush my hair this morning, to style it properly rather than just tying it back in a ponytail. When was the last time I even washed it? I look down at my feet and my legs, scruffy jeans and trainers, a food-stained T-shirt from lunchtime. Hardly the stuff to impress new men, I think, then wonder: why am I thinking about impressing new men?

We stand in silence again, pushing the kids on the swings. I can hear a pigeon coo, and a helicopter flies overhead.

'Helicopter!' I say to Johnny, and he looks up.

'It's a Chinook,' Adam says. He points up. 'The two rotors, the helicopter is called a Chinook.'

'Johnny loves helicopters,' I say. 'And planes and trains and police cars — typical little boy.'

'Dinosaurs?'

'Definitely dinosaurs.' I don't dare look at his face; just his arms alone are enough to render me tongue-tied. They are tanned, strong arms, a jumper pushed up to show the muscles as he pushes the swing. A few blonde hairs are scattered across his forearm, a stylish clunky silver watch on his wrist.

'Georgia loves dinosaurs,' Adam says. 'She has a good collection of them. Any time you want to come over so the kids can play, you and Johnny are more than welcome. We only live over there.' He points to the road behind the row of trees. 'Number thirty-three. Here, I'll give you my number so you can text to see if we're free.' He notices my hesitation. 'Or not? Hey, I don't mind. I don't want you thinking I'm some weirdo from the park. I just thought it would be good to have some adult conversation over a cup of coffee once in a while.'

'No, no, that would be lovely.' I pull my mobile out of my pocket. 'But only if you have tea.'

The kids jump off the swings and start running laps of the park while Adam and I exchange numbers. Adam beams at me, and I feel a little thrill as I enter his name in my address book, a fizz of excitement knowing it's something David doesn't permit: a friend he doesn't approve of. It's nice to know I have something that's mine.

We turn back to the children. Johnny has joined Georgia sitting on the grass. She is showing him daisies and he is pulling the petals off them.

'Daddeeee!' I hear Georgia call. Adam gives me an apologetic look and goes to join his daughter. She jumps up and grabs his hand in hers, pulling him away.

As I walk over to Johnny, I watch Adam from a distance. He is tall, with broad shoulders, dressed in jeans, trainers and a blue jumper, and the casualness suits him. Some men, like David, are built to wear suits, structure and bleak colours to match their stern expressions and slicked-back hair. Others are better suited to jeans. I wonder what Adam's wife is like. She would wear Boden, Joules or Jigsaw, hair falling in perfect waves even though she did nothing with it when she woke up this morning. She wears white jeans and stays immaculate all day, even with a toddler to look after. I expect Georgia dines on smoked salmon, lychee juice and hummus, always nutritionally balanced, no chocolate, never any sugar. This wife would smile all the time, be patient and tolerant, understanding towards her husband, putting out at least twice a week and giving blow jobs when she was too tired. Home-made cakes and roast dinners on a Sunday.

Nothing like me.

Through my pondering I haven't noticed that Adam has already left the park, his long strides following Georgia as she makes a run for home. I stare long after he has rounded the corner and gone out of sight.

* * *

Slowly I entice Johnny away from the park and cajole him towards home. Through the door, he runs off to find a train to play with and I take a moment to look at myself in the hallway mirror. Badly dressed, no effort, no make-up, no style. It's no surprise David doesn't pay any attention to me, I am a mess.

In my dreams I can look any way I choose, so why not in real life? Why shouldn't strange men look at me with interest in the park, rather than talk to me out of pity? I give myself a stern lecture. Time to wake up, Annie; time to get your shit together.

I take one final disgusted look, then turn towards the noise Johnny is making in his playroom. Bricks are being turned out onto the floor, bedlam created by a small boy. As I pass the office door, I try the handle out of habit, expecting the usual resistance.

But the handle turns. David's office is unlocked.

15

I step back from the door, my heart pounding. I can almost feel the adrenaline working its way round my body. I glance around, then try the handle again. It definitely turns: the room is open.

For a moment I wonder whether it's a trick, a test David has set up for me. He's never explicitly banned me from going in his study, but as it's always been locked, it's never been up for debate. Today, it's not.

'Daddy work,' Johnny says next to me, and I jump. I reach down and stroke his hair.

'Yes, pickle, it's Daddy's work room.' I crouch down to his height, face to face. 'So remember, we don't touch anything when we go in.'

Johnny's face adopts a serious air. 'No,' he says, shaking his head emphatically.

'Nothing,' I repeat.

I push the door open and a fine layer of dust is disturbed, scattering in the air. As the light shines through the window, I see it hanging, little flecks of skin and fluff, just floating, with nowhere to go. It's uncharted territory, a strange world in my own home.

Johnny is tentative at first, and then more confident, taking in the decoration and clutter he is unfamiliar with elsewhere. It is strange to see the level of crap David will tolerate in here, in his own domain, when he expects the rest of the house to be tidy and bare.

Johnny moves around the room slowly, exploring things with his hands as toddlers do, previous warnings forgotten.

'Don't touch anything,' I repeat, and he stops moving, his hands by his sides. I can see his eyes looking at all the trinkets at toddler eye height, shiny prizes to play with and keep.

I stand in the middle of the room and take it in myself. There is a bookshelf I remember seeing before, filled with management books designed to appeal to the super-ego: *Be the Man You Were Born To Be* and *Lead for Respect*. A few reinforcing unintelligible management speak: *Who Shot the Donkey?* and *Why Synergies are not Win-Win*. Scattered in amongst them are a few novels, masculine MI6 spy types, and then incongruous colourful Enid Blytons: the Faraway Tree and the Famous Five. I pull one out, old and worn, and open the front cover — 'For my perfect little boy, may your childhood be as joyful as this book'. And a squiggle underneath: 'From Dad'. I have never seen these before.

Across the higher shelves are glass and silver trophies, all embossed with the company logo. Trophies for winning money and clients, for long service and progression. I open the ugly world globe drinks cabinet and run my fingers over the whisky and the bourbon, expensive labels, all half drunk. Pushed next to the bottles is a small navy-blue metal tin, 'Cornish Fudge' embossed on the top, and I pick it up, remembering having given it to David as a silly gift one Christmas soon after we first met. Then, it contained expensive fudge; now, as I open it, I see a plastic packet of white powder, another of small white pills, and a black memory stick. I hold the bag of powder up to the grey light from the window. It looks like most of it has gone. Cocaine? Surely not heroin. And Ecstasy? Those nights when he is working with his colleagues are not as boring as he makes out. I replace the powder and the pills in the tin and pick out the stick. I stare at it for a moment, willing it to give up its secrets, before putting it in the pocket of my jeans.

Johnny has got bored and wandered back to his toys, where he's allowed to touch and throw. I can just see him through the open door, sitting on the floor, a plastic container of bricks next to him, carefully fitting one on top of another. Standing in the middle of the room, I ponder my next move. I leave and come back with a yellow duster and a can of Mr Sheen. Ruse in place, I continue my search of the room, running the cloth absent-mindedly across the surfaces, slightly disgusted at the level of grime, already rendering it black.

I turn my attention to David's imposing wooden desk. I know it used to belong to David Senior, but I can't pinpoint when it made its way in here. I can tell it was well looked after in its day: the wood still holds its polish and the brass handles are shining. I try the drawers in turn. The first two are locked tight, but the last one, a big, cavernous drawer meant for filing, opens easily. It's stuffed full of papers, with no order or thought, and I prod the piles tentatively, looking to see what's in there.

I lift out a heap; they look dull. Letters from our solicitor about the purchase of this house, land registry documents, bank statements. I cast a look at one of them, an account with only David's name on it, and the total is eye-wateringly high. I notice an A4 windowed envelope in the pile, and spot the red cover of a UK passport. I tip the contents onto the desk: old fully stamped ones of David's, and muddled among them, a pristine one that turns out to be for Johnny, and at the bottom, mine. I look at Johnny's — the photo is very early on, he looks like a tiny baby — and I wonder when David, or his PA, applied for it. We have certainly never talked about any foreign holidays. He took mine after our honeymoon, said he would put it away for safe keeping, and I gave it up without a second thought. I trusted him. I push the two passports into my back pocket.

I flick through the last of the papers, what look like documents and contracts from his work, all with the usual logo, all expensive, thick embossed paper and deep black ink. I find nothing else interesting so I put them back in the drawer, arranging them in the same higgledy-piggledy way they started out.

A worn and beaten-up cupboard stands behind David's chair. Like the desk, it is made of a dark wood and in its day it would have had pride of place in a dining room or hallway. It has two doors meeting in the middle, with an intricate design across them, and what looks like an old brass lock. I push at the doors and they give on their hinges, enough to jiggle the two sides of the lock apart. More mess and papers lie inside. A quick check to where Johnny is still occupied with his bricks, and I squat in front of the cupboard.

I sigh. What exactly am I looking for, digging through the minutiae of David's life, the stuff I don't normally see? The majority of it is boring and predictable, the paperwork that life accumulates: bills, council tax, P60s, payslips and letters from HMRC. I glance at a few in passing. For all his failings, it seems he pays our bills on time, and certainly earns enough money to cover my pathetic allowance. What does he do with the rest? I wonder.

As I start to close the cupboard door, a pile of letters and cards catches my eye. Stuffed down the back, just barely poking out the top, I can see the bright colours of greetings cards and unmistakable handwritten addresses. I pull them out, one by one, and lay them in front of me. By the end, there's quite a large pile. Birthday cards, Christmas cards, a few good luck cards, some still in their envelopes, opened roughly, some just out in the pile. Letters the same, some loose, some not even opened, but each with one unmistakable characteristic. All are addressed to me.

16

I stare at the stack of cards and letters, incredulous at the sheer number of people that have tried to contact me. I pick one up: 'We're sorry to hear you're leaving', it says, full of comments and notes from my colleagues at my old work. I look for a moment at the squiggles and signatures, in a mix of different pens and handwriting. I place it slowly to one side and select another. A group of birthday cards, one inside another, bundled up. Some gaudy and tacky, some tasteful and arty. I flick through and look at the names — Julia, Graham and Ryan, Sue and James, all people I thought I hadn't heard from in years. A few letters from a friend in Australia; a random postcard from an old lady, a neighbour I assumed had died; Christmas cards and congratulations cards when Johnny was born. Some of the Christmas cards distribute their glitter across the floor; a reindeer embossed in red smiles out with a happy grin. All people I thought had left me, all people I assumed hadn't given me a second thought.

I grew up lonely. A series of men journeyed through our tiny home, none of them staying for long, but otherwise nobody came to visit. I yearned for the sort of bustle and noise I found at Becca's, but I never knew how to behave with the affection at her house. Any attention was overwhelming; it didn't match the way my mother had always made me feel — insignificant and undeserving. I learnt to exist at the edge of the chatter and conversation.

At the bottom of the pile is a bundle of letters secured with an elastic band. Most of them opened and placed back in their envelopes; some untouched. All with handwriting I have known my entire life. I take off the elastic band and pull one out at random, written on light blue notepaper. I glance at random sentences, the words blurring in front of my eyes. 'I haven't heard from you in a while', 'I hope you and David are well', 'I miss you'. It's signed by Becca.

I sit on the floor, surrounded by the letters and cards from the people from my life before David. Some of them were there when we met and were encouraging and pleased for me. Some even lasted to our wedding. David said it was the natural way: you got married and had a child and moved on from the single life and your friends from before. People accepted that and left you alone. But now I'm not so sure.

My life was never normal as I grew up; I never had normal friends, except Becca. I found my confidence at work. I realised that by taking control of my life, and of the life of the MD I looked after, I could make a difference. I held my head up. I had a purpose. But that part of me disappeared with my job, so when I didn't hear from my friends, the people in my life, I adopted my old habits. I withdrew. I didn't bother to contact them. I was too unimportant.

But here they are, scattered around me. This is

what normal friends do — they send birthday cards, they send postcards, they try to get in contact with you after your mobile number changes because your husband accidentally dropped the old one in the toilet. These were my friendships and I had let them go, let them disappear.

I think back to the morning after our wedding. Sitting in bed in the honeymoon suite, hair still rigid with hair-spray, David turned to me and said, 'You need to stay away from Becca. She's bad news for you. Mother overheard her talking to that other friend of yours, the fat one in the pink?'

'Lisa?'

He was shirtless and handsome, the white sheets contrasting against his tanned chest. 'Whatever. She said something like 'I give it six months', and then the fat one said you looked like a six-year-old playing dress-up princesses in that dress, and then they both laughed.'

I looked over at the dress, laid out over one of the sofas. A mass of ivory lace and silk, the most beautiful thing I had ever owned, chosen on a wonderful day out with Becca. A lump formed in my throat.

David put his mug down and leant in close to me. 'You have me now, you don't need to worry any more.' He kissed me, his smell a mixture of manly early-morning warmth and coffee; it was everything I had ever wanted.

How has David kept these from me for all these years? Why did I so easily accept that we never receive post to the house? He said it was doing me a favour: one less chore for me to sort out every day. Why did I so quickly agree to redirecting it to the office when David has never done a selfless act in his entire life? How was that good? How was that normal?

The clock in the room chimes, announcing twelve o'clock. I jump, and scrabble around me, picking up the letters and cards, replacing them in their envelopes, trying to remember what went where, putting everything back where it belongs. But I keep the letters from Becca, pushing them into the waistband of my jeans. Quickly I wiggle the cupboard door closed and jump up, standing in the doorway, looking back at the room, seeing it through David's eyes. Apart from my poor attempt at cleaning, will he notice it has changed? I take a deep breath and close the door, looking around for Johnny. I can hear bashing and banging coming from his playroom and go in search of the noise.

Unchecked, my little boy has done what any self-respecting two-year-old would do — he's trashed the room. Toy boxes have been upturned, cars on top of trains on top of jigsaw pieces from any number of puzzles. He is sitting in the middle of it all, looking very pleased.

'Mummy!' he says, with a big smile. 'Tidy up?' he asks sweetly, and places one train into the empty plastic box by his side.

'My,' says a voice behind me. 'What has been going on here?'

I pull on my best happy face, and turn to face Maggie. Her keys to my house are still in her hand. 'Did you forget I was coming for lunch, dear?' she says with a smile, caustic enough to take off the wallpaper. A waft of talcum powder and floral perfume envelops me as she kisses me, her tissue-paper cheek a good centimetre from mine.

'No, not at all, Maggie. In fact, we were just tidying up ready for your arrival.'

Johnny smiles, and tips the single train out of the plastic box, back into the chaos.

'Let's get you comfortable while we clear up,' I say, ushering her away from the mess. 'Now, would you like a cup of Earl Grey?'

As she moves back towards the lounge, I pull my shirt down over the top of the passports and letters hidden in my jeans. I am desperate to take a look, but suddenly scared of what it might mean for my life, and for Johnny's. I feel my emotions teetering on a knife edge, terrified of which way the stark reality will tip me. But I will ignore it for now. There is time to look later. Time to think then.

17

I pop a plate with a slice of buttered toast and some baked beans in front of Johnny, and return to the hob to check on the soup. Maggie has brought lunch with her — a cuboid of grey leek and potato, rendered solid by the starch. It slides out of the Tupperware with a squelch and wobbles in the bottom of the pan, nervous of its fate. I attack it with a spoon as it heats up, and luckily it returns to something resembling soup, albeit smelling more of floral cleaning products than anything edible. I should be grateful for Maggie's show of effort, but suspect it comes from a reluctance to eat anything cooked by my own fair hand more than any sort of altruism.

The concoction starts to bubble, so I ladle out portions for Maggie and me and join them at the table. Johnny picks up his toast and takes a bite, carefully watching Maggie. She dips the edge of her spoon in the soup, tentatively. I begin to suspect it wasn't her that made it: her girl, perhaps, or maybe Waitrose, transferred into the Tupperware for show.

'Beans again, then,' she says, still looking at the soup on her spoon. She takes a sip, considers it, then picks up the salt, adding a generous few shakes.

'He hasn't had them for a week, Maggie,' I say.

'Still,' she replies with a shake of the head. She looks at me and puffs herself up, as if preparing for a grand announcement. 'I saw my charity ladies on Saturday. We're not sure how much longer we'll keep going as a group.' Johnny picks up a bean with his fingers, and I gesture at him to use his spoon. 'It's more of a chore nowadays.'

'I'm sure the people you raise money for appreciate it, though.' (Then, under my breath: 'Johnny! Spoon!' Johnny looks at me cautiously and slowly picks up his spoon, balancing a piece of toast on it with his fingers. 'For the beans, please?')

'Well, only so they can spend their money on cigarettes and beer. We turn up at the food bank, and look at them all, in their — what do you call them, the jumpers with the . . . ' She gestures, two hands by the sides of her head.

'Hoodies?'

'Yes, hoodies and trainers, stinking of cigarettes — surely, if you can afford cigarettes, you can afford a bit of Weetabix — and we never get so much as a thank you, or even a nod.'

I can imagine the scene, Maggie and her cronies turning up in their pearls and cashmere, expecting the common masses to throw themselves at their feet in gratitude. It's a miracle they don't get lynched.

Johnny finally takes a mouthful of beans with his spoon. He chews them slowly.

'It must be nice to spend some time with your friends,' I say, taking a sip of the soup. It has a slightly chalky texture and an after-taste of lemon washing-up liquid. Less Waitrose, more underpaid domestic assistant. I warm to her girl for her minor act of rebellion.

Maggie has polished off her soup and holds the bowl up to me, like Johnny would, asking for seconds. I get up and fill it from the pan. I plough on. 'I sometimes think I miss my friends. People to chat with about my day. Share funny stories and advice about the kids.'

'But you have David for that. And me.' She smiles, her lips a thin line as she takes the refilled bowl.

'Well, you know, it's good to talk to people, let off a bit of steam.'

'Sharing your family's dirty laundry with strangers?'

'But they're not strangers, they're friends. I had some great friends from school I'd love to see.' I'm rambling now, in the face of Maggie's piercing stare. 'I know David doesn't have any old school friends because it was a bit rough with all the bullying and drugs — '

'Rough? We sent him to one of the best schools in the country! The slightest hint of bullying and the little sod responsible would be expelled. There was none of that going on. Though David Senior thought it was a pity as it would have toughened him up a bit.'

'Oh, well David said — '

'Finished!' Johnny says next to me, holding out his bowl.

'Johnny you've barely started your toast. Have one more piece.'

He looks at me, then Maggie, and reluctantly picks up a square.

'Family are the only people you can trust,' Maggie says, placing her spoon in her finished bowl and dabbing at her mouth with her napkin. 'If you need someone to talk to, that's what your husband is for.'

I feel my lips press together, my muscles tense. I used to trust my husband, I did. Before the screwed-up receipt, the Christmas cards hidden in the back of a cupboard, the lies about his school. I stand up slowly and gather the bowls, the letters from Becca rough against my waistband. I place the dirty crockery in the dishwasher, then pause, knowing what I'm about to do but unable to stop it.

I pull the letters out and hold them in my hand, standing in front of Maggie.

'What are those, dear?' she asks.

'Letters. From my friend Becca.' She looks at them and turns away from me. I carry on. 'I found them in David's office. He'd hidden them from me.'

She turns to face me, her mouth a puckered cat bum of disapproval.

'Snooping in your husband's office?' She shakes her head. 'Put them back now, before he finds out.'

I take my seat again at the table, forcing her to face me.

'That's not the point, Maggie. He hid them from me. They're my letters, and my friends, and David hid them from me.' I wave them in her face. My voice is getting squeaky, and Johnny looks at me, distracted from the final bites of his lunch.

'I'm sure he did it for a good reason,' Maggie says.

Suddenly I realise. 'You knew. You knew what he was doing.'

'He asked my advice, yes.' She looks at me. 'He asked me what to do about these awful so-called friends of yours that kept on crawling out of the gutter. Distracting you, leading you astray.' She carries on, unflinching. 'What would be next? Drinking again? Nights out on the town? I agreed with him it was the right thing to do.'

'Right thing for you and David, or for me?'

'What's the difference, dear?' she asks. 'You're married now; you are one, together. Your thoughts don't matter, it's what's best for the marriage.' She tuts. 'Now, enough of this nonsense, let's finish our lunch. Does anyone want some yogurt?' she asks Johnny.

Johnny throws the piece of toast on the floor. It lands butter side down.

'Strawberry gogurt?' he says, with a smile.

I slowly place the letters on the kitchen counter, my hands unsteady.

'Please?' I say to Johnny, measured and calm, still facing away, feeling Maggie's gaze on my back. I take a very long breath in, trying to quell the flicker of anger burning in my chest, muzzling my screaming inner voice.

'Please,' he replies.

18

The click of the front door as it opens. David's footsteps as he comes into the house and closes the door behind him. I imagine him taking his coat off, hanging it up, smoothing down his suit and his hair in the mirror in the hallway, his keys still in his hand.

All of this makes my heart beat faster, my mouth go dry.

I hear the jangle of his keys as he goes to his office door. The grate of metal against metal as he puts the key in the lock and turns it. I hear a pause, when normally he would go straight in. I hear the door open, and a thud as David places his briefcase in the doorway. Another pause.

'Have you been in my office?' he says from the hallway.

My hands cling to a tea towel to stop them from shaking.

'I said, have you been in my office?' He is shouting louder now, his voice partly lost as he moves round the room.

'Yes, the door was unlocked, so I went in to clean.' I will my legs to move, to walk out of the kitchen. David is standing in the middle of the study, a striking figure in his black suit, his shoulders thrown back. He is rotating on the spot, looking slowly round the room.

I stand at the doorway, the tea towel still in my

hand. I smile, gently. 'I thought that's what you wanted.'

Another pause. David's face is frozen, his eyebrows knotted, scrutinising. 'You haven't done a great job.' He moves to the bookcase and runs a finger over one of the shelves. He shows it to me, grey with dust.

'No, Johnny needed me so I didn't have a chance to finish. I'll do it tomorrow.'

David rubs his fingers together. 'No. You're not to come in here again.' He walks towards his desk and pulls at the drawers, glancing up at me when they refuse to open: locked. He bends to the last one, which opens easily. He inspects the contents, then stands and looks at me.

'Did you go in here? Because you know this is none of your business. There is nothing in this room that is anything to do with you.'

'I didn't,' I lie. My inbuilt reaction. But a part of me hesitates; a part of me feels the anger start to build.

His eyes are on me, focused and intense. He pauses. 'Are you sure?' he asks, slowly.

* * *

As soon as Johnny was in bed earlier that day, I sat in my room, listening through his chattering for the sound of the door opening, of David coming home. I took the letters out of my pocket and laid them in front of me, the black memory stick next to them.

There were eleven in all. One dated as far back as four years ago, a few months after our wedding, the final one postmarked barely a month ago. All were written on the same light-blue stationery; heavy paper, envelopes matching the notecards. All were from Becca.

I started at the beginning. Becca's handwriting has always been neat, the letters round and familiar, small bubbles of her personality on the page. The first letter began with a single sentence: *I'm sorry*. I stared at those two words for a moment, remembering that evening, that argument, then read on, more apologies, more explanations. *I'm writing to you as I don't know how else to get in touch*, she wrote. *You're not on social media*. It's true, David doesn't want our business all over the internet; he says I should talk to people face to face. I agreed at the time, but of course, I never do. Becca had written her phone number down in big letters, underlined, asking me to call her, as she had tried to call me and my mobile had been disconnected. She signed off with four kisses. I put it back in the envelope slowly, then pulled out the next. Again the apology, but moving on to tell me about her new boyfriend, their first date, their first kiss. She said how she looked forward to seeing me, how she hoped I could forgive her.

Another letter moved her relationship with her new man forward. More dates, more kisses. Other things. Signed off a bit more urgently now. Slightly disgruntled, but still the four kisses.

The next: the boyfriend now moved in. A photo of the two of them together, with *As you're not on Facebook* written in biro on the back. I stared at it for a moment. Becca's face familiar but blurring with age, a few more lines, hair colour a bit blonder. The boyfriend: brown hair, stubble, warm smile. He seemed nice. I would have liked to meet him.

And so it progressed. Their relationship seemed to be going well, but Becca's tone grew increasingly annoyed, then angry. Accusing words, of me forgetting where I had come from, forgetting the people that loved me. The phone number again, underlined, with a few exclamation marks.

Two letters were unopened. I ran a finger under the top of the first envelope, and pulled the letter out. Along with the letter was a cream embossed card with fancy black lettering, inviting David and me to their wedding, Becca and Matt, with a date long since passed. I felt a knot form in my stomach. I had missed my best friend's wedding, the happiest day of her life, and I hadn't even known. I didn't need to imagine how she had felt, because she had written it all down in the next letter. An angry missive, full of exclamation marks and capitals. *I'm not going to write to you again,* it said, *I've had enough*.

I turned to my bedside table and pulled out the invitation to the birthday party, now buried under the books stored in there. I looked at the date, but it was gone, another significant moment missed.

Helen's disappointment in me made sense; she was quite right to be furious, and to try and protect her daughter and grandchild in the best way she knew how. In her eyes I had taken all the love and kindness they had shown me, and thrown it back in their faces. What must Becca think of me, ignoring her letters all this time?

I lay back on my bed, the letters around me, and took a few deep breaths, staring up at the ceiling.

* * *

'I'm worried about you, Annabelle. I'm worried about you and David.'

'What about me and David?' I asked.

Becca and I were sitting in our favourite restaurant. The lighting was low, the food was delicious but the conversation had been strange; stilted and halting. We'd struggled to find anything to talk about, let alone laugh over.

'It's just . . . ' she started, then put her knife and fork down. 'He seems very controlling. You never do anything without his say-so.'

'That's not true, don't be ridiculous. We're fine, I'm fine.' I was blindsided by Becca's comments, blustering in response.

Becca went to hold my hand, reaching across the table. I pulled away from her, sitting back in my chair, my arms crossed. 'He seemed lovely when you first met, but you're a different person now. I never see you, and when I do, you're desperate to get back to him.'

Becca was right, it had been months since I'd seen her, but that hadn't been David's fault. We had been busy: buying the new house, enjoying being newly-weds. I'd arranged to meet her, but each time something had come up: David had made plans, just the two of us, and couldn't rearrange, or he'd had a bad day at work and I hadn't wanted to leave him.

'Can you blame me, when you attack me like this?' I replied.

'It's just . . . I miss you,' she said, with a gentle smile, pulling her blonde hair away from her face and tying it back with a flick of her wrist. 'And I worry about you.'

'You don't need to worry about me. I'm married now, things work differently. I have to be there for my husband. You wouldn't understand.'

'Is he hitting you?' she asked, suddenly.

'For fuck's sake, Becca!' I stood up, and the chair hit the wall behind me. The other diners in the restaurant turned at the commotion. I leant forward as I pulled my coat round my shoulders. 'I am fine, we are fine. David loves me. And I don't need you acting like my fucking mother.'

'I am nothing like your mother.' Becca stood up too, matching my stance. The glasses on the table chinked together. 'Your mother didn't give a shit about you, but I do. That's the difference. And I can see when something's not right.'

'Oh, fuck off,' I hissed, and turned and stalked through the restaurant, heading home to my husband.

By the time I got in through my front door, I was properly crying, tears streaming down my face. It took me two attempts to open the door, then I collapsed on the sofa when I got inside, throwing my keys across the room in frustration.

David sat, beer in hand, and looked at me,

then reached for the remote, muting the football on the television. He placed his beer on the coffee table and came over, crouching in front of me.

'Fucking Becca,' I shouted, wiping my nose on my sleeve.

He took both my hands in his and looked up at me. 'What happened with Becca?'

'We had a fight.'

'What about?' David's eyes were wide and open. I was reluctant to tell him; I didn't want to hurt him, to ruin his evening in the same way Becca had ruined mine.

'Tell me,' he said. 'You can tell me anything, it's okay.'

I started crying again, and David reached up and wiped my cheek with his finger. 'It was about you,' I blurted out through the sobbing. 'She said awful things about you, said you're no good for me.'

David cocked his head to one side and rested his arms on my knees. 'What a strange thing for a best friend to say.' He thought for a moment. 'Is she still single?'

I nodded, and sniffed.

'Well, there you go, she's just jealous of what we have. Perhaps she fancies me for herself.'

He rested his chin on my knee and looked up at me. I ran my hands through his hair and he knelt up and kissed me gently on the lips. 'Can you blame her?'

I smiled. 'No,' I said and kissed him back.

'I can't stand to see you so miserable,' David said. 'You don't have to see her again, not if she makes you feel like this.'

And I didn't. I didn't call, and weeks turned into months, and then years. At the special times — my birthday, Christmas, when Johnny was born — I wondered why I hadn't heard from her. 'You obviously weren't that important to her,' was all David had to say on the matter. 'Don't dwell on people who aren't worth your time.'

But of course now I knew why. What an idiot I was, how stupid and blinkered. Why hadn't I listened to her, the person who knew me better than anyone else in the world?

Johnny's room was quiet. He had gone to sleep, and I suddenly grew nervous, expecting David home from work at any time. I didn't know what I was going to do. I knew Maggie would tell him about our conversation; maybe she already had. My stomach turned over, making me feel slightly sick. I put the letters back in their envelopes, and bundled them up with the elastic band before placing them in my chest of drawers, under some socks. The contents of the memory stick would have to wait.

* * *

'Are you sure?'

Am I sure? What about the letters from my best friend, David? What about the invitation to her wedding? Who else is stuffed in that cupboard, David?

My heart is thumping, and I can feel my cheeks turning red. All those lost fucking years.

The anger overtakes me. I feel my muscles tense and my fingers contract into fists.

'Actually, David, I did have a quick look, and do you know what I found?'

He stands up straight and stares at me. I look at him, and in that moment, my charming husband has disappeared; his eyes are icy, hypnotic. I have no idea what he's thinking.

'You did what?' Quiet, slow.

'I had a look in your desk, and in that crappy old cupboard behind you.'

He glances quickly over his shoulder, then turns back to face me.

'And?'

'And I found something.'

'Please enlighten me, Annie. What exactly did you find?' David's voice is still, calm and measured. He hasn't moved from his position behind the desk, his arms by his sides.

'I found all my post. Cards, letters, postcards, all addressed to me.'

'Did you?'

'Yes! Loads of them; piles and piles of them. I didn't have time to look at them all. Why did you take them, David? They were mine! They were from my friends!'

Suddenly, in two great strides, he is next to me in the doorway, his face close to mine.

'Your friends?' he shouts. 'Friends?'

I hold my ground, wincing from the force of his voice.

'Yes, my friends. What right do you have to keep them from me?'

And then, *bam*. Out of nowhere, something

hits me on my right cheek. It hits me so hard my ear bounces on the door frame on the left-hand side of my head. Then the pain starts, in my ear, my cheekbone, to the side of my eye. Blood rushes to my face; I feel light-headed and put my hand to my cheek. My hand feels cold in comparison.

David is still standing next to me, his right hand raised. And that's when I realise: he hit me. Took the back of his hand and whacked me.

'What *right*?' he says, spit freckling my face. 'I am your husband, that's what right. *I* say who you can talk to, *I* decide who you're friends with, and it's certainly not the bunch of alcoholics and deadbeats you used to hang out with.'

My hand is still next to my cheek, my mouth open, tears slowly running down my face.

'I saved you,' he continues, shouting, barely an inch away from me. 'When we met, you were nothing. You were drunk every night, chain-smoking, out of control. But I saw you, who you really were, who you could be. My wife.' He softens, and steps back from me, his face changing. He moves his hand towards mine, and I flinch, backing out of the door. 'Oh now, don't be like that. I'm sorry. You drove me to this; only you can make me so angry.' He smiles, taking my hand away from my face and enveloping it in both of his. 'Those people have no place in our lives now. Friends wouldn't have let you behave in that way. Sleeping with unsuitable men, wasting your life. You're better than that, you know that now, don't you?'

I nod.

‘Good. Now go tidy yourself up for dinner and let’s not talk about this again.’

He lets go of my hand and points me towards the bathroom. I stumble towards it, my feet barely leaving the carpet, and shut the door behind me.

I look in the mirror and an unfamiliar face stares back. My mascara has run under my eyes, and a large red mark takes up the whole of my right cheek and cheekbone, from under my eye to the side of my mouth. I can taste blood where I have bitten my tongue.

I touch it tentatively and I can feel the swelling already starting to take hold. I take a flannel out of the cupboard and run it under the cold tap, before slowly folding it in four and putting it against my face. The coldness soothes me.

Is he right? In the time before I met him, I certainly had my fair share of hangovers; there had been more mornings with missing memories than I care to remember. Every Saturday night, getting pissed with friends; one occasion in particular when I passed out on the pavement outside the club in a pile of my own vomit, waking up with a strange man leering over me. But wasn’t that what your twenties were all about? Was I better off now, with him and Johnny?

I take the flannel away from my face and wipe my forehead and my eyes, carefully rubbing away the stray mascara. I retie my hair, stand up straight, and take a deep breath.

‘Come on, slowcoach, dinner is getting cold,’ David calls from the kitchen.

I turn quickly as my mouth fills with saliva. Vomit rises in my stomach, and I retch uncontrollably into the toilet. I throw up what was left from lunch, the cup of tea, the biscuit I ate with Johnny. I retch until my stomach is empty, my hands either side of the seat, hair falling in the way, tears in my eyes. I drop to my knees, holding onto the toilet for support, and spit a sticky ball of whatever is left in my mouth into the lurid yellow splattered mess in the bowl. I gulp down a few deep breaths, then sit back on the carpet, my legs folded under me, my body shivering.

My limbs feel weak, my head stuffy, and my eyes and face are stinging. I am uncontrollably tired. I pull myself up on the sink, wipe my face down with the flannel again, and go to open the door. It takes two attempts to turn the door handle and a further few to pull the door open and go out into the hallway.

'David,' I call, forcing my voice to sound breezy. 'I'm not feeling well. I think I might just go to bed.'

I hear David's chair scrape back and he walks to the door of the kitchen. He smiles.

'You're not looking so good,' he says, walking up to me. I jump as he raises a hand to gently touch my forehead. 'Go to bed, and have a good sleep. I'll see you in the morning.'

He kisses me on my sweaty forehead, and goes back to the dining table. 'This lasagne is great, by the way. I'll save you some for tomorrow,' he calls over his shoulder.

I turn, stunned, and drag one foot after the

other up the stairs towards my bedroom. As I go, I look back. The door to his study is still open, light from the hallway casting a ghostly glow into the room, and it reminds me of the memory stick, still unchecked, hidden among my socks.

I glance down the hallway, then shut my bedroom door behind me. I dig in the depths of my wardrobe, pulling out an ancient laptop from my old life, opening the lid and switching it on. The screen flickers, then dies, its battery long neglected.

Plugged in and working again, it boots up, and I look at the empty desktop, the memory stick clutched in my hand. It's a Pandora's box, an insight into my husband that once I wouldn't have wanted to see. But now, things are different.

I plug the memory stick into the USB port.

19

The old laptop rattles, ancient circuit boards trying to load the data. A small icon appears on the desktop — an image of a disk drive with 'DAVID' underneath. I click, and it whirrs, red lights flashing.

A new window appears, showing a long list of folders, all with two- and three-letter acronyms. I click on the top one, labelled AS, and it opens to show a screen of files, all random numbers, all ending .mov. I pick one, and double-click.

It's a video file, grainy and flickering. The screen shows nothing but black, and for a moment I am disappointed. Then a chink of light shines through and I can just make out a bit of movement, shadows in the darkness. A light is switched on, and I can see it's the master bedroom in our house, David's bedroom now, although there's nobody in shot. I squint and work out that the camera must be on top of the wardrobe. The shot is from above, capturing the bed and the bedside table on the left-hand side.

The door opens and David comes into view, and I gasp as I see him leading me by the hand. He glances directly into the camera for a second, then back at me. I am laughing. I am wearing red lacy lingerie, underwear I remember from way before Johnny was born, now shoved to the back of a drawer somewhere. My hair is longer, and even in these bizarre circumstances I note that I am in good shape. The video must be three or four years old.

I can't stop watching although I know what happens next. I remember this particular night, the first time David wanted to do something a bit more adventurous and teased me for being a prude. I was unsure — I can see this now in my face — but went along with it. Handcuffs, a blindfold, a bit of a slap here and there. Nothing extravagant, given what David has tried since.

My mind wanders back to the other files. AS — Annie Sullivan? Is this folder all about me? I click off the film, and select another few files at random. Some were taken in David's room, some in the spare room where I now sleep, but all are of me with David; different times, different positions, different props.

I hear a noise from downstairs and get up quickly, my heart beating hard, opening my bedroom door a fraction and glancing outside. I can hear the television has been turned on, and the sound of football drifts up the stairs.

I go back to the laptop. If I am AS, then who are all the other folders? There are at least twenty on this drive. My hand jumps to my mouth. I feel sick as I click on another; it opens to show five files, and my hand is shaking as I load one up.

It seems to be a hotel room, with bland furniture, generic artwork on the walls and a large double bed in the middle of the room. This time the camera angle is lower; the edge of something wooden takes up a centimetre at the bottom of the screen. A woman I don't recognise comes into shot, laughing and joking with David. She is young and confident, turning and kissing David, undoing his shirt and trousers while he pulls at her dress. They work through a variety of sexual positions, and after a while I fast-forward through the film. The other videos of PB are similar — same hotel room, same woman, but getting more and more adventurous: the handcuffs in one; in another they snort a line of cocaine. In the final one, he holds her hands above her head with one hand and slaps her round the face with the other. She leaves crying, her clothes balled up in her hands as she runs out of the room.

The video comes to an end, pausing on a blurry image of David's face, smiling as he turns away from the camera. I open the next, JK, and immediately see Jane, his pretty doe-eyed PA, in front of the camera. The background looks like an office at David's work, the blinds closed and the film taken from the angle of a desk, by a webcam on a laptop maybe. She turns around and David comes up behind her, one hand undoing his belt, the other groping under her skirt, making no effort not to be rough. I watch, stunned, as my husband fucks his PA as though she is little more than an object to him, a commodity to be used and taken as he wants. I watch the familiar expressions on his face change, then sag as he discards her and she rushes from the room.

More videos, more folders and files: different women, different hotels. My body is shivering and my cheeks are wet. I feel numb from what

I've seen, a tiny proportion of what I can only imagine the rest of the files must hold in their code. It isn't just one affair, one trip to a restaurant; it is many. He hasn't just slept with one woman; it is systematic, regular abuse — and the bastard records them all, to play back for his own pleasure whenever he feels like it.

As I click on the files, something niggles in my mind. I go back to the AS folder, the videos of me, and select a later film, ignoring the embarrassing display in front of me and instead studying the shot, the perspective of the camera. I glance up to the top of the wardrobe, to the small gap between the wardrobe and the ceiling, then back to the film. Grabbing a chair, I pull it across the carpet and move it to the wardrobe, pulling myself up so I am in line with the top. I can just reach into the gap, and I grope around in the dust, my fingers touching plastic. I grab it and pull it forward, but it's attached to something at the back, so I tug it round to the front of the wardrobe.

It's a camera. It's small and black, with a lens that takes up most of the front, and a long black cable coming out of the back. The cable that I must have caught with the vacuum cleaner all those months ago; It has been here all this time. Watching me. Monitoring me.

I suddenly feel very tired. I pull the cable out from the back of the camera and hear it drop behind the wardrobe. My face is aching. My eyes are dry from the light of the laptop. I eject the memory stick and close the lid, my mind still playing snippets on a loop. I stare at the camera again, barely able to make sense of what I've seen.

David's betrayals mount up into a sociopathic playbook; he bears no resemblance to the man I thought I married. I can't process the truth; my mind is a jumble of disconnected thoughts and memories. I hide the laptop under my bed and put the memory stick and the camera in the sock drawer with the letters. I feel tired, so very tired.

I fall into bed still clothed, and instantly disappear into a deep, bottomless sleep.

Blank

Annie opened her eyes to perfect white. She blinked for a moment, then looked down to her hands, her torso, her feet. She was wearing simple blue jeans and a white T-shirt, her feet bare. She was here, she was dreaming, but there was nothing around her, no floor, no ceiling, nothing. Her mind was blank. She was empty.

But she knew who she wanted to find.

She took her time, appreciating the calm and the sheer nothingness of her dream. She thought back to her childhood, to the places she had gone when her life seemed overcrowded and scary. A disused corridor at school — a patch of cold, grimy tiling, empty lockers and worn radiators where she could sit and read in peace. Becca's house, the chaos and noise from her family demonstrating the love and care within its four walls. And her local library, with its labyrinth of books, alternative worlds and escape within their pages.

Annie thought of that library now. Closing her eyes, she imagined it around her: the smell of the old books, the stamp of the librarian checking out a novel, the worn but comfortable chairs where she'd spend hours with nobody to disturb her. She opened her eyes and there it was, every detail she remembered, down to the little rows of Dewey Decimal numbers on the spines of the books.

She picked a book from the shelf and ran her finger over the pages. It was a simple hardback cookery book, but the act of holding it in her hands was soothing. It was nice to have something solid to look at, something to distract her.

She couldn't see Jack; she wasn't sure how she was going to find him. She felt a sudden panic swell in the pit of her stomach. Try another location, go somewhere else.

She moved. Conjuring up an image, she found herself at the edge of another park, this time at night, and stuffed with the stalls and rides of a fairground. A huge big wheel towered above her on her left, while the dodgems bashed and bumped on her right. A large cylinder twirled into the air, people standing in cages all around the edge, screaming as it spun and rose at ninety degrees. All around her bright lights flashed; she heard the thud of a bass line and the twinkle of a Wurlitzer jingle.

The noise and lights baffled her. Everything moved faster than she could comprehend, blurs of pinks and streaks of yellow. She moved slowly into the arena, and there he was — David. He was still wearing his black suit, waiting in a queue for a shoot-'em-up game. He hadn't seen her, his attention diverted as the dodgems stopped and the people spilled out, laughing and joking, jostling Annie to and fro. He moved away, towards the big wheel. She could tell by his movements he wasn't in control. He flowed, almost hovered as he moved. No hesitation, no thought, his subconscious in the driving seat.

And what a subconscious it was, truly outdoing itself, pulling together a woman dressed in a tight-fitting red dress, hair styled from the fifties, red lipstick, bright red nails. She stood square in the middle of the walkway, other dreamers needing to move to get round her. Dream David was staring. The woman saw him and slowly walked over, stopping and running a finger up his arm. His expression was transparent and dopey; this subconscious was being run by one organ and one organ alone. Her plump lips pursed as she whispered something in his ear, then she turned his face with her blood-red fingernails and kissed him.

Annie flinched as they locked themselves in a passionate embrace. All groping hands and sucking mouths, but nothing really compared to what she had just seen in real life, on the laptop. The woman whispered in his ear again, idly chewing on his ear lobe at the same time, and then hand in hand, they walked towards the big wheel, skipping the queue and getting straight on. Annie didn't follow them; she had seen enough for one night.

She looked around again, still no sign of Jack. 'Damn it,' she muttered under her breath.

She caught a sudden waft of an amazing hot, sugary smell, and turned to locate it. A fresh doughnut stall shone out behind her, the man inside tossing a bunch of freshly fried rings into the tray of sugar. She paid for a bag, enjoying the warmth seeping through to her now greasy fingers. She moved out of the way of the other fairground goers and took a seat on a bench to the side. She smiled, picking one of the hot gooey doughnuts out of the paper bag and taking a bite. It soothed her, filling her hollow shell of a body.

What now? Still no Jack, and she would have to get up soon to attend to Johnny. She imagined him in his cot, probably lying on his side with his feet tucked up close to his tummy. Rabbit would be clutched tight in his chubby little hand, his eyes screwed shut. His hair would be sticking up at angles, his cheeks a perfect glowing pink as he slept snug in his sleeping bag. A faint snore would be audible from his lips. She envied the sleep of the baby, so pure, unsullied by adult life. She wondered what Johnny dreamt of; whether she could find him one day here. Did he dream of chocolate buttons and his Rabbit, of Fireman Sam and Thomas the Tank Engine? Or was it monsters and scary things, of being alone and lost? If he did, he certainly didn't show it in the morning. She would ask Jack when she saw him.

She sighed and sat back on the bench. What a wasted night this was.

'That took you a while,' said a voice to her right, making her jump.

Jack was sitting next to her, smiling, the lights from the entrance to the roller coaster casting his face in an eerie shadow as they switched from pink to green. He reached over and took one of her doughnuts, handling it delicately between his thumb and forefinger.

'Jack! What happened, what did I do?'

'What were you thinking about before I appeared?'

Annie stopped for a moment. 'Johnny, and what he dreamt about. And then I thought I needed to ask you about it — is that it?'

'Yes, maybe.' He took a bite of the doughnut, chewed for a moment. 'It's different for everyone, I think, so whatever works for you.'

'And here you are.'

'Here I am.' Jack smiled again and Annie realised how much she had missed him. She had missed having someone to talk to who actually seemed interested in her, who made her a person in her own right. She hoped Adam could be a friend too one day, but she barely knew him at the moment. She was tired of being David's wife, or Johnny's mum; sometimes it was good to just be Annie. Even if she didn't truly know who Jack was.

'Tell me something about you,' she said. 'Where do you come from, what do you do?'

He smiled. 'I'm a software engineer. I write little twiddly bits of code and make computer programs. Is that what you expected?'

'I guess I saw you as a bit of a mad-scientist type, conducting experiments with strange women by night, and testing it all out on locked-up monkeys by day.'

'Mad engineer, maybe, but monkeys, no, sorry.' He grinned. 'I'm not that interesting.'

'Girlfriend, wife?' Annie asked.

'Girlfriend,' Jack said. 'Lizzie, been together two years.'

'Right,' Annie said, suddenly very interested in the life of this person she knew so little about. 'How do I know what you're telling me is true?'

Jack smiled. 'How do you know it's not?' He gestured at the scene in front of them. 'Nothing here is real, or so I'm telling you. How do you know that this is a dream?'

She pointed at the neon signs, a mess of bizarre lines and circles, every single word incomprehensible.

He finished the doughnut and wiped the sugar from his fingers. 'Just so long as you know.' He stood up and brushed the sugar from his coat. 'Thank you for the doughnut.' He gave a quick salute, two fingers of his right hand to his head, and faded from view.

Annie sat alone, the bustle of the fairground escalating, growing louder by the second. The flashing, the dazzle, the bombardment of colour. Too much of an assault on her already fried brain. She left and went back into the endless white, the blank nothingness, and then finally into a long, dreamless sleep.

20

In the morning I wake, and for a moment I forget. I forget who I am now and I look in confusion around the room. My head is still dozy from sleep, and I expect to be back in my old flat, floor strewn with clothes, discarded glasses and wrappers by the side of my bed, head fuzzy from a hangover and lungs aching from too many cigarettes. But then I hear a little voice in the next room and it all comes back to me — my life, my husband, my son.

I remember the smack around the face, the hidden letters, the snide comments and the belittling remarks. I remember the memory stick: the breasts, the buttocks, the blow jobs. The camera watching me, all this time. I sit on the edge of my bed and screw up my eyes. I'm not ready to deal with this now, to face this reality. Surely this is something that happens to other people. Not me, not this boring middle-class wife. I have no fucking idea what to do. And in the absence of an alternative, I do what I have to do, and prepare breakfast.

* * *

Later, after a morning of distractions and play, I walk into my bedroom and take in the crisply made bed, the dust-free windowsill and the evenly stacked pile of books. I turn round and look back into the hallway, where the curtains hang in the window, just the right shade of white against the painted walls, not a trace of cobwebs in the architrave, no dust on the skirting boards, carpets still showing the tracks from the vacuum that morning.

I move and stand in the doorway to Johnny's room. The curtains are closed as he takes his midday nap, the whole room hidden in shadows. I quietly walk in and stand over his cot. He is sleeping on his back, his arms thrown out above his head, Rabbit's ear clasped in his tiny grip. His cheeks are flushed, his hair tousled and messy. So much innocence and love wrapped up in one tiny precious bundle. My chest aches just looking at him.

I move around his room, opening drawers quietly and slowly gathering up two pairs of trousers, two pairs of socks and two T-shirts. A jumper joins the pile, along with five muslins and Johnny's spare coat. His baby blanket. His summer trainers.

I turn back into my own room, softly closing the door behind me, and open my wardrobe, removing a dress from its hanger and placing it on the bed. I open a drawer next to it and take out a pair of jeans, folding them in half and putting them on top of the dress. Next I take out three basic pairs of black cotton pants, then reconsider and put another two there, with five pairs of socks.

I'm moving slowly, almost on autopilot. A jumper. Two T-shirts. A scarf and a woolly hat. A pair of pyjamas for me, then back into Johnny's room to get some for him.

I'm moving faster now, and quickly run downstairs, pulling the sofa away from the cupboard door and digging out my old trundle case, a battered-looking thing with a broken strap. Dragging it upstairs, I pull off the old airport luggage tag, allowing myself a moment to think about the last time I used the case. Four years ago, on our honeymoon, when my husband seemed like a completely different man.

I still don't think about what I'm doing, I still don't let myself acknowledge what I'm considering. I carefully place each item in the case, filling it to the top, then throw in a few more bits and pieces for good measure. Toiletries: shampoo, conditioner, a spare toothbrush from the cupboard for me, and one for Johnny. A tube of moisturiser and a stick of mascara. A chequebook from a bank account I don't use any more. My engagement ring. Johnny's birth certificate. Our passports.

I stop, and sit heavily on the bed. I push the heel of my hands into my eyes, then open them, looking at the passports. Most of the pages in mine are blank, but a few hold the exciting reds and blues of a stamp from a foreign country. The trip to Los Angeles David and I took together, when he patiently hiked up to the Hollywood sign with me just because I was desperate to see it up close. The trip to Egypt where I got food poisoning and David sat by himself by the pool while I chucked my guts up in a five-star toilet, emerging flat-stomached and ready for the all-inclusive two days later. And the stamp for the Maldives — the blissful two weeks of our honeymoon. All that sex and lying around: reading books, talking, scorching our skin in the sun. All those memories, our life together: am I really prepared to throw it away? I wound David up, I made him angry. I just need to be more careful and follow the rules.

I tentatively move my fingers up to my face, and gently press on my right cheekbone. It's still tender, and I explore around the bruise, seeing how far it spreads. The redness has gone, replaced by a dirty-looking mark sweeping from the bridge of my nose, under my eye and along my cheekbone.

David took his cup of coffee with barely more than a murmur when he saw me this morning, but he hesitated, his eyes staying slightly too long on my face. He gave me a gentle kiss on the other side when he left but said no more about it. We moved on, the argument forgotten. But I noticed the door to the study was locked, once again forbidden territory.

There is a shout from Johnny's room. He yawns loudly and I hear the thump of his legs against the side of his cot as he gently wakes up and gets himself ready for the excitement of the afternoon. I envy the simplicity of his life. I can hear him now and I imagine him sitting in the semi-darkness, holding a conversation with Rabbit. I can make out sentences and words, mixed in with the garbled jargon of a two-year-old, commander of his world. Would I really take Johnny away from his home, his father, everything he has ever known? He is such a happy, easy-going little boy; what would become of him if I dragged him away?

I look at the suitcase, open in the middle of my bed. A few things spew out of it, a hotchpotch of belongings, suddenly looking inadequate just for me, let alone for a two-year-old as well. The case is small, too small. I push a jumper sleeve inside and tuck our passports into a pocket at the front. Maybe not now, I think, and close the lid, zipping it shut.

I pick up the case and open the door to my wardrobe, pushing my clothes aside and tucking it in behind a massive pile of shoes at the bottom.

Johnny's chattering has evolved into a regular shout of 'MUMMY MUMMY MUMMY,' desperate to get out and crack on with the day. I go into the room, and he laughs when he sees me, a big smile across his face. I open the curtains and peer out at the grey weather that has overtaken the springtime sun. No trips to the park today.

I turn back to Johnny and pull up the zip to get him out of his sleeping bag. A pair of chubby, wiggly legs pop out of the warmth.

As we go downstairs, Johnny ready for a busy afternoon of trains and tea parties, I glance back at my closed bedroom door. The packed suitcase and the memory stick lurk behind it, preying on the unease in my mind.

* * *

The day done, I retreat to my bedroom. I've already tidied the lounge, straightened the sofa cushions and lined up the coasters on the coffee table, all in a row, symmetrical and neat. The washing-up is done; David's wine glass has gone with him into his beloved study and I listen to him now, moving around in the room below me. I feel restless, my legs twitchy even before I take myself off to bed.

Insomnia is a problem that happens to other people; not me, not ever. I lie with my head resting comfortably on my pillow, warm under the duvet, window open to make sure I don't get too hot. Food in my belly, teeth clean, ready. But nothing. Not a flicker.

For the first time, I feel hesitant about going to find Jack. There's so much I can't reconcile, so many unanswered questions. Why has my subconscious thrown me Jack to talk to? Who is he? Why does he remind me so much of myself?

My head refuses to empty. It swims with images: Jack sitting on a deckchair on the beach, David screwing his PA, all those women, so many women. Johnny playing with Georgia. Adam.

What is it about Adam? I think about his arms as he pushed the swing earlier that week. Light hairs against the tan of his forearms, strong as he flexed his muscles, pushing Georgia as he chatted to me. His hair, dirty blonde, blowing in the warm breeze, falling messily onto his face. His eyes as he spoke to me, crinkling at the edges as he smiled. Those arms. Oh for Christ's sake.

I turn over in bed, trying to get comfortable. I can go anywhere in my dreams, but could I find a real person? I saw David, so how about someone else? I know where I want to go tonight. I want to see Adam.

I roll over onto my back and stare at the ceiling. Am I brave enough? I glance at the clock, glowing in the gloom. 12:56. He will definitely be asleep. Could I? Would it even be possible?

Only one way of finding out.

Marlboro Lights

As the bedroom drifted away, the park came into view. Annie's usual park; the starting point from which everything else had grown. She sat on her bench, watching the dog walkers, a couple picnicking on the grass, feeling the sun on her face. She closed her eyes and thought of Adam. How she had felt when she spoke to him, how he had looked at her, her feelings of regret, shame, interest, lust.

She opened her eyes. She was in a dark narrow corridor with rooms off at every angle, lots of people and music blaring. Some sort of house party. The wallpaper was patterned and dated, peeling off in strips, with posters stuck over the top. A bicycle leant against the radiator near the front door.

She could smell cigarette smoke, mixed with something else. A tinge of burnt leaves, something slightly sweet and herby. It smelt of misspent youth; cold evenings in the park, smoking illicit joints behind concrete public toilets.

She moved into the kitchen, the epicentre of any good party, stuffed full of people. She looked around and didn't recognise the room or anybody there. Someone had their head in the fridge, and a large bowl of something green and liquid sat on the counter next to her. The room hummed of old beer and sweaty bodies — more reminiscent of a student party than anything since adulthood. Plastic glasses and cheap decorations. Tiny bottles of inexpensive French beer, boxes of horrible sour-tasting wine.

The people around her were no more than mid-twenties. They had an air of carelessness about them: they drank alcohol with no worries about hangovers, and wore tight tops with no risk of excess chub. She moved out into the hall and took a look at her own reflection. Badly bleached hair, styled to within an inch of its life, eyeliner expertly applied but undoubtedly not subtle, and bright red lipstick. Yes, this was Annie in her twenties. She looked down at what she was wearing. Short denim skirt, white crop top, no bra! Look at that stomach, flat as a pancake. Long woollen cardigan thing over the top. Shockingly awful, but somehow it worked. She was bloody gorgeous.

Ha! she thought. If I am here, and about . . . what, twenty-two? I might as well enjoy it. She grabbed a plastic cup and a ladleful of whatever was in the green bowl and took a sip. She nearly choked. Advanced cocktail mixology it definitely wasn't.

She took a look around. Perhaps her skills had fallen short; perhaps it wasn't possible. Maybe Adam wasn't here at all. She scanned the kitchen again, and seeing nobody she knew, moved on to the garden.

Someone had rigged up some dodgy-looking fairy lights on a tree, and Annie could see figures dotted around the lawn. Some sat on the grass, some lying together, and a group at the back clustered around a rickety-looking table on a neglected paved area, healthy green weeds pushing through the gaps in the paving stones. Rather glum-looking stoners occupied the rusty chairs, passing a joint back and forth; one guy was smoking a cigarette. Adam.

Annie pulled a chair up next to him with a loud grating noise as the rusted metal dragged over the concrete. She sat down heavily and looked over. He seemed happy within himself, enjoying his cigarette, deep in his thoughts.

'Can I bum a fag off you?' she asked. It had been nearly a decade since she had quit, but she was back in her twenties and feeling brazen.

He nodded and reached into his shirt pocket, pulling out a box of Marlboro Lights. He passed one to her and held out a lighter, flicking it into a flame with expert precision. She leant in to light the cigarette and took a deep breath. Her head was instantly fuzzy with the unfamiliar toxins. She sat back in her chair and exhaled slowly.

'Who are you here with?' Adam asked. 'Are you a friend of Fiona's?'

'Honestly, I'm not sure,' Annie said, and he laughed. 'I just sort of found myself here.'

'Enjoying it?'

'It's improving,' she replied and looked across at him.

Like her, he had decreased in age, ending up, she guessed, about mid-twenties. His face was smooth and unlined, his jaw strong with a trace of stubble on his chin, and he had a thick head of hair. There was a youthful look about him, full of hormones and energy, his eyes bright. His shirt was rolled up to his elbows, showing his forearms, and they were just as muscular and desirable as they were fifteen years on.

He leant forward and stubbed his cigarette out in the pot plant in front of them. It had obviously been doubling as an ashtray all evening, judging from the brown fag ends around it.

'Do you fancy a drink?' he asked, and gestured back towards the house. Annie nodded and stubbed her cigarette out in the same way.

He held out his hand and pulled her up from her chair. To her surprise, he held on and led her back into the house. Through the kitchen full of people, grabbing two beers on the way, through the sitting room, where people lay snogging in the darkness, out into the hallway, and the staircase. He never let go of her hand, his warmth beating into her.

Away from the party, the music was quieter, the doors and walls muffling the familiar retro sounds of Oasis whining on. Adam sat down near the top of the stairs, and patted the space next to him, screwing the cap off one of the beers and offering it to her.

'So what shall we do?' he asked her, a grin forming on his lips. She wondered what it would be like to kiss them.

'Talk?' she said quietly, suddenly scared.

She didn't have time to deliberate any longer. Adam took her chin in his hand and turned her to face him. With a smile he leant in and kissed her. Gently, but deliberately. He tasted of beer and cigarettes and something else. Annie liked it.

A few people climbed past them on the stairs as they behaved like the couple of teenagers they weren't far from being. They snogged like they were twenty again, before things got complicated and marriage and kids were thrown into the equation, when snogging was done just for the fun of it. She could feel his hands in her hair, on her neck, her waist, and then on her boobs, her bum, under her clothes. Annie did the same, sneaking her way under his shirt and making the most of the time she had. Here was a body untainted from hours in boring boardrooms with too many pastries. A body before all that pesky male testosterone got involved and things became too hairy. Smooth, muscled, taut. She felt her own body warm into him, moving with the same motion as his. She wanted to be a part of him, she really wanted him naked.

He moved away from her.

'Shall we find somewhere to go?' he asked. His voice was quiet and husky.

Annie nodded, not trusting herself to speak.

He took her hand again and they went up the stairs, trying one door after another. First the bathroom, and then a bedroom, both already occupied, their residents glancing up guiltily as they were disturbed. Then another door, this time quiet and dark, and nobody anywhere near. It seemed to be a student house, and this was somebody's room. *Pulp Fiction* and *Reservoir Dogs* posters dominated the walls, a huge triple CD player taking up space on the desk, next to a pile of academic textbooks. There was a clip frame on the wall full of photographs of grinning teenagers, and a more formal frame on the desk of a girl and her mother and father.

Annie felt Adam's hands on her waist from behind her, creeping up her top again, cupping her breasts. She could feel his warm skin against hers; this was everything she wanted, but she needed to see him, to feel his eyes on hers, his lips on hers.

She turned round, forcing him to look at her, and he smiled, before kissing her again. She ran her hands through his hair and over his body, every inch of it different from David's, every moment a different experience, something to relish.

The desk seemed sturdy, so she pushed backwards, sitting the edge of her bum next to the textbooks and a pot of biros. She tried not to giggle, the experience was so surreal. This was a dream, but was it Adam's dream too? Poor man would wake up in the morning and would remember — what? Not a lot? He certainly wouldn't know it had all been down to her, that she had orchestrated it.

Reassured, she kissed him again, pulling him forward and fumbling with his belt and the buttons on his trousers. She hitched her skirt up and pulled her knickers down and off, over her trainers. He pushed into her and they moved together, her Converse locked round his waist, holding tight onto him, her face pushed into his shirt. The smell of Marlboro Lights, sweat and sex was overwhelming.

When it was over, both of them half dressed,

sweaty, gasping for breath, he rested his head on her shoulder, Annie still sitting on the desk, Adam still inside her. After a second, he lifted his eyes and said, 'Nice to meet you.'

She grinned. 'Nice to meet you too. Now should we get off this poor girl's desk? She has to work here.'

Laughing, he pulled out and at the same time grabbed a tissue from a box nearby, expertly mopping himself down and removing a condom Annie had no memory of him putting on. We don't get pregnant in dreams, do we, she thought, but it was nice to know he was a responsible boy.

He screwed it up and put it in his pocket as he adjusted himself and pulled up his trousers. Then he held out his hand and she shuffled off the desk, yanking her top and skirt down, her knickers back up.

A girl opened the door, and stopped in her tracks.

'Oi, who are you? This is my room,' she said, her words slurred and broken.

Adam held up his hands. 'Our mistake, we're just leaving,' he replied, and grabbed Annie, pulling her away.

Out in the hallway, he kissed her on the lips. 'I have to go.'

'Really?' Annie said. 'That's a pity, no time for one more drink?'

'Drink?' he laughed. 'Is that — '

Wakeupwakeupwakeupwa —

21

I can't breathe, I can't breathe. There is something stopping me. I try to open my eyes but there is only dark. I try to reach out but my arms are pinned to my sides. Something heavy is on top of me. I smell laundry detergent and my own sweat, my own fear.

My lungs ache. My body strains to get oxygen. The pressure on the tops of my arms continues, pushing down. I frantically kick my legs, but I can't gain any purchase on the soft cotton of the bed. I am confused; my brain can't understand what is going on. I am losing strength; my legs grow heavy.

And then it stops, with a cool breeze on my face and an intake of sweet fresh air. I gasp and take in a few deep breaths, my body straining to inhale as much as possible. Whatever was on top of me has moved, my arms are free, and I push myself up, eyes watering and vision blurry.

A light snaps on and I am blind. I blink repeatedly, but only see flashes of bright light. I am dizzy from the shock of taking in so much air; I gulp and hyperventilate, slumping back on the bed.

Slowly my vision returns to normal and my breathing slows down. I wipe the tears from my eyes and look around.

I am in my bedroom, in my bed. My duvet is thrown around me; my legs are tangled up in it.

A pillow lies to my left, discarded. David is standing to my right, his hands at his sides. He is wearing his normal night-time garb of a T-shirt and shorts.

'David? What . . . what is going on, what happened?' I am still confused; my brain can't seem to make sense of it.

'What,' he hisses, 'is this?'

I look to where he is pointing, and see my case. Packed and ready to go. He has opened it and flung the contents out onto the floor.

Everything thuds into place. The case. The pillow. David.

'I . . . I . . . ' I stutter, still trying to comprehend what he was doing. He was trying to kill me. He was sitting on top of me, suffocating me with a pillow.

'Why have you been packing, Annie?' he says, quieter now, his voice serious and full of threat. 'Where are you going?'

'Holiday,' I say weakly. 'For when we all go away.'

David laughs. 'All go away? Seriously? We never 'all go away'.' He says it in a high-pitched voice, mocking me. 'Don't even fucking think of walking out that door.' He moves closer to me, and I jump backwards in the bed, still tangled in the discarded duvet. 'You are mine, and he' — he jabs a finger in the direction of Johnny's bedroom — 'is mine.'

He leans in and grabs my chin, holding it tightly between his thumb and forefinger, pulling me towards him. My eyes are wide, my body frozen.

'You go and I will track you down. You will never see your darling little boy again.' He says these last few words staccato, spitting them out as he holds my face in his hand, shaking it back and forth with the force of each syllable.

He pushes me back, then leans forward and slaps me across the face. The force of his hand shoots through my jaw and I feel my teeth rattle. I fall back. My legs scrabble and I propel myself to the far side of the bed, as far away from him as I can get.

He stares at me for a moment, revulsion on his face.

'You need me. You need someone telling you what to do, running your life. Your mother did it first and now you have me.' He pauses. 'Do you understand?'

I am still frozen, paralysed.

'DO YOU UNDERSTAND ME?' he shouts, his eyes bloodshot and bulging.

I nod. 'Yes,' I say.

I can feel tears running down my cheeks. He nods at me, bends down and takes the two passports and my engagement ring from the front pocket of the case. He waves them at me, then snaps off the light, plunging the room into darkness.

I fall back onto the bed, my head bouncing on the mattress where my pillow should be. I can feel my lungs contracting, my heart pounding in my chest. I feel alone, and scared. Everything I thought I knew is collapsing around me. For a moment I want Jack there to soothe and protect me, and then I realise I need someone real, someone flesh and blood and solid.

My hand reaches to my phone, and without thinking, I dial the last number to have been inputted into the memory. I hear the phone ring, and then a male voice answers — sleepy and disorientated. Blood rushes in my ears. I am still hyperventilating, trying to talk but only managing to exhale deep racking sobs down the phone.

The voice is awake now and I can hear him shouting my name. I choke out another sob and the line goes dead.

I hold the phone in my hand, staring at the glowing screen. What the hell have I just done? I press the call button again, but this time nobody answers, the call goes to voicemail. I redial, willing him to pick up.

Panic takes over as I jump out of bed, pulling the curtains aside to look out into the blackened street. For a while, nothing, then through the darkness I see a figure coming up the path and into our driveway. I rush out of my room and down the stairs, as quietly as my thumping feet will allow.

I open the front door, edging the bolt as gently as I can, and see Adam's face come into view. He's out of breath from his sprint, wearing no more than a T-shirt, a pair of jeans and trainers.

'Annie! Are you okay?'

I put one finger to my lips to shush him and he lays a hand gently on my arm. 'What's going on? I was worried, you sounded so upset. I came as soon as I could.'

'You have to go,' I whisper, my voice panicked. 'You have to go now. David — '

'David what?' A hand pulls me back into the hallway. David opens the door wide and stands in front of me, a human shield. Adam takes an automatic step back, then, sensing the source of my fear, squares up to David, his shoulders back, legs apart.

David does the same, taking up the entire space of the doorway. Two stags, gearing up for a fight. Both men standing at six foot, broad shoulders, hands balling into fists.

'I suggest you leave now,' David growls.

'I just want to know that Annie's okay.'

'I'm fine, Adam, please go,' I plead, as David pushes me further back into the house.

'I'll call the police,' Adam says.

'Go ahead. This is my fucking house and you are trespassing. I could beat you into a pulp right here, and the police wouldn't bat an eyelid.' David sounds eerily calm, his voice measured and low. He takes a step forward out of the front door, and Adam backs off, holding his hands up, palms out.

'Okay, okay.' He tries to look past David, but I shrink back into the darkness of the hallway, mute and ashamed.

I hear the rustle of feet on gravel as Adam retreats, and David closes the front door slowly, the lock clicking back into place. My feet are frozen to the spot as he turns to face me. I start to gabble, words falling out of my mouth in a waterfall of apologies.

He is shaking, his face red and his eyes bulging. The veins pop out of his forehead as he puts his face close to mine. His hands find my neck and close, pushing me up against the wall.

'You ever pull a fucking stunt like that again, you whore,' he is talking very slowly and deliberately, his hand pushing against my throat, 'and I will kill your little boyfriend, and then I will kill you.'

I am starting to get dizzy; I can't breathe, yet my hands stay motionless by my sides. I'm resigned to my fate; I know this is it. My whole life of crappy choices, reduced to this final moment, dead in my own hallway. My mind plays out a silent apology to Johnny: I'm sorry for leaving you here, little man, I'm sorry for leaving you alone.

But then I'm breathing again, coughing and choking, discarded in a heap at the bottom of the stairs. David stands over me, then rotates his shoulders and his neck, clicking joints back into place. He bends down and pushes against my forehead so my bloodshot eyes are looking up at him.

'You're mine,' he says, and I nod.

* * *

I drag myself up the stairs on all fours, and crawl into bed. Every part of me is shaking as I pull the duvet over me and roll into a ball, my knees up to my chest, crying silently.

The clock blinks: 4:02.

22

The next morning, David comes downstairs with coffee in one hand, BlackBerry in the other. He puts his empty cup on the sideboard, picks up his jacket and walks out. He ignores his breakfast, waiting for him on the table: two fried eggs, two slices of bacon, two slices of brown buttered toast. One glass of orange juice, ice cold. He doesn't say a word to Johnny or me; he doesn't even glance in our direction.

We don't talk about it, we never talk about it. What is there to say? The gradual creep, the changing tide. I should never have called Adam, that mistake was on me, and my insides screw up just thinking about it. David has never tolerated competition, even when it is against his own son.

My mind goes back two years, to when Johnny was a tiny baby, barely out of hospital. He'd had a bad night, squalling and screaming, unable to sleep, refusing to feed, and I'd sat in the bedroom, tears rolling down my cheeks, impotent and useless as he'd thrashed with his furious baby fists. Hour after hour had rolled by, and at last, at seven a.m., he'd collapsed out of exhaustion. Now he was sleeping in his Moses basket in the living room as I made breakfast for David.

I put two plates on the table — the same for both of us, eggs, bacon, toast — then gently lowered myself into a chair, the incision from my healing C-section causing me to wince. David glanced at both plates, then across at me. I must have looked a sight — face puffy from lack of sleep, scraped-back hair, oversized T-shirt and old maternity trousers — and he frowned.

'This is late,' he said. 'How am I going to get to work on time if my breakfast is late?'

'Perhaps you could make it yourself next time, if it's so bloody important to you,' I snapped back.

He paused, put his cutlery down and stared at me. From the silence of our kitchen I heard a car drive past outside, its radio blaring. David looked down at my breakfast, then placed two fingers on the edge of the plate and slowly pushed it across the table. He left it teetering on the edge for a moment, and then, with one final push, it fell, spinning, crashing in a pile of crockery splinters, orange yolk and bright red ketchup.

The noise woke Johnny up again, and he started to cry.

'You shouldn't be eating this stuff now,' David said, calmly. 'It's time you lost some weight.' He took a mouthful of egg, the yolk dripping down his chin. 'And I can't sleep with all the screaming. I think you should move into the spare room; you can do all your baby stuff in there.' He pointed back towards the living room, where Johnny still lay bawling. 'Sort the baby out; what sort of mother are you?'

I stood up to go to Johnny, but David put his arm out in front of me. 'Clear that mess up first,' he said.

I stopped, my mouth hanging open. David's gaze didn't waver, and I saw something in him I hadn't noticed before: a lack of hesitation, a certainty in his manner that made me uneasy. I picked up a cloth and knelt down slowly, my C-section wound screaming. David looked down at me, on my hands and knees, while Johnny howled in the next room, and pointed with his fork towards the newspaper on the counter top.

'Pass me the *FT*, won't you?' he said.

* * *

The front door slams, dragging me back to the moment, and I hear the BMW start up and drive away into the distance. I release my trembling hands from their grip on the kitchen table and breathe out, all in a rush.

At the time, I didn't like sleeping in separate rooms; it felt like a divorce of sorts, a failure in our marriage. But it was easier with Johnny and it meant David could have a good night's sleep. And then it simply stayed that way — even after Johnny slept through the night. David didn't mention it, and then, one day, I realised I didn't want him to. Something had changed.

I look up and see Johnny staring at me from his chair. Breakfast finished, he is waiting quietly, taking in the expression on his mummy's face, reflecting it on his own. His bottom lip quivers, and he reaches for Rabbit, left to the side of his high chair.

I force a smile onto my face and pick him up, pulling him towards me. For a moment I get a waft of his smell, and hold him close, taking in his warmth. His pudgy little arms go round my neck, and he rests his head on my shoulder.

'Hugs, Mummy,' I hear him say from my neck. He is warm and sticky, and beautiful and reassuring.

I stand in that kitchen — the glorious, perfect kitchen, with the American fridge freezer, the blender, coffee machine and six-slice toaster — and watch my son toddle out into the lounge, clutching Rabbit. He pauses for a moment, looking at the floor, then crouches down, his hand outstretched to something small in front of him. He touches it, and I see a spider scuttling off, darting this way and that, then stopping, trying to be invisible. Johnny laughs, his gurgling belly laugh, and stands to go after it, stopping slowly where the spider has stopped and reaching out a small finger. The spider, sensing the danger of a large toddler, legs it under the sofa and Johnny laughs again, standing up and turning back to me in the kitchen.

'Gone now,' he smiles. 'Spider.'

Johnny doesn't care about eight-piece dining sets or special bowls for chips and dips. He doesn't care about what James at the office thinks or how much Daddy's car cost. He finds a spider hilarious and a piece of paper and a biro entertainment.

A tear rolls down my cheek and I brush it away. He needs his mummy; he needs to be safe. He is so innocent. How can I let him grow up in this house? How can we stay?

I pick up Johnny's bowl and spoon. I put them

in the sink, using the cloth to wash them up. I place them on the draining board. I dry them up, then put them away, wiping my hands afterwards and folding the tea towel carefully.

I pick up my bag, full of the usual essentials — nappies, wet wipes, wallet, spare muslin, two plastic cars — and I put Johnny's shoes and coat on him. I sit on the stairs and put on my own trainers and coat, then pick up Rabbit and coax Johnny to leave the house.

I start the car and point it towards the motorway. I don't think. I drive away from the house, north. North up the M3, the A34, the M40, the A43. Anything that says north, I take. We eventually stop on the M1, three hours from home. There's only so much sitting in a car a small boy can take. We climb out and make our way towards the grubby lights of the Welcome Break service station.

* * *

For a moment I stop and look around the room. A tired-looking mum nurses her tiny baby, her overexcited toddler bashing the floor with a small plastic Minion. On the other side of me, a scary-looking man with a skinhead and tattoos sits in sombre silence with his overweight girlfriend, the two of them concentrating on eating the burgers in front of them.

'More?' Johnny asks, and I break off another piece of my cake, nut-free, placing it on his plate. I pick up my cup of tea and take a tentative sip.

The chair is green plastic and worn. A line of

dead black flies lie upside down on the windowsill to my left. The table was sticky when we arrived and I carefully wiped it down with a wet wipe. The PVC windows are covered in condensation, their double-glazing blown. Disenchanted employees patrol the tables, wiping grumpily and ineffectively, moving trays slowly back to the kitchen, covered in paper and cold chips.

I lean back in my chair and it moves too much, in a way that makes me think it's going to fall apart. Johnny has finished his cake and has transferred his affections back to his box of raisins, digging into it with his tiny fingers. Triumphantly he picks out the last one and shows it to me, discarding the box on the floor in front of one of the employees, who scowls.

'Thank you,' I say sweetly, and the man moves away without a word, mop in hand.

Service stations are, by nature, transitional. You don't stay long. You're in, then out, and back to where you're trying to go. Which is where? I pick up my phone and google *women's refuge centres Birmingham,* clicking on a website full of smiling women and their kids.

I look over at Johnny, happily playing with his water cup, turning it over and letting it drip on to his high chair. He looks happy, bashing his hand in and out of the water. He is my boy, and nothing else matters.

I think of the beaming smile that transforms his face when he sees me come into his room in the morning. Nobody else gets a smile like that. The soft warmth of his little hand when he reaches up to put it in mine. The sudden realisation that only I know what he likes to eat for breakfast. I know which specific one he means when he says 'dinosaur book', and only I can translate his strange jumbled jargon into what he's trying to tell me. How unhappy would Johnny be if I wasn't around? Who would kiss his knee better when he fell over?

David has money, he has contacts, but more importantly, he's determined and doesn't like to lose. I walk out today and that would be it. His smug face would be on the news, talking about kidnapped children and dangerous wives. He would find us, and he would take Johnny. Best case, social services wouldn't know who to believe and Johnny would end up in care with strangers.

It would be my childhood all over again. I remember the loneliness, the strange people that came to the house who I knew not to trust, the official-looking women with their clipboards, sitting on the edge of our sofa. I can't do that to my boy.

'Home now?' says Johnny.

I nod, slowly.

There has to be another way. We leave and get into the car, ready for the long drive south. I will think of something. I won't let my little boy down. It isn't over yet.

As I drive, tears roll quietly down my cheeks. I am angry with myself for getting in this position again. I escaped once and now, somehow, here I am, life on repeat. Prisoner to the person I loved, helpless and trapped in the very place I am supposed to feel safe. How have I been so stupid?

* * *

I pull into our driveway and the walls close in. I switch off the ignition and Johnny twitches in his car seat, keen to get out and play with his toys. For a moment, I can't bring myself to open the car door. I sit frozen as he complains.

What I believed to be the marriage of my dreams has turned into a living nightmare. And slowly it occurs to me. I don't move. I stay in the driving seat, my hands motionless on the steering wheel, my brain whirring and processing the little snippets offering a glimmer of hope. What if there *is* a way out? What if I look beyond the obvious, beyond the land of the living? If I can't solve the problem while I am awake, what can I do when I am asleep?

23

The door slams, followed by silence. I take a deep breath and hold it, my heart pounding in my chest. Slamming doors are not a good sign, but if the briefcase is put down lightly, things could be okay.

We have been home a few hours, and Johnny is sitting in his high chair, a spoonful of spaghetti bolognese close to his lips. For such a messy dinner, for once he is doing quite well, the tomato sauce only slightly smudged round his mouth. He pauses when he hears his father, waiting for a cue from me. I am standing across from him at the kitchen counter, knife in hand, preparing the vegetables for our dinner.

I hear a loud thud as David's briefcase hits the door at the bottom of the stairs, thrown from a distance, and I reach across to Johnny in an instant reaction, wiping the red stains off as best I can. I take another deep breath and try to remain calm. Dinner is prepared and Johnny is clean, tidy and quiet, as am I.

David hurls open the kitchen door, bashing it against the wall, and stomps into the room.

'Fucking shareholders, fucking imbeciles who don't have a clue about what the fuck they are doing,' he shouts. I reach up into the cabinet and pull down a wine glass as he picks out a bottle of red. 'Honestly, it's a wonder I make them any money.'

I murmur something quiet and soothing, at a loss for the right words to say.

'I'm in charge,' he rages. 'Me! Yet I get called into my own boardroom to answer a whole load of fucking stupid questions to make sure they are happy. Christ! I have better things to do with my time. And then they have the audacity to question my answers and say I'm being flippant. Flippant! Of course I'm being flippant, they're fucking stupid people with fucking stupid questions.'

'What did you say?' I ask, opening the bottle quickly and pouring him a glass.

'I did what I'm paid to do,' David says, and stops, peering into the glass. He sticks his finger in. 'What, dearest wife,' he says quietly, with a sneer, 'is this?' He holds out the finger, with the tiniest piece of something brown on the end of it.

'David, I'm so sorry, let me sort that out.' I go to take the glass away from him, desperate to dispose of the offending piece of cork.

He pulls it back, out of my reach.

'This is a 2011 Château Haut-Brion. Do you know how much this costs?'

'No, I'm sorry, David.'

'Fucking seven hundred pounds a bottle. And you've fucked it in one quick move by getting fucking cork in it.' He throws his wine glass into the sink and it smashes; pieces of glass flying close to Johnny, red wine splashing like blood across the white ceramic.

'Careful, David,' I say instinctively, as Johnny starts to cry, the noise scaring him.

In a second, David is up close to my face, eyes

bulging and nostrils flaring. 'Don't you tell me what to do. You are my wife!' he spits. 'You do not tell me what to do!'

'I'm sorry — ' I start, then stop as the back of David's hand smacks across my face. It makes my head spin round, my teeth clatter together, my hair fall over my face. He grabs the top of my arm and pulls me round roughly so I am facing away from him, pushing me over the kitchen counter.

'You're all out to fuck with me,' he shouts, grabbing the back of my neck and pushing me forwards, my face pressed roughly into the chopping board, my arms trapped behind me. 'I am in control, me! Only me!'

I can't see much: the outline of the carrots I was chopping, the knife next to them and the spice rack in the distance. I am turned away from Johnny, my cheek pressed into the hard wood, David's hand on my neck, pushing me down. I can hear Johnny crying, properly now, and imagine his face, screwed up and red, mouth open and wide, as he watches what is going on, not understanding, just wanting his mum.

I hear a metallic chink, and feel David's hands roughly pulling up my skirt and pulling down my knickers. Material rips, skin chafes, and I gasp in shock as he rams himself into me, bashing, pushing, forcing his way in. My hands flap uselessly behind me, my head pushed down, hair over my face, nose running, tears obscuring my vision. He thrusts against me, not caring what damage he does, and it hurts, it really hurts, more than it has ever hurt before. This is nothing new, but he has never been so severe, so determined to punish, to use me as something to fuck and make me know my place.

Johnny's crying has risen to a scream, and I can hear the plastic scrape of his high chair as I imagine him trying to get out, to get away. I feel the bile rise inside me. I want to be sick. The pressure on my neck makes it hard for me to breathe. My anger grows as the pain increases. I feel something wet run down the inside of my leg, and through the haze, I realise I can move my arm, bit by bit, each time he withdraws and bashes into me again, getting closer and closer to the knife on the counter top. A knife newly sharpened.

Fuelled by anger and fury and pain and survival and the overriding urge to protect my tiny son, I push and reach. The handle is inches from my fingers. I imagine myself gripping it and flaying round, random, panicked, determined to make contact with something, anything, to make it stop. It feels so real, I see an arc of red, David's shocked face, and can imagine warm, sticky blood on my fingers.

But then with one final thrust, David hurls me against the counter and lets go of my neck. My legs are wobbly and weak and I fall to the floor, coughing, back to reality, the knife clattering out of my hand. David stands above me, clutching his penis in front of my face, small drips of cum glistening on the end.

'You should clean me up while you're down there, you bitch,' he spits, but then turns, pulling his trousers up. 'Sort out this fucking child,' he says, standing by the kitchen door. 'I'm going out. The sight of you makes me sick.'

The front door slams, and I drag myself upright, adjusting my clothing, then crawl over to my shaking son and pull him out of the high chair into my arms.

We sit on the kitchen floor, Johnny and I, both stunned into silence, Rabbit now clutched to his chest and Johnny clutched to mine. We sit there surrounded by the mess, the glass, and red wine, until the pain subsides, replaced by something stronger, something more permanent.

'He's going to go soon, Johnny, don't you worry,' I say, stroking his hair, my arms tight around him. 'He'll be gone soon.'

Winter's gloom

She found him sitting on a bench overlooking the sea. He was wearing a large black overcoat, the collar pulled up to his ears, covering his mouth and half his face. His hair stuck out the top, curly and unruly in the sea wind. He was watching the passers-by, a slight smile on his face. She sat down next to him, pulling her own coat tightly around her.

'Do you ever wonder about all of this?' Jack said, not turning to her or acknowledging her arrival with even a hello. 'Why are we able to control what we do, but they can't?' He shook his head. 'They don't have a clue.'

Annie listened to him with barely a flicker of interest. She knew what he meant, she had often wondered the same thing herself, but she didn't care right now. They looked out from the bench to the sand, thick and wet, and the dark forbidding sea, tossed with huge waves. The grand pier stood to their left, overlooking them all. The pink neon from the arcade shone out, a modern lighthouse in the winter's gloom.

'How come we realise we are dreaming, but they don't?' He frowned. 'Think what they could do. Think where they could go.'

'You know you said that if you die in your dreams, you might die in real life?'

He turned to her for the first time since she had joined him. 'Yes?' he said tentatively.

'How can we find out if that's true?'

He looked at her and studied her face closely. 'Why?'

'If you killed someone in their dream, would they die?'

He raised an eyebrow. Slowly, he asked again: 'Why?'

'Because I want to kill my husband.'

Part Three

The test

'I want to kill my husband.'

Jack took a deep breath and studied Annie's face.

'Right,' he said. He didn't ask why.

'Is it possible?'

He paused for a moment. 'Do you want to hear my theory?' he asked, and Annie nodded. Jack turned back to the people rushing along the promenade, braced to the wind. 'I tried early on to interact with others, to influence people in the dream with me. But they weren't like you and me, they were lost in their own heads. I could move them a bit, if it was something fun, but otherwise it was impossible. I couldn't change their minds from the path they were following.' Annie stayed quiet. Jack turned on the bench to face her, slotting one of his legs under the other. 'I think it will be hard to do something that someone doesn't want to do — something their subconscious won't like.'

'Isn't our subconscious the same as us?' Annie asked.

He screwed his face up. 'Not really. The subconscious is more concerned with the basics — food, water. Think of it as a survival mechanism. Have you ever noticed that in your dreams you wake up before you hit the ground, or if something is chasing you, they will never catch up?'

Annie nodded.

'That's your subconscious protecting you. It won't take the risk that you might die. Because if you die, it will die.' He shrugged. 'That's my guess, anyway.'

'So can I do this?'

He pushed his hair out of his face with a sweep of his long fingers. He looked at her for a long time, then frowned. 'You really want to?'

'Yes.' Annie was sure.

'Then you will have two problems: your subconscious won't let you do anything nasty to someone, and the other person's won't let anything nasty happen to them. So you'll have to make it sneaky, and do it fast, so he's not expecting it.' He rubbed his chin with his hand. 'And finally, we don't know if it will work.'

He reached over and slipped his hand underneath her upper arm, twisting the soft, unprotected skin between her elbow and her armpit. She jumped, pushing his hand away.

'Ow!' she said. 'Why did you do that?' She rubbed her arm furiously, trying to make the sting go away.

'A little test,' Jack said. 'When you wake up tomorrow morning, let's see if you've got a bruise there. You should, it was hard enough.'

It started to rain, big droplets making small indents in the sand. Jack produced a red and white umbrella and held it over them, protecting them from the downpour.

'So how could you do that to me?' Annie asked. 'Assuming you're not some sort of sadist who enjoys pinching people?'

'I convinced myself it was for your own good, so my subconscious was happy.'

They sat for a moment, looking out to the ocean. Large, ominous black clouds had formed on the horizon, blending the line from sea to sky. A couple passed on the promenade in front of them, riding the wave of their dream, moving effortlessly in the way she had seen so many times before.

'So I have to tell my subconscious that David being dead is a good thing for me?'

'Don't you know that already?' Jack said, turning to her again. 'Or why would you be here?'

24

The alarm goes off with its usual shrill, and I jump awake, my heart thumping. Outside, it's still dark, the birds haven't started their rude chirping, and the rest of the street is sound asleep. Exactly where I should be, I think. How different things would be if . . . I sit up quickly with a jolt. Reaching over to silence the buzzing, I flick the light on and blink in the sudden illumination. Slowly I wait for my eyes to adjust, then I pull my arm free of the covers and twist it round to see if anything lies underneath. It feels sore and tender where I am pulling at it, but I can't see a bruise, just pale, pink flesh.

My heart sinks, and then I feel silly. Such a ridiculous thought — so much for Jack's theory. Neither of us knows anything about how this dream thing works, and at the end of the day, that's all it is. Dreams don't really come true. Not for me.

I fall back in the bed, lying there for a moment. Dread floods my body. Johnny and I are still here, we're still stuck, with no way to escape. Nothing but this man, this life, this fear, for the next twenty, thirty, forty years.

I pull myself out of bed, sliding my slippers onto my feet. Even with summer round the corner, in my light T-shirt and pyjama trousers the house feels freezing. I go downstairs, flicking the kettle on and overriding the heating.

So morning duties, here we go. Breakfast for the boy, breakfast for the man. Two fried eggs, two slices of bacon, two slices of brown buttered toast. At least if the dream won't kill him, perhaps the cholesterol will. One glass of orange juice, ice cold. Coffee: fresh and hot, black, no sugar. I pad up the stairs quietly, open the door and place the coffee by the side of David's bed. The room is still in darkness, and a stale smell fills the air. Male sweat, alcohol, garlic, all compressed into a noxious fug. David is lying on his back, his mouth open, a loud snore emitting from his lungs. I close the door behind me quickly.

For a moment I stand at Johnny's door, my ear to the gap, listening to the contrast of my son's light breathing. I feel my heartbeat return to normal, and decide to let him sleep for a while longer.

Lay the table, ready for the both of them. Weetabix for me, bread in the toaster, ready for Johnny.

Make tea.

Tidy up the living room. Straighten the sofa cushions; pick up the red wine glass, the whisky tumbler and the finished bottle. Put his laptop in his briefcase and leave it by the front door. Straighten the coasters on the coffee table, all in a row, lined up with the edge of the table. Symmetrical, neat.

As I hear the shower start, the baby monitor next to me springs to life. A little chirp, then more chatter fills the usual hiss, making the blue lights dance. Johnny is lying with his legs vertical up the side of his cot, Rabbit clutched in his paws, his little eyes shining in the dark. He is always pleased to see me, and this morning he claps his hands with delight.

He smiles, a cheeky little grin that lights up my day. That grin can see Johnny through any of his mischief, make me forgive him anything: hands in the spaghetti hoops, a thrown train, days when his only word seems to be *no*.

I get him dressed and go downstairs. I put him in his high chair. I take a quick swig of my tea, now practically cold.

I hear footsteps on the stairs, and feel myself physically recoil, my body hunched. David walks into the kitchen, face looking down, staring at his phone. He makes a call and finishes his coffee in the other hand. I take a step back, turning away. I want to be invisible; I don't want him to see me, to talk to me. I can't bear it if he touches me.

Johnny watches him silently while I butter the toast, trying to seem normal.

David hangs up and tosses the phone into his pocket. He picks up his breakfast and eats it with a fork, plate balanced on the palm of his hand. Shovelling it in, like a peasant from the Dark Ages.

The plate is returned to the table, fork tossed nearby, and he turns his attention to Johnny, who is still staring. 'Be a good boy,' he says. 'Don't let anyone give you any shit.' He laughs at his joke and turns to me. 'Mother is coming over on Thursday night to celebrate her birthday. She's going to phone and tell you what she wants you to cook.' No question, just a certainty that that is what's happening. 'I'm eating out tonight, so don't prepare dinner.' I nod. 'And what the hell have you done to your arm? Be more careful; you don't want people thinking I did that to you.'

With a smirk he swings out of the room, his aftershave lingering.

I look at my arm but still can't see anything. I rush into the living room and hold it above my head, looking in the mirror. There, where Jack pinched me, are two large bruises, turning black and brown, clear against my pink skin.

25

Summer has at last arrived in our part of the world, and the park is now a mass of white and pink cherry blossom, with the smell of newly cut grass. A few white clouds scud across the sky as we walk, and for once I actually look half decent, rather than like an escaped patient from a mental home. A pair of scuffed denim jeans and a T-shirt, with towel-dried hair, works in the sunshine. I could have just rolled off a beach in the Mediterranean.

We are so engrossed in our little world that I don't notice our companions until it's too late. Johnny runs ahead to the swings, and instantly my cheeks are bright red. I'm cringing with shame, remembering the last time I saw Adam, how stupid I was to phone him, to put him in that position with David.

He is standing next to the slide, watching Georgia climb up the steps, and he turns as Johnny and I arrive. As usual, he looks like he has stepped out of a Crew catalogue. Blonde hair just the right side of wind-blown, wearing a T-shirt, jeans and flip-flops. I glance down: he even has nice feet. I can feel him looking at me, but I can't meet his gaze.

'I'm glad you're here, I was worried about you,' he says, trying to catch my eye.

'I'm so sorry, Adam, I'm sorry I got you involved. I should never have phoned,' I ramble, still looking at the floor.

'I was going to call or text, but then I thought I might make things worse.' He puts a hand on my arm. 'How are you?'

I look up, and he smiles at me, dimples in his cheeks and the beginnings of a tan highlighting long dark eye-lashes. In that moment I feel a choir of angels is singing in the sycamore trees above us; that Cupid himself is sitting cross-legged in the bramble bushes. I cringe internally, thinking something so embarrassingly cheesy. I feel ridiculous around him; just remembering the dream from the other night is making me blush: what we did, what I orchestrated. Honestly, I tell myself, this crush is getting out of hand.

'I'm fine,' I mutter, 'really.'

We sit down on the grass next to each other, watching the kids. Johnny is hitting a tree with a stick, cackling with laughter, as Georgia looks on, more hesitant. She sits down next to him and starts picking the daisies in the grass around her. Adam abandons his flip-flops, stretching his legs out in front of him.

I decide to be brave. 'What's your wife like, Adam?' I ask.

'Wife?' he asks, looking at me with those big brown eyes.

'Georgia's mum?'

He laughs, quietly. 'Sadly, no. Georgia's mum left us when she was a baby. So now it's just the two of us. Me and Georgia against the world.'

'I'm sorry,' I say, feeling nothing of the sort.

He smiles. 'It's okay, we get by. Better that than being with someone who doesn't want to be there.'

I nod and put my hands behind me on the grass, holding my face towards the sun, closing my eyes and enjoying the warmth. I like the quiet; I like being with someone with no demands, no expectations.

'I dreamt about you, that night.' I turn to look at him and he glances away from me, embarrassed. 'It sounds crazy, but that's why I came over so quickly when you phoned. I had this feeling something was wrong. It woke me up.'

'What were we doing? In your dream?' I ask. I can feel the red creeping up my neck, the sun hot on my face.

'I don't really remember.' He frowns. 'We were at a party, I think. I felt very close to you . . . ' He shakes his head. 'Dreams are funny, aren't they? Some you remember for years and others fade as soon as you wake up.'

He turns back to the children, happily absorbed in a playhouse under the slide. They seem to find great mirth in running round, ducking and hiding from each other behind the simply constructed walls.

'Do you . . . do you ever wish for a different life?' The words are out of my mouth before I can stop them.

Adam turns to look at me, then back to the grass, picking a daisy and rolling it around in his fingers. In the silence, I regret my honesty.

'I would never wish for a life without Georgia.' He stops, and pulls up a handful of grass, letting it fall between his fingers. 'But would I have made some different choices along the way? Yes, I think I would.'

'What would you do differently?'

He sighs. 'Georgia's mum, for a start. I'd stay away from her. But then I wouldn't have Georgia, and that's unthinkable.' He smiles, an expression that transforms his whole face. 'It's hard: we are who we are because of the choices we made. You can't turn back the clock; you can only be more careful about what you do in the future.' He pauses. 'What about you?' he asks softly.

'Well, you've met my husband, and he's just lovely.' I try to laugh, but a strange sound comes out instead. My eyes feel hot. I clear my throat. 'It's knowing what choices to make in the first place that's the difficult thing.'

Adam nods, and passes me one of the daisies he's been holding. 'Any time you need anything . . . '

I nod, not trusting myself to speak.

'Is it? It is something you want to go through with?'

Jack and Annie were sitting together somewhere new: Jack's choice, an old-style pub, dark and atmospheric, with worn sofas and aged wooden benches. Jack had a tankard of beer in front of him and Annie a glass of white wine. There was a hum of music in the air and a buzz of conversation around them. They were near the sea, Annie guessed, from the smell of salt in the air, and it must have been winter. A fire burnt enthusiastically in the fireplace next to them, and every now and again someone would blow in from outside, rubbing their hands together to warm them up from the chill.

Annie nursed her wine. 'There's no guarantee it will work, is there?' she said.

'No, but there's no guarantee it won't, either. This isn't going to be easy, it's not going to be a try-once-go-back-and-redo-it-later sort of thing. We just don't know. You try to kill your husband in his dreams — in your dreams — and you might have actually done it.' Jack was looking at her intently, trying to read the look on her face. He was worried.

'He's a bastard, Jack. He's a cheating, womanising, horrible man.' She held back, leaving out the worst part.

'Divorce him, then.'

'He'd never let me divorce him, it would ruin his reputation.' She shook her head. 'He would take Johnny. He'd take my son and have that awful woman bring him up, and they would destroy him.'

She looked at him, trying not to let her emotions come out in her voice. 'Johnny's such a sweet, loving child. They would take all of that from him. Bring him up to be a man, whatever that is. I'd certainly never see him again, and I couldn't stop David. He has money. Lawyers. I wouldn't stand a chance.'

'Is he really that bad?' Jack asked quietly.

'Worse. All he cares about is his reputation and his money.' Annie looked at Jack. 'To him, they're the same thing. He wants people to see him as the powerful man he is — powerful men don't have wives that walk out on them, and they certainly don't have wussy little boys. I need to stop it now, while I still can.'

'He'd be without his dad, though. Surely a bad dad is better than nothing.' Jack stopped for a moment, staring into his beer. 'I grew up without a father. It's no fun, you know.' He waved the statement away with a swipe of his hand. 'I'm just saying, make sure you're certain.' He took a final swig of his beer. 'Another one?'

As Jack left to get another drink from the swarming bar, Annie cupped her hands round the cooling glass of wine and thought about what he had said. Was a crappy dad better than nothing at all? Maybe it was; maybe she wasn't doing what was best for Johnny, just what was best for her.

As she pondered, she reached over into the fireplace and plucked out a flame. She swirled it around in her hand, feeling its warmth but knowing it wouldn't hurt her. She rolled it into a ball, watching the reds and yellows flicker inside, then popped it into her mouth. It tasted of smoked paprika; of burnt toast, and barbecues.

Jack came back, another tankard of beer in his hand.

'I've thought about what you said, Jack,' Annie said. 'About whether a bad dad is better than no dad.'

'And?'

'I don't think it is. Johnny shouldn't grow up thinking it's okay to treat women as David does. He needs to know that people are more important than money and that he is the top priority in his dad's life, not the third or fourth. David sees him as a commodity, as something to show what a great *man* he is.' She spat out the word with distaste. 'He sees Johnny as an accessory so he can demonstrate how he has it all: the son, the wife, the house, the car. He doesn't see us as people. Johnny needs to be encouraged and praised, not shouted down and terrorised. He needs love and cuddles and to be able to throw baked beans on the floor like any normal toddler. He doesn't need David in his life. And nor do I.'

She paused, her hands grasping the edge of the table. 'He's worse than you could possibly imagine.' Her voice cracked and she swallowed, taking a gulp of wine. 'I found videos, films he had taken, him with other women. He shags anyone he likes, he abuses . . . ' She felt ashamed; she couldn't look at Jack. 'He hits women. He hits me.' She stopped, cheeks wet and mouth dry.

Jack nodded and reached over, wordlessly wiping the tears from her cheek with his thumb. He took her hand gently, and squeezed it. A gesture of solidarity, of understanding. 'Okay then,' he said. 'So what are we going to do?'

26

Maggie phones in the morning to give her formal decree for the birthday dinner.

'Beef Wellington,' she declares. Crap. 'It's so kind of you to offer to make it all from scratch. Nothing beats that home-made touch,' she finishes, sealing my fate.

She knows bloody well I can't make pastry, let alone all the bits and pieces that go into a Beef Wellington. Steak? What sort of steak? That mushroom stuff round the edge? Something to do with ham or bacon, and pastry — short-crust or puff? I scowl at the beautiful pictures online; it all looks horribly complex. Johnny stands next to me, fat fingers smudging the screen.

'Sausage roll,' he says, looking up at me.

'If only,' I mutter back.

* * *

Thursday evening rolls around and David comes home to an immaculate kitchen, Johnny bathed and sleeping peacefully in bed, and a Beef Wellington on a baking tray, ready to go in the oven. The buttery puff pastry is glazed with egg wash, the side crimped to a perfect zigzag, ready to be cooked at 180 degrees for a crisp golden finish. Vegetables are chopped and in a saucepan, kettle boiled and ready. Roast potatoes already cooking in the oven. A chocolate cake with a mirror glaze of ganache stands on our crystal cake stand, one silver candle in the centre. The table is laid with our best plates and cutlery, ironed white napkins folded precisely, wine glasses rinsed with hot water and shined.

He looks at it all and grunts, taking his jacket and tie off without a word. He hands me a small purple jewellery case. I open it and gasp, seeing a delicate bracelet shining on a velvet pillow. Tiny diamonds glisten all round the diameter, refracting in the bleak overhead kitchen light, throwing out triangles of colour and sparkle.

'Wrap it quickly,' he says. 'Mother will be here soon.'

I snap the top shut. David forgot my last birthday. For the one before, he got me a steam mop.

The doorbell rings, Maggie forsaking her key for a bit of formality. I hear their cooing salutations as I come back into the kitchen, placing Maggie's present on her place mat and tweaking the ribbon.

'Annie,' she says, holding me at arm's length and air-kissing me on both cheeks. 'It looks like you've outdone yourself.'

'Only the best on your birthday, Maggie.'

'Still, the proof is in the tasting, isn't it?' She smiles.

'Dinner will be in about thirty minutes,' I say, and turn to put the Beef Wellington in the oven.

'Thirty?' Maggie reaches out a bony finger to prod the pastry as the tray passes her. 'I would normally go for forty-five. Still! You're the chef, Annie, who I am to interfere?' She laughs, a little girlish tinkle.

‘Come and sit down, Mother,’ David says, bored of the talk of cooking. ‘And open your present, I think you’ll like it.’

* * *

Maggie’s face when presented with the steaming Beef Wellington is something to behold. David cuts thick handsome wedges, and for the first time I can breathe with relief. It is bloody perfect: beef cooked on the outside, rare in the centre, delicate flakes of pastry, precise layers of mushroom and ham.

David gives little moans of pleasure as he eats it; Maggie picks at her plate, chewing slowly, her nose wrinkled.

‘We’ll make a good wife out of you yet,’ David says, not meeting my eye. ‘What do you think, Mother?’

‘Delicious,’ Maggie agrees. She looks at me, ready for the kill. ‘You’ll have to tell me your secret, Annie. Who is your caterer?’

David’s head snaps round to face me. ‘Someone else cooked this?’

‘Of course not,’ I say smoothly. ‘All done by my fair hand. Even the pastry.’

‘Well then, you must tell me how,’ Maggie replies.

‘A good chef never reveals her secrets.’

‘Don’t be ridiculous, Annie. Tell Mother how you made it.’

I take a deep breath, and step by step recite the method for making puff pastry. How much butter, how many turns and how long in the fridge to let it cool. How I made the mushroom duxelle, how many slices of prosciutto and how long I pre-cooked the beef.

'How much flour?'

'Two hundred and fifty grams.'

'What sort of beef?'

'Aberdeen Angus, fillet.'

Maggie quizzes me like a prize interrogator, her face screwing up into a grimace each time I answer correctly.

'How much white wine?'

'Just a splash.'

'And where's the rest of the bottle?' David chips in.

'In the fridge,' I reply, pointing unnecessarily.

Maggie gets up and walks across to it, pulling out the bottle and looking at the little bit gone from the top.

'Mother, are you doubting Annie?'

She giggles and comes back to the table. 'Not at all, David. Just want to know so I can make it for my girls next time they're over.' She spears another mouthful and chews, her expression as if I've served up a plate of bush tucker and dog scraps.

I smile. 'I hope you're enjoying it, Maggie. I wouldn't want it to go to waste after all my efforts.'

She narrows her eyes. 'The roast potatoes aren't as good as mine.'

'No, no, they're not, of course.'

We sing 'Happy Birthday' and Maggie blows out the candle, her eyes screwed shut. We eat delicious moist slices of cake and David prepares the coffee as Maggie and I move to sit in the lounge. On the way through, she catches my arm, holding it surprisingly tightly with her spindly fingers.

'I know you didn't make that dinner.'

I look down at my arm, and slowly prise her fingers away, one by one.

'But I did, Maggie. Haven't I proven that already?' I reply sweetly. I'm feeling brazen. 'Check the bins for the wrapping, look for the receipts, do whatever you need to do: you'll find no evidence.'

'I have,' she says abruptly, then clamps her mouth shut. She continues in a whisper, glancing back to where David is humming in the kitchen. I can hear the whirr of the coffee machine and the clink of mugs. 'Don't think you can edge me out. I am here to stay. I am the most important person in his life. You don't deserve either of them; if it wasn't for my David, I'd worry about how that little boy was being brought up. This is what I do best; you are nothing but a pathetic copy of me, a substitute.'

I raise my eyebrows. 'Except tonight I wasn't, was I, Maggie?'

'I know you didn't make that dinner,' she says again. 'I know you didn't.'

I sigh, and slump down on the sofa. 'Whatever you say.'

My apathy makes her mad. 'He is my boy!' she spits. 'Mine. Look at this!' She waves her scrawny wrist in my face, the bracelet glistening in the light. 'He bought me this because he loves me the most. What do you have? Nothing!'

'What are my girls talking about?' David interrupts, coming into the room and placing the tray of coffees on the table. Maggie moves away from me and sits on the sofa opposite, smiling smugly when David sits next to her, offering her the first mug and putting in the cream.

'Just chatting about you,' I reply. 'It's always about you, David.'

He laughs. 'And so it should be.'

Mad old cow, I think, as I sip my coffee. All that effort, and she doesn't appreciate it one iota. She just doesn't understand what I'm good at: lying like a seasoned grifter, memorising procedures and recipes from YouTube videos, working through every possible move to hide my tracks. Of course I didn't make the sodding dinner.

Staring despairingly at the photos earlier that week, I remembered a shop I'd seen months ago when I was out shopping one day with Johnny — 'Home-prepared meals cooked just for you'. A professional-looking place, disregarded at the time, but a lifesaver now. Johnny and I raced into town. Beef Wellington? Chocolate cake? Sure, no problem, they said. Keep it quiet? Of course, discretion is our middle name.

And sure enough, it arrived this morning, delivered in a nameless van by a disinterested bloke, all laid out perfectly in two brown cardboard boxes. I paid by cash, as underhand as any dark alleyway drug deal, and disposed of the cardboard in the public dog bin on the way to the park with Johnny. There, done.

I look over to the pair of them, David

mid-conversation. Maggie glares back at me, saving her fight for another day, shrivelled up in her corner of the sofa. I can't bear the sight of them, with their arrogance and entitlement. They believe they can do anything they want to me; they believe they own me, and that I am too weak, too stupid to stop them.

I smile and take another sip of my coffee, enjoying the moment.

Because tonight it's all going to be over. Tonight I'm going to kill my husband.

Evergreen

Annie found him quickly. The hatred that ran from her connected them like a bungee wire; she practically flew to his dream. All she had to do was imagine his smug smiling face, the feeling when he arrived home, the fear, the uncertainty, the dread in the pit of her stomach, that slightly sick, retching lurch, and suddenly, there she was.

Today, the dream was cold. It was winter, with tall evergreens dusted with white, and a pale-blue sky; Annie heard nothing but the crunch of her boots as she stepped through the snow. It was deep, at least a foot, and hard going as she walked through the clearing towards a picture-book old-fashioned log cabin. It had a pitched roof, a small red-brick chimney with smoke coming out of the top, and a red front door. It was David's dream, but the pretty scene seemed at odds with the filth she knew to be in his subconscious. She hesitated and looked round; she needed to take him by surprise.

She knew she would have to be quick, and sneaky. She thought about Johnny, about his future, about his life as a grown-up and how much better off he would be without David around. Without David, she would be able to bring her son up in a better way, with respect and love, free from worry or fear. At the moment David paid Johnny little regard, but what happened when Johnny developed a mind of his own? Would he copy his father, take on the same misogyny and distaste, or would he rebel? Would he become his father's ally, or worse, another recipient of his temper?

Annie took in her surroundings. She was wearing warm fur-lined boots and a thick coat. Black technical-looking gloves over her hands and a woolly hat on her head. She lifted the hat slightly from over her ears and listened; she could just about hear a repetitive sound of metal against wood. Faint, but there it was. Thud, then a pause, and then another thud. She looked around. There was nothing except more trees and forest; a few snow-capped peaks dominated the horizon, but there were no people, no other trace of habitation.

She slowly moved closer to the cabin and peered through an icy window. Inside she could see a fire blazing in the log burner and a large bed in the centre of the room. A long feminine leg poked out of one side of the sheets, with blonde hair obscuring the face on the pillow. Ah, Annie thought, David's subconscious: there it is.

The noise continued from the other side of the cabin. Thud, pause, thud. She started moving again, slowly, round the house, getting closer, then poked her head round the final corner.

At last, there stood a figure, axe in hand, a pile of logs to one side and a pile of chopped-up wood to the other. He had his back to Annie, and was wearing a black T-shirt, no coat, no gloves and no hat, despite the freezing weather. It was David at his most macho, proving his worth as a man.

He raised the axe over his head again and took the impact as he connected with a log. It broke in two perfectly. He moved the chopped wood to the side, then rested the axe against a workbench, standing up straight and stretching out his back. Even Dream David, despite seeming in much better shape, was obviously not used to the physical demands of wood chopping.

He picked up a mug, a rustic enamel creation, and took a swig of what seemed like coffee. In the cold of his dream world the mug steamed, piping hot, and he stood for a moment, king of his domain, looking at the scenery. Annie moved closer, slowly approaching where he stood, but still out of his line of sight.

David put his coffee down and started stacking the logs in an ordered pile. Annie moved closer now, and picked up the axe. It was solid but heavy in her hand; it felt big and reassuring.

She thought about him fucking his PA. She thought about him smacking her round the face, she thought about him raping her in front of her son. She thought of the hotel rooms, the videos, and all the other women. She thought about the blood, the snot, the pain and the fear. Feeling scared and lonely all the fucking time. Everything she had pushed down and suppressed for oh so very long. But most of all she thought about Johnny. She heard her son's cries as he sat captive in his high chair; she heard him alone and ignored at Maggie's house. She thought about the future, when David might hit him, when he might lay his hands on her perfect boy.

She thought about Johnny's future, picked up

the axe and swung it into David's head.

The dream resisted her, as she knew it would. She felt the push back as everything moved in slow motion, leaving a blurred vapour trail behind. She summoned all her strength to lift the axe and heave it down. She pushed her subconscious away, replacing it with anger and the love for her son. She felt the muscles in her arms flexing and pulling, she felt her body tense, she saw the look on David's face as he turned and saw her. At first recognition, then confusion, then sudden understanding, surprise and fear.

He was too late. The axe connected; she felt the contact of metal with bone, and suddenly the world returned to normal speed. It jarred in her hand as it made its connection, vibrating all the way down her arm to her shoulder, but she held fast. The blade caught in his skull and stuck in the hard ridge of the thick bone. She let go, and he stood there for a second, axe embedded in the middle of his forehead, staring, shocked. Then the consciousness left his eyes and he fell forward heavily into the snow, his head hitting the ground last. The axe remained stuck, pushing his head up at a strange angle, so he was still looking at her, eyes wide, empty.

Annie took a step back, her hands still in front of her. Before she had picked up the axe, she had cleared her mind, deliberately stopping herself clicking on to what she was about to do. But now that she was free and she could think what she liked, her mind still seemed empty.

What had she expected to feel? They were married, after all; once they had even been in love. She sat down on the log where he had been chopping wood and took a look at his face. When they had met, she had thought him the most handsome man she had ever seen. Masculine, commanding, confident, all the things she had since come to hate. He had been kind once, too, although somehow she couldn't remember the times when he had been good to her.

A slow, thick stream of blood was leaking out of the hole in his head, running down the handle of the axe onto the snow. It pooled round the pile of chopped wood and she watched as it diluted into the pristine white of the snow. She had expected him to disappear or for her to be pulled away, to return to the land of the living, but nothing had changed. Perhaps something still flickered in his mind; a part of his subconscious remained. Around her the scene was silent. She could hear nothing but the gentle rustling of the birds in the trees. Her own subconscious had given up: it was obviously thinking, well fuck it, look what you've done now.

Suddenly she heard footsteps and turned quickly, expecting a similar fate for herself.

'You did it then?' Jack stood behind her, his hands stuffed deep inside a smart wool coat, a comical multi-coloured woolly hat with a bobble pulled down hard, blocking out his unruly hair. A matching stripy scarf was tied round his neck, pulled up to meet his hat.

Annie took her gloves off and put them in her pockets, feeling suddenly warm. 'I guess so.'

'How do you feel?' he asked.

‘No idea. I mean it’s not like it’s real yet, is it? Haven’t I just dreamt about killing my husband? How will I know if it’s worked?’

He shrugged, blowing on his hands to warm them.

‘Wake up.’

* * *

Jack took a step back as Annie disappeared. He saw the body in front of him, the blood a ghoulish red halo in the snow. He tentatively poked it with the toe of his shoe and it shifted slightly, the axe dislodging and the face falling forwards with a thud. He jumped back, his heart pounding. What the hell was going on?

When he woke up, back in his bed, the sun was low in the sky, a soft glow highlighting the edges of the furniture and the gentle lines of Lizzie sleeping next to him. He stared at the shadows on the ceiling, feeling muddled and confused. Lizzie stirred in her sleep, turning over and facing him. Her hair had escaped during the night and was falling over her face, and he gently moved it away, tucking it behind her ear. He very rarely complimented her — something inside held him back — but looking at her even now, face sagged with sleep, mouth open, hair a mess, she looked beautiful.

It was her confidence he’d first admired. She had the air of someone who knew her place in the world and was comfortable in it. It was a trait he recognised in others and envied because it was so absent in himself. His parents had been amazing, always telling him they loved him, and he'd wanted for nothing, but as a small boy, being adopted had always made him feel like an outsider, like something or someone was missing. Piecing together his childhood had helped a bit, but it wasn't until he met Lizzie that he found someone who could truly create a home. This house, with her, was his life, and he was always grateful for that. He should tell her, he resolved, he should tell her every day how he felt about her. He would try harder to push away the feeling that there was something, someone, missing, and let go of the worry that he would lose another person he loved.

He got up carefully, tucking the blue bunny affectionately back under the duvet with Lizzie, his hand pausing for a moment to stroke its tattered ears. He reached down and put on a sweatshirt lying next to the bed. The weather didn't get cold nowadays, even in the middle of winter, but he needed the comfort of something round his shoulders. He fitted his feet into his slippers and walked quietly down the stairs to the living room.

Their house was tiny, but perfectly proportioned. Lizzie wasn't one of those women with acres of shoes or clothes or handbags, but she did have an eye for interior design and colour. She had decorated the whole house pretty much single-handedly, with him on hand to do the grunt work, and she had done an incredible job: creating a cosy nook but without twee kitsch; functional and fun but not too girlie.

She was an amazing woman, he thought, as he

sat on the sofa watching the sun come up. Why the hell hadn't he asked her to marry him yet? Why hadn't they talked about starting a family or making things more permanent?

He stood and went over to the bookshelf, taking out an old copy of *One Flew Over the Cuckoo's Nest*. The book was orange, with yellowed pages; a photo of a young Jack Nicholson grinning out of the cover. He liked the irony of hiding it here, in this book. Thumbing the worn pages, he pulled out a flimsy white envelope, the handwriting on the front scrawled and messy, just giving his name, a name he didn't use any more. He didn't get the letter out; he didn't need to. He had read it a thousand times before and knew every word by heart. He held it in his hand for a moment, then slipped it back into its hiding place and put the book back on the shelf, lining it up with the others so it looked perfectly in place.

He hadn't known who she was at first — just another person in his dreams — until slowly the niggle of recognition turned into a dawning realisation. He hadn't even known it was possible. He was confused. He knew what had happened in his past, what his parents had told him, so what was going on now? The line between reality and dream was blurring.

So she had killed her husband. Or had she?

27

I wake with a jolt. The light is still dim; I slowly register it's morning as my eyes open to the sound of Johnny talking to Rabbit next door. I lie still for a moment, smiling at the chatter. Still time until the alarm will wake David. Will usually wake David. Who knows what will happen now.

I remember the dream. I remember the axe, and what I've done. I put my hand over my mouth and giggle slightly — from the shock, or the anticipation of what might happen next. I know I should feel guilty, but my only concern is whether it's worked. I feel twitchy, my hands desperate to do something, anything, to distract me.

I put on my dressing gown and go into Johnny's room, opening the door to the sight of my grinning son. I pull him out of the cot and he immediately demands to be put on the ground. He waddles off towards the doorway, the John Wayne of baby walks, his nappy full and in the way of his pudgy little legs.

I pick him up, Rabbit in his arms, and carry him to the changing mat. 'Thomas, watch it?' he says.

'Maybe, after Daddy's gone to work,' I whisper. 'Let's get you changed first.'

Changed, dressed, clean and sweet-smelling, we make our way downstairs. Empty dishwasher, tidy living room, coasters in a line, briefcase by the front door. Tea, Weetabix, toast. Coffee made for David. I hold myself back from rushing. Slow and measured as I go about my routine, like any other day. Part of me is desperate to know what waits for me in the master bedroom and the other part can't bear to find out. If he is alive, would I be disappointed? What does that say about me? And if he is dead, what then?

Coffee in hand, I leave Johnny downstairs with his toys and take the stairs slowly, hesitating at the door. I push the handle down as quietly as possible and go into the darkened room. His curtains are still shut, so my eyes adjust slowly, looking for the light in the darkness. I put the coffee cup on his bedside table and stand for a moment watching him. I can't see any movement. I can't see if his chest is going up and down, if there is blood pumping through his veins. There certainly isn't any blood on the pillow. I move closer. I can't tell if he's breathing. I lean down towards his face; I just want to see if he's warm, if there's air going in and out of his lungs. I slowly reach out a finger to touch his cheek.

'What the fuck are you doing?' David's voice throws me a metre back from the bed, and I stand against the wardrobe, my heart lurching.

He sits up in bed, head intact, breathing steadily.

'I just . . . I don't know,' I stutter. 'I was going to give you a kiss.'

'Stupid bloody woman,' he says. 'Go and make my breakfast.'

I stumble out of the room, hitting my hip and shoulder on the door frame as I go. My head spins. It hasn't worked, I didn't kill him, he's still alive. Will he remember the dream? What will I do now? Try again? Run away? Take Johnny and just leave?

I sit on the sofa for a moment, stunned, with Johnny in front of me slowly lining up his toy trains on the coffee table. He takes them one at a time from the box, turning them around so the magnets connect. Today he seems keen on the bigger trains, discarding others for the ones he clearly prefers. He puts Edward back in the box and connects Gordon to the back of Spencer. He is oblivious to everything going on, so innocent. How can I protect him?

A loud noise from upstairs disturbs me from my thoughts. A thud and a crash of falling crockery. Something smashes against the door to the living room and Johnny and I both look towards the sound. Johnny looks back at me, train clutched in his hand.

'David?' I call.

I stand up slowly and open the door. David's BlackBerry lies in pieces on the floor in the hallway, the back and the battery at my feet. Halfway up the stairs there is a brown stain and a piece of coffee cup, the rest scattered as my gaze moves upwards.

'David?' I call again. I look at Johnny. 'Stay here.'

Slowly I walk up the stairs, glimpsing David's socked feet, perpendicular to the ground. As I get closer, I can see his body, half dressed in suit trousers and an untucked shirt, more untidy than I have seen him in months. He is lying on the floor, eyes open, mouth gaping, a gash on his head gently seeping blood onto our pristine cream carpet.

Without a word I retrace my steps back down the stairs and pick up my mobile.

'Ambulance, please,' I say calmly to the emergency operator. 'My husband has collapsed.' I adjust the tone of my voice. 'Please come quickly,' I add, a trace of hysteria creeping in. 'I don't know what to do.'

I hang up slowly and sit back down on the sofa. I pick up my tea and take a sip. It's getting cold.

28

The ambulance arrives with a scream of sirens loud enough to rouse the curiosity of the road. Men rush in, big green bags in hand, and I point up the stairs, wiping away my horrified tears with a tissue. Johnny attaches himself to my leg and I pick him up as he starts to cry in response to the noise and bustle. I bury my face in his warm shoulder, providing a welcome distraction from my strange demeanour. I'm not sure what to go with; nothing feels natural. Quiet and shocked, or hysterical and wailing? Quiet and shocked is easier, so I opt for that.

They bash about at the top of the stairs, scuffing the paintwork with their equipment and bags. One of the paramedics goes downstairs to the ambulance and returns with another piece of equipment. I watch wordlessly from the doorway, Johnny still attached to my neck.

Another car pulls up in our driveway, black and white, a police car, this time the sirens mercifully silent. My heart jumps. What the hell are they doing here? Are they here for me? Two officers climb out of the car, one in uniform and one in a suit, and walk slowly to the house, deep in conversation for a moment. They look over and see Johnny and me at the doorway, straighten their shoulders and approach the front door.

Johnny has stopped crying, mesmerised by

actual policemen arriving at his house.

'Mrs Sullivan?' the plain-clothes officer asks, and I nod. 'Can we come in?'

I move aside and they step through the doorway, wiping their feet on the mat. I force myself to calm down; there is nothing for them to know, I tell myself. I follow them into the living room, pulling Johnny onto my lap and cuddling him, his familiar warmth and toddler smell instantly reassuring.

The first policeman sits opposite me on the other sofa, while the second stands uncomfortably in the corner of the room.

'Would you like a cup of tea?' I ask, remembering my manners.

'No, no, you stay there,' the plain-clothes officer says, gesturing towards his colleague and then the kitchen. The policeman in uniform scuttles off, and I can hear the sound of my kettle being filled under the tap and switched on, then a clattering of teacups and cupboards opening and closing.

The officer puts his hands together and leans in towards me. I notice the noise upstairs has stopped, just a gentle rustling and moving of heavy boots replacing the previous frenetic thumping and talking.

'Mrs Sullivan, my name is Detective Sergeant Coleman. I'm here because in cases like this, we need to investigate what's happened,' the man says.

'Cases like this?' I echo.

'When the accident is sudden, with no obvious cause.' He clears his throat. He's obviously not completely comfortable, fidgeting in the chair and running his hands through his salt-and-pepper crop. It's receding fast at the front, showing a large expanse of wrinkled forehead. He's not unattractive, but this, combined with his large nose, gives him the appearance of a wise eagle, care-worn and beaten through life experience. 'I know this is hard, but can you tell me what happened?'

He gets a small black notebook and a biro out of his pocket and sits with it in front of him, poised. Johnny, realising that nothing interesting is happening, slides off my lap and goes to his toy box, where his cars live. He extracts a small black-and-white American-style police car, placing it on the floor and looking back at the officer.

'Um . . . ' I stop for a moment, thinking back to the morning. 'Nothing out of the ordinary. I got up, and Johnny and I went downstairs to make breakfast.'

'Where was your husband at this point?' DS Coleman interrupts.

'In the other bedroom, asleep,' I say. He raises his eyebrows but says nothing. I continue. 'I made him his coffee and took it in, then I could hear David get up and use the bathroom, and then this thump, and then nothing.' I look at DS Coleman, scribbling in his notebook. 'I went upstairs to see what had happened and saw David on the floor, so I called 999.'

'Did you attempt CPR?'

'I don't know how to do that sort of thing,' I reply.

He pauses for a moment, and makes another note.

‘And how would you describe your marriage?’
‘What do you mean?’
He hesitates and clears his throat again. ‘I mean, does your husband always sleep in a different bedroom to you?’
The noises in the kitchen stop and the other policeman comes back in, cup of tea in hand. He has used the good china, our wedding china. He hands me the cup and I sit with it in my lap.
DS Coleman looks at me pointedly.
‘Um, yes, he does. He has a busy job and doesn’t like being woken by me in the night if I have to get up for Johnny. There is nothing wrong with our marriage,’ I add.
A paramedic appears in the doorway, and DS Coleman gets up to speak to him.
‘What’s going on?’ I say, standing up and spilling a bit of tea on the carpet. ‘Can you tell me what’s happening with my husband?’ My voice rises an octave in a satisfying way, and Johnny looks at me in alarm.
DS Coleman leaves the room with the paramedic and I can hear whispering outside. ‘He’ll be back in a moment,’ says the other officer. He is still standing on the far side of the room. He shifts his weight from his left foot to his right and back again, desperate to be involved in the big-boy conversation.
I sit down heavily and take a sip of tea. It’s weak and sugary, obviously taught on the most recent soothing-the-hysterical-wife course; it’s disgusting. The police officer taps his foot.
DS Coleman returns and takes a seat next to me on the sofa. He’s big and heavy and it makes

me lean slightly towards him. He smells of a flowery aftershave, and I wonder who bought it for him; who did he leave behind at home this morning?

'I'm really sorry, Mrs Sullivan. The paramedics have done all they can, but they were unable to save your husband.' He pauses. 'Unfortunately they think the injuries he sustained were too serious for him to recover from.'

'He's dead?' I say quietly, and DS Coleman nods. I don't know how to react. 'How could he be dead? He was just here a minute ago.'

'We don't know, I'm sorry.' He is sorry for a lot of things, this policeman, none of which are his fault. 'We will need to take the body away to find out exactly what has happened.'

'The body,' I repeat. 'Right. Can I see him before you go?' I ask quickly. I need to be sure. I want to see it with my own eyes.

'Yes, of course, follow me,' says DS Coleman, gesturing to the other policeman to watch Johnny.

We go up the stairs slowly. Past the paramedic waiting at the bottom, past the wedding photos on the wall, me leading the way and DS Coleman following behind. A second paramedic stands on the landing, packing equipment away in a large green bag. At first I can only see David's feet, and then gradually more of him comes into view. His suit trousers, perfectly dry-cleaned, with a crease down the front, still neatly fastened. His shirt, pin-striped blue, ironed by me, ripped open at the front, revealing his pale white stomach, the little scattering of chest hair, pads stuck on where I assume they have tried to revive him. Then up to his neck to his perfectly shaved chin, his open mouth, his nose, eyes, his hair in disarray. Not the David I know, not the David I remember. This isn't the man who terrorised his wife, scared his son, fucked every woman in sight and threatened his friends. This man is no danger to me any more; he is unmistakably, most emphatically, dead.

I put my hand over my mouth quickly and dive into the bathroom, locking the door. My body shakes and tears run down my face. Tears of anger, of joy, of relief, of shock. How has this ridiculous plan worked? But whatever the bizarre circumstances, one thing is clear: David is dead and Johnny and I are free.

29

Luckily, the sound effects of a good old bout of hysteria are similar whether they are tears of joy or sadness. When I emerge out of the bathroom, a bit of toilet roll clutched to my face, DS Coleman and the paramedic are waiting for me.

'Mrs Sullivan,' the officer says, 'can we take him away now?'

I nod. 'Yes, yes, please do.' Can't just leave him there on the carpet, I want to add, he'll make a hell of a stain. Instead I say, 'What happens next?'

'We'll take the body to the hospital for a post-mortem, to find out what happened to him. We can do all the official stuff there,' he says.

The body. How quickly someone moves from being a person, to the patient, to a body. I nod again, and go back downstairs. The paramedic there pulls the same face DS Coleman's been wearing all morning: a rumpled forehead, lips pressed together in a thin smile, more of a grimace. Head tilted slightly down. The I'm-sorry-for-your-loss face.

In the living room, the uniformed policeman has Johnny enthralled. He's down on all fours, police car in hand, running it over the coffee table and floor, making a loud *brmming* sound. Hardly the sort of behaviour normally taught at police school, but heart-warmingly sweet, especially when Johnny's own father never did anything remotely similar. Upstairs, I hear talking and instructions being dictated, then a few thumps and the sound of men struggling to lift the body. I don't envy them. David isn't a light man: all that wine at late-night posh dinners with his mistresses.

Out of the front door they go and into the ambulance, under the prying eyes of everyone on the street. DS Coleman follows and shuts the front door behind them, gesturing me back into the living room. The police officer jumps up quickly and guiltily hands the car back to Johnny.

'What's the best number to call you on?' DS Coleman asks me, and I tell him; more scribbling in his incomprehensible handwriting. As an afterthought he adds: 'Is there anyone you want us to notify?'

Oh Christ, I think, Maggie. Her only son. How would I make that call?

'Could you tell my mother-in-law? Margaret Sullivan?'

DS Coleman nods, and I give him her address and number.

'We'll be in touch,' he says and gestures to his colleague that it's time for them to leave. 'We're sorry again for your loss.'

The front door closes and Johnny and I watch their car through the living room window.

'Police car,' Johnny says, looking at me.

'Yes, it was, little man,' I say, and pull him onto my lap for a hug.

The house is quiet again, save for the drone of *Fireman Sam*. Johnny is transfixed by the images on the screen, completely unaware of the emergency playing out in his own life.

But what now? I haven't thought beyond this point; I didn't know if it would work. I don't even know if we have life insurance, or any way to support ourselves. Have I been crazy? I know David had money, but where the hell is it? I only have access to my pathetic little allowance, but I guess I can always sell the ring, if I can find it again. As I feel the stirrings of panic begin to build in the pit of my stomach, I think at least this is a normal reaction for someone who has lost her husband, rather than hysterical laughter or a smirking grin.

I get up, placing the cup and saucer on the side in the kitchen, ready to be washed up delicately by hand, then reconsider and bung it in the dishwasher. Johnny still engrossed, I go back into the hallway, observing the scratches on the hall paint made as our visitors left. I notice a piece of David's smashed coffee cup hiding behind the hallway table, and pick it up, turning it over in my hands. I put it on the table, then gather up the disconnected battery and shell of his BlackBerry, piecing them back together. The battery cover has smashed, but I press the on button out of curiosity. Lights come on and it springs to life.

Standing next to the front door, I hear the chatter from a mum and daughter walking by the edge of our drive. As I look their way, I notice David's BMW is blocking in my Audi and wonder where the key is to move it. I pick up his briefcase and place it in front of me on the hallway table. I open pocket after pocket, looking for his keys, eventually finding them in the front, a big ball of metal and importance.

Taking the mobile and case with me, I stand outside David's study, trying key after key until one fits and turns easily. I open the door, and the smell of David hits me like a blow — cigars, whisky, stale sweat and testosterone. I go over to the window and push it open, letting the breeze billow the curtains out and knock over an award on the windowsill. It's a cheap block of engraved plastic; it falls off into the waste-paper basket and I leave it there.

I put his mobile on his desk and it starts vibrating angrily. I look at it impassively and it stops. Somebody misses him at least.

I feel kind of blank, rather than a loss. Something has fallen away from me, to be replaced by a big gap, a gaping void. Someone has erased a small part of the picture of me, but hasn't decided what colour to fill in the space.

Everything feels different. I am a widow now. Not officially, as I realise there are still a hundred calls to make and forms to fill in, but technically, I am a widow. No husband. I am single — a single-parent family — and Johnny has no father. Instantly I am reminded of Jack's words about his own lack of a dad. It must be hard growing up as a boy with no man in your life, but better, surely, than the alternative. Maybe I will find another male influence for Johnny; maybe Adam, or perhaps someone new is round the corner. Maybe not. That will be fine too.

I place the briefcase on the desk and start pulling open the expensive leather sides and the pockets, placing piles of paper and folders on the desk. There is his laptop, and a sheaf of boring-looking documents with numbers and columns and rows on them. A few project proposals, one with a big red cross carved on its front. I feel sorry for the poor soul who had to present that to him, and relieved that he or she might never know its fate.

Out of pure curiosity, I carry on looking through the papers, interested in what my husband did with all the time that he was supposedly at work. None of it looks that complicated or impressive — an excess of perplexing PowerPoint and Excel documents, a few dog-eared copies of the *Financial Times*, stray Post-it notes with messy scribbles in a handwriting I have seen before and assume to be his PA's.

A red folder at the back catches my eye. Unlike the rest, which are battered and manhandled, it is neat and pristine. The hairs on the back of my neck bristle as I open it and look inside. The top page is a form, with a large logo of a stag in the right-hand corner. That school, that bloody boarding school again. He was planning two years in advance to put our little boy in boarding school.

I can feel my hands shaking, and sit down in the plush leather chair on the other side of the desk. I take a deep breath, then slowly rip every page in the lovely red folder into quarters, putting them in a small pile in front of me. This done, I place my hands on the desk, palms down, and take another deep breath. In and out, in and out.

The phone in front of me buzzes again and I pick it up. The green answer button leaps around excitedly, wanting to be selected. *Answer me*, it says. I do.

'Hello?' says the voice at the other end of the line. I am silent. 'David, are you there?'

'Who's this?' I ask, slowly and calmly. 'This is David's wife, Annie.'

A very long pause. 'This is Jane,' says the voice, and I imagine her pretty young face from when I saw her on screen being screwed doggy-style by my husband.

'Hi, Jane,' I say. 'How can I help?'

'I'm looking for David,' she says. I can hear the uncertainty in her voice. The wife answering the phone is not something she has ever encountered. 'Do you know where he is?'

'He's dead,' I say, without hesitation. 'Died this morning.'

'Oh God, oh Christ, oh my dear Lord.'

'Easy on the blasphemy,' I say, my voice dry and still.

'What happened? Oh my God, what do I do now?' Jane says, hysteria starting to creep into her voice.

I sigh. 'Get over it, Jane, you'll find someone else to fuck you soon,' I say, and put the phone down.

30

In the back of my mind, I know I have to face Maggie. I did the cowardly thing by sending the police officer over to tell her the bad news, and now I am hiding in my house, avoiding her. We have had lunch, and Johnny is down for a nap. I am standing in my own bedroom, contemplating a sleep myself to see if Jack is doing the same, when I hear the sound of a car on gravel and go to the window to watch Maggie's BMW 1 Series park up on the drive. From upstairs I wait for her to get out of the car, and eventually the door opens and she totters to the front door.

I rush downstairs and open it before she has a chance to use her key. She grabs me and holds on; I realise she is shaking. Her tiny body contorts with sobs, her face thrust into my shoulder, her legs weak and collapsing under her.

I stand half in, half out of the doorway, unable to imagine what she must be going through. Her husband is dead, her only son is dead. I can empathise but am unable to summon any tears.

After a while, I manage to manoeuvre her through the doorway and into the living room, sitting her down on the sofa. She is still gripping onto my arms with spindly fingers. She looks up at me with bloodshot eyes and I see her for the old lady she is. Her grey hair is like cotton wool, soft and spun into a neat chignon; her skin as thin as tissue paper — I can see her arteries and the veins on her hands.

'My darling, I'm so sorry, what must you think of me? You've just lost your husband and here I am sobbing in your doorway.' She smooths down her blouse and mops delicately at her eyes with a white handkerchief.

'Would you like a cup of tea, Maggie?' Now *I'm* doing it, all these cups of tea.

'Earl Grey,' she says, as if she hasn't met me before.

I stand up to go through to the kitchen, picking up Johnny's discarded toys on the way.

'Where is David Junior?' asks Maggie, perching on the edge of the sofa.

'Johnny's having a nap.'

'Of course, Johnny. I just thought . . . I don't know.' She looks down into her handkerchief, then sniffs. 'Does Johnny know about his father? Was he . . . was he here?'

'He was, Maggie, but I don't think he knows what happened. I'll sit him down soon and make sure he understands. I'll go get your tea.'

I click the kettle on. The top cupboard door where the tea bags live is open slightly and things have been rearranged as the police officer tried to find what he needed. The used tea bag sits on the draining board, perched on a teaspoon. Strange to have someone you don't know touch your things in that way. Disconcerting.

The kettle clicks off and I make the tea just how Maggie likes it. The proper cup and saucer. Handle to the right, lemon slice cut in half on the side, with a teaspoon. Normal builder's tea for me, in a big ugly mug. No sugar this time.

I hand her the teacup and she sets it down on the table next to her. She looks at me. She's pale and her cheeks are sunken. 'I can't believe my beautiful boy is gone,' she says, dabbing at her eyes. 'It was such a shock when the policeman came round, such a nice man, so understanding. Of course, it would have been better to have heard it from a family member rather than a stranger.'

'I'm sorry, Maggie, but I was no use to anyone, and I had to stay with Johnny.'

'Of course, of course. Did you see him?'

'When . . . ?'

'When he died, were you with him when he died?'

'We were downstairs. He was unconscious by the time I got to him.'

'Oh, my poor little boy.' She starts crying again in great racking gasps, her head in her hands. I move to sit next to her and put an awkward arm around her shoulder.

Your poor little boy indeed, I think, running through the time when he fucked that woman over the boardroom table, or half murdered me with a pillow. Your poor little boy.

She looks up at me, pleading. 'Of course, you'll come to stay with me now. David mentioned you were having some problems, so I'll be happy to support you both.'

'Problems?' My voice has taken on a strange squeaky tone.

'He said you had been sleeping all the time, that you were,' she clears her throat, 'depressed,' she adds in a theatrical whisper.

'No, Maggie, I'm fine. There is nothing like that.'

'I'm not saying there's anything wrong with it, just that David mentioned it to me. We are family after all,' she says with the smile of a snake weighing up its ability to digest a small pig. 'I wouldn't want you to be alone, and for Johnny to have any problems.'

'Johnny won't have any problems. We'll be fine, Maggie. We'll come round all the time, and you can see for yourself.'

'Yes, yes, and I'll pop round regularly.'

We finish our cups of tea in silence, conversation over. I feel for the old lady, I do, honestly, but I can't wait to get away from her. With her there, a part of David lingers, haunting me. Why did he tell her I was depressed? I will have to get my daytime naps under control.

Maggie sets her teacup down on the coffee table and places her hands on her knees.

'Well, make sure you keep me updated on any news. The policeman said he would phone me, but you can't be too sure, can you?'

'No, of course.'

'And I'll arrange the funeral. I know all the right people to make it a wonderful celebration of his life.' She smiles like a switch has been flicked; it seems strange, forced and unnatural. I wonder if she's still in shock.

She gets up. 'Did he have a will?' she asks, one hand on the doorknob.

'I don't know. I'll phone our solicitor.'

She moves forward to hug me again, then

thinks better of it and pulls away, patting my arm instead.

'Take care of yourself, my dear, and David Junior.'

'Of course,' I say. Johnny, damn it, I think.

31

The first knock is controlled: a quick ring on the doorbell, followed by a tap with the knocker. No answer. My arm starts to ache, so I put Johnny on the doorstep and he immediately buries his head in my leg. I adjust the heavy bag on my shoulder and knock again, this time with more force.

'Okay, okay,' comes a voice from behind the front door, and I breathe out in a big whoosh of relief, not realising how long I have been holding my breath.

I hear the door unlock, and at last it's opened, Adam standing in front of me, effortlessly gorgeous in a basic grey T-shirt, jeans and bare feet. He is holding a tea towel, drying his hands and glancing back into the living room, where Georgia is playing.

'I'm really sorry,' I gibber at him, words coming out in a jumble. 'But I mucked up and I don't know what to do.'

'Come in, come in,' Adam says, seeing my flushed cheeks, sweaty forehead. 'Hello, Johnny,' he adds, ushering him inside.

I walk into the living room, Johnny behind me, hand in mine, and plonk the bag at my feet.

'I'm sorry to bother you, I wouldn't normally . . . '

'It's fine, sit down. Would you like a cup of tea?'

I almost laugh. 'No, I'm fine, no more tea. I just wondered if you could look after Johnny for an hour or two? I know it's a big ask . . . '

'It's fine.'

'It's just I need to go to the morgue, and the policeman called and I said okay, fine, but then I forgot about Johnny and you can't take a two-year-old to a morgue, can you?' I pause and catch my breath, glancing up at Adam. He looks confused.

'The morgue? Why do you need to go to the morgue?'

Three days on, and Johnny and I have fallen into a chaotic existence. Without David forcing structure and routine on us, I've been a bit disorientated. I haven't really noticed the time. Get up when we want, eat breakfast and lunch on the sofa, watch endless *Thomas the Tank Engine*, have a bath when we notice the smell, and generally forget about the trappings of domestication.

So when DS Coleman rang, we were in the middle of fish fingers and chips for lunch for the second day in a row, both still in our pyjamas, Johnny with a smudge of chocolate round his mouth from an earlier post-breakfast snack. We were enjoying our freedom.

'Mrs Sullivan,' said the voice at the end of the phone. He paused, and I heard the background chatter of a busy office. 'Your husband's post-mortem has been completed and we would like you to come to the hospital to discuss the results and identify the body.'

'Discuss the results?' His words woke me with

a jolt. 'What do you mean?'

'We just like to talk these things through. Is two p.m. this afternoon okay?'

'Yes, yes, of course,' I said, but of course it wasn't. I didn't have any childcare for Johnny and I couldn't bring myself to call Maggie. So my new friend Adam it was.

Adam's face changes instantly as I explain the events of the past few days. His cheeks flush and he moves backwards slightly, away from me.

'How did David die?' he asks quietly.

'We're not sure. The policeman is going to explain what they've found. I am so sorry,' I say, 'but I didn't know where else to go.'

'It's fine,' Adam says. 'Johnny can stay here, it will be fun.'

I notice something in his tone is forced, but there is nothing I can do. I hastily run through Johnny's routine. Snacks, park, Rabbit, nap if possible; he's had his lunch, water bottle is here. Johnny stays by my side throughout, quietly watching Georgia, who ignores us, playing with her toys. Adam nods as I go through it, paying attention but saying nothing.

'Thank you for this,' I say at the end. 'I won't be long, I promise.'

Adam turns to Johnny, bending down on his knees in front of him. 'Do you remember us from the park? Would you like to play with Georgia?'

Johnny nods, looking to me for approval, and I gently encourage him. I glance at my watch: I am late already.

I wave goodbye as I rush out of the house,

trying not to look behind me, trying to stifle the guilt at leaving Johnny alone with someone I've only just met and know nothing about. All my instincts tell me to keep him close, to keep him next to me at all times, but not today, not at the morgue. I resolve to get it over and done with quickly and be back with him as soon as I can.

I run to my car, and swerve out of Adam's road. My phone cheerfully tells me at regular intervals where to go, tracking the roads and turns. At every T-junction I feel my stomach drop a little further as the panic takes hold.

Down squeaky white corridors stinking of bleach and disinfectant under buzzing luminescent lights. Down to the bottom floor in an impossibly slow and clanky lift, to more corridors and increasingly glum-looking faces.

Finally, I walk up to the metal swing doors of the morgue, and without another thought push them open.

The room is as generic as any other NHS waiting room. Scratchy worn-out green chairs circle the edge, a few magazines scattered on a small table. A reception desk sits on the left-hand side with a doorbell sticky-taped to the wood. I press it and it plays a discordant tune, 'Camptown Races', I think. Doo-dah indeed.

With my ringing on the doorbell getting no response, I wait a moment by the desk, taking in my surroundings and fiddling with the biro attached to a string next to the bell. There is one other person in the room with me, an ageing gentleman who seems cheerful, incongruous in such depressing surroundings. He sits in one of the green chairs, tapping his foot in time to the tune he is humming under his breath. He looks up at me as I stand at reception, and smiles. I nod, then turn back to the empty desk.

The swing doors I came in through open with a whoosh of air, and a woman in a nurse's uniform glances around.

'Oh, Mr Barker, there you are,' she says, looking at the older gentleman with her hands on her substantial hips. She glances in my direction.

The man jumps up with an enthusiastic childlike leap and practically skips over to the nurse, who takes his hand. She squints at me again.

'Are we expecting you?' she says.

'I got a call this morning to come in and identify my husband. David Sullivan?'

She stands with the man's hand still clutched in hers. 'I didn't know we had anything . . . ' she coughs, 'anyone down there.'

She moves with the gentleman to the reception desk next to me, and leans over the wooden barrier.

'Maureen!' she bellows, and I jump.

A shuffling of feet heralds the arrival of Maureen.

The nurse nods at me, then leaves with the cheerful man trailing behind her.

Maureen raises an eyebrow. 'Did you ring the bell?'

'I did.'

'I didn't hear it.'

There was a pause. 'I'm sorry,' I say.

Another pause, and Maureen looks at me.

'And how can I help you?' she says, in the unwelcoming tone one would normally expect to receive for taking a sticky toddler to a posh clothes shop, whilst wearing tracksuit bottoms.

'Um, I was called by DS Coleman to come here,' I mutter, and hate myself for my lack of confidence.

'Name?'

'David Sullivan.'

She looks down at the clipboard in front of her, then back at me.

'DS Coleman's not here yet. Take a seat, and I'll let you know when he arrives.'

I do as I am told and sit down on one of the scratchy chairs. They are as uncomfortable as they look. I pick my phone out of my bag and flick through photographs from the past few months. Shot after shot of Johnny smiling, reaching to grab the phone; Johnny with food round his mouth, Johnny with food in his hand; Johnny and myself grinning in a selfie. All of Johnny, none of David. I have never had an opportunity to take a photo of the two of them together. I think there is a posed one of them when Johnny was born — David looking stiff and forced and Johnny's face contorted into a cry — but not much else.

In the silence while I wait, I wonder how Maggie is getting on with the funeral arrangements. When my mother died, there was barely enough money to buy food, so a funeral wasn't exactly a priority. The council took over, burying her in a cardboard box somewhere. I don't care where; I don't have any motivation to find out.

Maggie phoned yesterday to ask what church we went to, and I managed to avoid saying the name of his golf club. I muttered something about non-practising Christians, and she got off the phone before I could ask any more. I need to get more involved; I need to be a better grieving widow. This mess and disorganisation has to stop, and I need to pull myself together. I'm Johnny's only parent now, and I have to start acting like it.

An overhead luminescent tube starts to flicker, casting an eerie glow. I've just picked up one of the magazines when a man clears his throat in the doorway.

DS Coleman looks exactly the same: his suit crisp and clean, buttons done up smartly, his shoes shiny. He holds a taupe folder under his right arm. His adherence to the importance of his profession reassures me; this is a man who knows how to do things right.

He escorts me wordlessly into another bland room. It has similar chairs, but blue this time. The one I am sitting on has a hole in the seat cover and I can see a bit of yellowing sponge seeping through, trying to escape. I poke it back in with my finger.

'Sorry to keep you waiting, Mrs Sullivan,' he starts, fingering the folder in front of him. He smiles awkwardly. 'We have the results here from your husband's post-mortem.' He doesn't open the folder, and I imagine all sorts of photos of David's insides within its pages. 'The pathologist found that he died of an extensive brain haemorrhage affecting the frontal lobe of his brain, the prefrontal cortex, resulting in significant cerebral oedema. Simply put, he had a huge amount of bleeding in his skull when more than one artery burst. He wouldn't have suffered,' he added. 'He died very quickly.'

I nod. 'Do you know why?'

DS Sullivan opens the file a tiny amount, concealing the inside from me. He looks at me again. 'We found no external trauma to the outside of his head, except for a small cut to his forehead that we believe happened when he fell. When we referred the report to the coroner, she concluded it was one of those unpredictable events, something that might have always been there that no doctor could have foreseen happening. Was your husband's health generally good?'

'I don't think he ever went to the doctor, for anything.' Too much of a proud bastard, I feel like adding.

'And did he look after himself?'

'He played golf every Saturday. But he did drink and smoke, and he ate a hell of a lot of red meat.'

'You can't blame yourself, Mrs Sullivan. Annie,' he adds, and I look up in surprise. 'No wife can stop her husband doing the things he loves.'

I snort and then hide it with a tissue, shaking my head in mock grief.

DS Coleman places one hand on my arm. 'Don't worry if you don't feel up to it today, but as soon as you can formally identify the body, we can release it for the funeral.'

I look up, my eyes clear. 'No, that's fine, we can do it today.'

We walk down yet another featureless corridor, lit overhead by the same strips of luminescence. DS Coleman marches in front of me, his shoes squeaking on the tiled floor. He stops by a closed door and waits for me before turning the handle and opening it, escorting me in with an outstretched hand. The door closes behind us.

The room is thin and long, smelling of cleaning fluid, bleach and metal. It has a wide window stretching the length of it with wire inside the glass, reminding me of the reinforced windows from my old school. I wonder what they expect people to do in here, how people react. Through the window I see what looks like an operating theatre, all steel and silver, with something on a trolley in the centre. It's covered with a large navy-blue sheet, and a man stands next to it, looking at us, his hands clasped in front of him.

DS Coleman glances at me and I nod, then he nods through the glass. The man slowly removes the navy sheet from the end of the trolley, and I see David in front of me.

The sight takes me by surprise and I start, my hand flying to my mouth, naturally this time. He is face-up on the trolley, his hair slicked back. His face has a waxy, yellow pallor, his eyes mercifully shut.

'Is that your husband, David Sullivan?' DS Coleman asks.

'Yes,' I say, but somehow the word comes out

as a croak. 'Yes,' I repeat.

DS Coleman knocks on the glass gently and David's face is hidden for the last time.

We say our goodbyes and I stumble slowly out of the morgue and back into the normal part of the hospital. Without concentrating, I wander, and find myself in a part of the building I don't recognise. I didn't come this way earlier. I stand for a moment in front of one of the signs, looking for the way out, my vision blurry and my mind racing.

This isn't theory any more; this isn't a game. My husband is dead. Properly on-a-slab-in-the-morgue dead. And nobody knows it was me, nobody even suspects I had anything to do with it. But the fact is there, staring me straight in the face: I am a murderer. It was my actions and my actions alone that put him there. Sure, he was a wife-beating, PA-shagging grade A bastard, but I killed him. Or did I? Standing in that empty corridor, I try to convince myself that perhaps I had nothing to do with it, perhaps it was just one of those random events as the police officer described. Nothing but coincidence and happenstance rolled into one bit of truly bad timing. Perhaps.

I take a deep breath and steady myself for a moment, one hand on the wall in front of me. Whatever the truth, the reality is I have a small boy waiting for me. A small boy who needs his mother and nothing more. I dig into my handbag as my mobile beeps, showing the symbol for a new message.

I laugh as a photo comes through. Johnny is

standing on a chair next to a kitchen worktop, wooden spoon in his hand, chocolate cake mix all over his mouth and a big grin on his face. He is doing normal things, making cakes, in a normal kitchen. With a normal man.

Johnny's going to be fine. We're going to be fine. I'll make sure of it.

Part Four

White

Annie opened her eyes. She lay still, taking in her surroundings, disorientated. This room, this featureless box, wasn't anywhere her subconscious would have taken her. She didn't recognise it, she didn't understand. She sat up slowly, swinging her legs over the side of the metal-framed bed, touching the pillow and sheets gently with her hand.

The room was basic and still. The walls were white, with some scuffs and scrapes across the paintwork but otherwise no distinguishing marks. There was the bed, and a small bedside table made out of cheap wood, its top scratched and worn. A second bed and table mirrored her own on the opposite side, pristine and bare, but otherwise nothing else. Above her, a light bulb was enclosed in a plastic box pinned to the ceiling. She looked down. Her clothing was as bland as the room: a white long-sleeved top and grey tracksuit trousers. Her feet were bare.

She stood up and walked to the door, no more than three steps to get there. Like everything else it was white, with a stainless-steel handle and a small window in the middle at the top. She stood on tiptoes to look out, but could only see a patch of wall on the opposite side of a corridor. She tried the handle; it moved but the door wouldn't budge. It was locked.

She sat back down on the bed and closed her

eyes. She conjured up the park — the gentle rustling of the trees, the feel of the grass between her toes, the concrete path, the wooden bench. She smiled and opened her eyes, but the white room was as present as it had been before. She frowned, and tried again, this time thinking about the beach, asking Jack what was going on, hearing the seagulls, the roar of the ocean. Again, the white room.

She took a deep breath. She could feel her breathing quicken as the walls started to close in. She felt trapped in this strange dream, the silence, the endless white. She struggled to understand why she was here. Was this Jack's doing? If so, where was he? And where the hell was *she*?

Wake up, she thought, wake up and go home and start again.

Wake up.

But she was still here. The white walls, the silence.

She stood up and tried the door handle again: still locked. She pushed her whole weight against the door, then pulled it towards her. It didn't budge an inch. She could feel the panic buzzing in her veins and she hammered her fists against the door, screaming.

Wake up.

She heard the squeak of shoes on a polished floor, more than one person running, getting closer. She heard frantic shouts, and a face appeared in the window. She screamed louder. The door opened, followed by a barrage of bodies charging at her. They threw her onto the bed, pinning down her arms, her legs. Heavy weight on her chest. She screamed and thrashed, then felt a sharp prick in her arm and her body went limp.

Everything went dark.

32

I wake with a gasp and sit up suddenly in my bed, the duvet tangled round my feet, the pillows thrown to one side. I put one hand on my chest, where my heart is frantically beating, and lean back, trying to get my breathing under control. My throat feels scratched and sore, and I wonder if I have been screaming, playing out the nightmare in real life.

I listen, but Johnny still seems to be asleep. I think about the dream, but unlike previous ones, the remnants of it are fading from my memory. I take another deep breath and pull the duvet back over me and the pillows into place, curling up in the warmth. It just goes to show what control David still has over me. His legacy remains, inducing claustrophobia and fear when I least expect it. I doze as the light trickles into daytime, still too wary to fall back to sleep.

* * *

In the morning, we get up when we want. Johnny normally wakes about half six, and we take our time. We have breakfast — Cheerios for Johnny and Weetabix for me — and I enjoy my cup of tea while Johnny watches *Fireman Sam*. I slouch about in pyjamas until I feel like getting dressed, then take a shower and put on whatever I fancy for that day. Usually jeans and a top, the track-suit bottoms consigned to the bin. Johnny, however, is comfortable in tracksuit trousers and a T-shirt. Then the day is ours. We go shopping and buy meals for one in Waitrose if I can't be bothered to cook. Some days the house stays messy, covered in garish plastic toys until way past Johnny's bedtime. I watch trashy American shows in the evening, hand in a bag of popcorn.

I pile up the heap of paperwork you need to complete when someone dies, untouched. Everything needs to be completed in black ballpoint pen, the same details over and over again. Copies of the death certificate, descriptions from the coroner's report, National Insurance numbers, proof of who I am, who David was, what he died of and when. Someone's life reduced to a few numbers in a mountain of bureaucracy. I never get round to even picking up a pen: my attention span is short and I'm easily distracted when faced with the endless unintelligible text, the letters swimming in front of my eyes.

I debate getting in contact with Becca. I even pick up a pen at one point, to write her a letter, but I don't know what to say. I missed it all — her wedding, her pregnancy, her baby's first birthday. David hid her letters from me, that was true, but I didn't try to contact her either. I could have called her at any time; I could have gone to see her, but I didn't. I was too wrapped up in my own life, too weak, too brainwashed. Just thinking about it makes me curl up inside with humiliation. I am desperate to see her but I haven't got the strength for the conversation I know we need to have, the apology I have to make. I put it off, still frail, still ashamed.

David does have a will, and to my relief, I can get hold of the money. The solicitor, a stale but efficient man, sorts it all out without fuss. I speak to a surprisingly nice lady in the HR department at David's office. She phones me one day and calmly talks through the policies and procedures that apply to David's death. I listen, one hand on the phone and the other replacing the food from lunch in the fridge.

'I'm sorry for your loss,' she says. 'David was . . . ' She pauses. 'David was an important part of the office here.'

'Thank you,' I say automatically, and then stop, the phone still to my ear, standing with a slab of cheese in my hand. 'Did you know, about David's . . . '

Silence from the other end of the phone.

'About David's . . . ' I try again.

'Undesirable behaviours?' she suggests.

'Yes.'

'We had heard a few things. We were . . . ' she pauses, 'investigating.'

* * *

We go to the park, often our schedules corresponding with Adam and Georgia's.

'So, did you phone back?' he asks me once the children are happily running loops on the muddy grass.

'Yes, eventually,' I reply. Last time I saw Adam, I told him about a call I'd received from an old workmate who'd managed to track me down. 'They're looking for an assistant; it's just an admin role, less than I used to do, but it sounds okay,' I tell him. 'Part-time, too, so I can still spend time with Johnny.' I fidget with my hair. 'I've got to apply yet, and have an interview, so it's far from certain.'

Adam smiles and reaches over, touching me gently on my arm. 'I'm sure you'll get it.'

I look at him. He's turned back to watch the kids and I take in his profile. A nice face, softer than David's was, more crinkles and creases than jutting jawline. His hair is getting a bit long, starting to curl slightly behind his ears and at the nape of his neck, and I cross my arms, holding myself back from touching it.

I look at Johnny again, who is now lying on the grass laughing, his legs in the air. I am sure the job will be dull, full of filing and binding and typing up minutes from interminable meetings, but it will be mine. I remember the cards and letters David squirrelled away, reminding me of the friendships I used to have. Going to work isn't just about earning money. I had friends, I had a life. I need both of those.

'And how did the funeral go?' Adam asks.

* * *

It rained. Great globlets of downpour pooled in the streets and flooded the car park, forcing the mourners to jump like billy goats around the puddles. Contrary to the latest thinking about funerals, where people are asked to wear bright colours to celebrate the life of the deceased, Maggie opted for a strict 'black only' policy. Strangely appropriate, I thought.

That morning I dressed in the only suitable outfit I had, a ubiquitous black wrap dress from Marks and Spencer, pulling it over forty-denier tights and black heels I was unused to wearing. I wobbled slightly as I came down the stairs, one hand gripping the banister, the other holding a large black handbag that would have to carry everything we needed for the day.

Maggie had refused to accept that a funeral was no place for a two-year-old, and insisted that Johnny attend.

'What would people say if he wasn't there?' she said, one hand fluttering round her crepey throat. When I replied that I didn't care what people would say, she shook her head, looking close to hysterics again. 'He must pay his respects to his father,' she replied, and turned away from me, her omnipresent handkerchief going up to her eyes.

I still didn't know what that meant, but capitulated with a scowl when Maggie brought round a tiny black suit with elasticated tie. He did look sweet, I thought, once I had persuaded him into it, though how I was going to get him to stay quiet through the service, I didn't know.

One eye on the time, I quickly stuffed all manner of provisions into my handbag: nappies, wipes, cut-up grapes in a little Tupperware box, banana, raisins, a spare muslin, T-shirt and trousers, Rabbit, a few Thomas books and a couple of cars. As an afterthought, I put in a packet of tissues, for me, just in case.

The doorbell rang and I answered it, nearly falling over my own feet in the impractical heels. An unfamiliar man stood under a large umbrella, dressed all in black, face solemn and silent. I glanced over his shoulder to the driveway, where a massive black limousine was parked, another man standing next to the open door, Maggie already waiting for us inside. Oh crap, Maggie, I thought. What have you done, how awful is this funeral going to be?

The question was answered as we drew up to the church. The drive behind the hearse had been excruciatingly slow, Johnny fidgeting on my lap, Maggie uncharacteristically mute. It was the same church David Senior's funeral had been held at, but this time the attendees were few and far between. When David Senior had died, the church had been packed, with people standing at the back and all down the sides, reciting affectionate and humorous anecdotes before the service started. Today, everyone was silent, clustering together in small groups, cowering out of the rain. They all looked over as we arrived, Maggie clutching my arm on one side and Johnny on my hip on the other. I walked through a large puddle, the water freezing my feet, but I barely noticed.

Maggie had pulled out her best Jackie O ensemble once again, and sniffed occasionally under her black veil as we took our seats at the front of the church. A lone violinist played as we entered; something oppressive, screechy and grating. Maggie seemed rather dazed, her eyes glazed with the zombie stare of the overmedicated, something I had seen only too often growing up. Johnny perched on my lap, stunned into silence by the massive glossy photo of his father staring out from the front of the pulpit. Dressed in his trademark black suit, his eyes followed you wherever you went; even in photographic form he was intimidating.

The church reverted to a stony silence as the coffin, a shiny black motorcar of a box, was slowly carried inside and placed at the front, a huge bunch of lilies on top. I took solace knowing David was in there, and would soon be in the ground.

'A beacon of dedication, David Sullivan rose through the ranks at Melville Wright without hesitation. He commanded respect, attention to detail and hard work from his colleagues, and those who worked for him knew his unwavering demand for perfection would only work to their benefit.

'God works in mysterious ways, and we can only guess at His plan for taking David away from us so soon . . . '

At this Maggie clutched my arm tighter and sobbed into her handkerchief. I wasn't sure if it had been God's plan or mine and Jack's that had put David in his coffin, but I knew He hadn't done much to help me out when I needed Him the most.

There was no mention of friendship or love as the eulogy continued, and nobody else got up to make any comment. I had gently implied I hadn't the mental strength to make a speech at my husband's funeral; Maggie said it wasn't her place. Nobody murmured an agreement or laughed at a joke as the vicar spoke, and he fidgeted in his pulpit and frowned at the piece of paper in his hands, looking as uncomfortable as we all felt.

I had managed to keep Johnny quiet as he jiggled in my lap, in the end offering him a packet of chocolate buttons to get us through the last ten minutes. Maggie glanced over and pursed her lips, but made no comment. For the final hymn ('He Who Would Valiant Be'), I let him down and he ran up and down the aisle, arms waving. Maggie looked at me pointedly, then, when it was obvious I wasn't going to do anything to stop him, tried to grab him, but ended up snatching at air. Johnny hooted with laughter and headed off up the aisle, stopping when Jane, the infamous PA, crouched down next to him. Through the din of the singing ('to BE a pil-grim') she said something to him, and he showed her the plastic cars clutched in his hand, coming to sit next to her in the pew. She looked at me and I smiled and nodded.

A row of muttered 'Amens' and a sign of the cross from the vicar signalled the end of the service; discordant organ music sparked up and we shuffled out to the back room, towards the rows of curled-up sandwiches on paper plates and warm wine in plastic cups. Most people took the opportunity to make their exit, as Maggie's ladies crowded round her, patting her arm and offering their sympathies.

I watched Johnny out of the corner of my eye.

He had clearly taken a shine to Jane, and I waited as they made their way over to me, Johnny leading her by the hand, Jane barely making eye contact as she approached.

'Thank you for coming,' I said as I picked him up. 'And thank you for distracting Johnny.'

'He's a lovely little boy,' she said. She shuffled her bag and umbrella in her hands.

'He is,' I said. She was young, now I could see her properly up close, perhaps no more than mid-twenties, slim and pretty. She was wearing barely any make-up and her hair was scraped back off her face, but I could clearly see how attractive she could be, and how she deserved more than my husband had offered.

'I'm sorry,' she said, blurting it out in the silence. She looked like she was going to cry.

'It's okay. Just look after yourself a bit better, eat some cake.' I gestured towards the table, and the lack of people to eat the food.

She smiled, and bit her lip.

'And stay away from shits like my husband,' I added, and she widened her big Disney eyes in surprise.

Johnny, bored at the conversation, tapped me gently on my nose. 'Mummy?' he said with a charming smile.

'Yes?'

'Chocolate cake?'

'Of course, sweetie, whatever you want.' I turned away, Jane staring after us.

While Johnny covered his shirt in chocolate icing, I watched the wake from a distance. Nobody seemed keen to talk to me, and Maggie continued to enjoy the attention from her gaggle of ladies, her elegant hat now discarded and a glass of wine in her hand, merrily mixing her sedatives. As people slowly slunk out of the door and back into the rain, I shuffled in my plastic chair, Johnny on my lap surreptitiously starting on a cupcake just within reach, and watched the rain pour down the metal window, breaking through the frame and pooling on the window-sill.

'Wasn't it a wonderful representation of his life? So nice so many people came.' Maggie wobbled next to me, her lipstick slightly smudged.

'It was, Maggie, so good of you to organise, thank you.'

'I'm going to head off with my girls.' She gestured towards the old ladies in the corner of the room, one of them hiding something in her handbag in a napkin. 'The burial is at two tomorrow,' she added. I nodded. 'I'll leave the limo so you and Johnny can get home.'

'That's fine, don't worry, we'll get a cab.'

'No, it's yours.' She leant forward and gave us both a hug. Some of the chocolate icing from Johnny's face transferred itself to her dress. She touched his head lightly, then turned and was folded back into the mass of black.

For a moment I envied her. She had friends to look after her. Their motives might not be as pure as they should be — I sensed some were there for the drama, and others the cake — but they would look after her and keep her busy over the next few weeks. Who did I have?

I looked down at Johnny, who was quietly finishing off his cupcake.

'Come on, little man, enough now.' I reached into my bag and pulled out the wet wipes, fighting his resistance and cleaning the mess from his face. 'Let's go home.'

Johnny picked up his plastic cars, and I stood, taking his sticky little paw in mine. My heels in one hand and his hand in the other, I walked in my stockinged feet towards the door, past the pretty pictures about baby massage, the Alpha course and yoga. I looked up, and I stopped.

She was standing in the doorway, shaking the water off her umbrella and wiping the back of her hand across her dripping face. She looked older and more grown up but she was the exact same girl I had known all those years ago. She glanced up and saw me, a nervous grin spreading across her face.

'Hi, Annabelle,' she said.

'Hi, Becca,' I replied. Johnny pulled at my hand, anxious to get moving again.

'This must be Johnny,' she said, bending down to put her face at the same level as his.

'Hello,' he said. 'Chocolate cake.'

'Did you have chocolate cake?' she asked. 'Was it nice?'

Johnny looked up at me. 'Yes.'

Becca stood up again. 'I'm sorry about David. I saw the funeral notice in the paper.'

I shrugged, feigning an ambivalence that she would never believe, then felt my legs buckle slightly. Becca grabbed me, holding me tight around my middle as I gave way to an avalanche of relief, sadness, grief, regret, anger; everything I had held inside released in a tsunami of tears and snot and dribble. Seeing me, Johnny started to wail and Becca steered us all onto the plastic chairs lined down the side of the corridor. I pulled Johnny onto my lap in a big cuddle, taking the tissue Becca offered and blowing my nose.

'He was a bit of a shit,' I offered.

'I thought he might have been,' Becca said, wiping her own eyes and mopping down the mess I had transferred onto her shoulder.

'I'm sorry I didn't get in contact,' I muttered into my hands. 'David took your letters but I should have called, I should have got in contact. I should have done something. I just . . . I just let you go, and I shouldn't have. I'm so sorry.'

Becca nodded and took my hand. 'It's not your fault. I should have done more too. I should have come round, I should have knocked on your door.'

'You weren't to know. I don't think I realised myself, not really. Not until recently.' I blew my nose again, and pushed the decimated tissue into my pocket. 'Are you busy now? Johnny and I are heading off home. Do you want to come back with us?'

'I'd like that. Do you need a lift?' A small green Ford Ka was parked at an angle at the end of the path. I could see the child seat in the back.

'And I'm sorry I missed Rosie's birthday.'

Becca smiled. 'Mum said she saw you. I can imagine she was less than friendly.' She gestured towards the car and I picked Johnny up. 'Let's

go, we have a lot of catching-up to do.'
I smiled back. 'We do,' I replied.

* * *

'It was okay,' I say to Adam at the park. Cold, stressful, boring, glad it's over. 'An accurate reflection of his life.'

Face-down photo

The house was clean and tidy, decorated in muted browns and beige. Here and there sat a small ornament in turquoise: a vase or a candle-holder. The curtains were accented in blue, the cushions fawn, brown and navy stripes. It was night, and a few table lamps at the corners lit the room. All perfectly co-ordinated, but with a slightly messy air, relaxed and homely.

Annie wandered the room, unclear as to why her subconscious had dumped her here, but glad it wasn't the white room again. It had all the usual things you would expect — a bookcase, but with titles Annie didn't recognise, a spider plant cascading from one of the shelves. A posh television dominated the room, more technical-looking than anything she had ever experienced.

There was a display of photos across the mantelpiece, some facing outwards — a handsome older man and woman hand in hand smiling out — but the majority face down. Annie went to pick one up.

'Annie?'

She paused, and turned to face Jack. He stood in the doorway of the living room, his hands in the pocket of his jeans.

'What are you doing here?' he asked quietly.

'I was looking for you.' Annie smiled and went over to him, taking his hands in hers. 'We did it, Jack, we did it. He's dead.'

Jack smiled back and gave her a hug. '*You* did it, Annie.'

'And it worked!' Annie moved and sat down on one of the beige sofas. 'He's gone. Everything's going to be fine now.' She looked up at Jack. 'Johnny's going to be fine.'

Jack slowly moved round and sat next to her. He rubbed his eyes and took a deep breath in. 'He is, Annie. Johnny's going to be fine.'

Annie's energy was palpable; she fidgeted and twitched, happy to be sitting with Jack, her husband gone, her son tucked up in bed, safe and warm at home. In contrast, Jack was very still, his face cast to the floor. He produced a mug of coffee and held it in both hands, cupping it for warmth.

'Do you have kids, Jack?' Annie asked.

He smiled. 'No. It's just me and Lizzie. We're too young at the moment.'

'How old are you?'

'Guess.'

Annie studied him, taking in his cheekbones, the stubble that didn't quite cover his chin, the lack of wrinkles, the full head of hair. 'Twenty-two?' she said tentatively.

He laughed, and some of the tension disappeared from his face. 'Close, but I'll take it as a compliment. Twenty-five.'

'Ah. And what about me?'

'Thirty-two,' he said, without missing a beat.

'How did you know?'

He smiled. 'Good guess.'

'And where did you meet Lizzie?'

'At work.' Annie raised her eyebrows and Jack

sighed. 'Why so interested all of a sudden?' he asked.

'I know so little about you. I'm just curious.'

Jack looked at his mug of coffee. 'We both work for the same company. She is part of the systems engineering team and I am part of software. We started on the same day.'

'Good, we're getting somewhere.' Annie was enjoying herself. 'Does she know what you get up to at night?'

Jack laughed. 'You make it sound like I'm out with prostitutes! No, she doesn't.'

'Why haven't you ever told her?'

Jack sat up in his seat and frowned. 'I've thought about it, but what would be the point? I've found her a few times and she doesn't have the same ability as you or me, so she wouldn't understand. And I don't want to freak her out.'

'Do you think it would?'

'Wouldn't it you? 'Hey, love, at night I can move around and spy on people's dreams.' Wouldn't you think you were dating a crazy?'

Annie nodded. She thought about a mug of tea then brought it into her dream, with a packet of chocolate digestives for good measure. She opened them and held them out to Jack, who took one.

'And your family?' she continued, eating a biscuit of her own.

'You don't give up, do you?' Jack said, through a mouthful. He chewed thoughtfully. 'My mum lives in Camberley. She has a nice little house there and a small dog — one of those yappy things, you know? She seems happy. My dad died when I was seven. Cancer.'

'I'm sorry. What was he like?'

'From what I remember, wonderful. Did all the usual things with me — played football, helped with my homework. We used to go for these long rambly walks when he would tell me the Latin names for all the plants and trees, and show me animal tracks and make me guess what they were. I found it boring then, of course. Would love it now.' He rubbed the side of his nose with his middle finger. 'It's a bugger, cancer.'

They paused for a moment, quiet in each other's company. Unlikely friends in unlikely circumstances.

Jack looked over at Annie, and placed his empty mug on the coffee table. 'Annie?' She looked at him. 'Does anything feel odd?'

She raised an eyebrow and gestured around the room. 'Everything always feels odd. I'm only just getting to the point when odd feels normal.'

Jack smiled. 'Yes, but . . . I don't know. Like you've forgotten something.'

Annie looked puzzled, then listened and heard the unmistakable chatter of a small boy, awake and ready to start the day. 'I'm being called,' she said with a smile, and faded out of the room.

Jack got up and walked over to the mantelpiece. He picked up one of the photos lying there and looked at it for a long time. Whatever he needed to do, it would have to wait. Until when, he didn't know.

33

The rain eventually stops, and the sun returns to our part of southern England. On this particular morning, Johnny and I have nothing planned. We eat our breakfast; we tidy up the kitchen. I put some washing on and hang it out to dry in the garden, a gentle warm wind blowing about. Johnny decides his toy cars are the way forward, so we are carefully putting the final pieces in place of a rather impressive road layout (figure-of-eight, with two bridges, a T-junction and a pedestrian crossing, no less) when I hear the jiggle of a key in the door. It scratches and tries to turn a few times, the handle going up and down redundantly. I sit in my position on the living room floor and watch.

The doorbell rings twice in quick succession, so I pull myself to my feet with a sigh.

'There seems to be a problem with your locks,' Maggie says as I open the door, handing me her jacket.

'No problem, Maggie. I just had them changed.'

'Whatever for?' She stands in the middle of the living room, one foot on the edge of Johnny's road. A small white battery-operated car swoops round and hits it, overturning next to her. Johnny runs over and taps her foot in protest.

'What?' she says to him, and he holds up the car.

'Crash,' he says.

'You're standing on his road,' I point out, and

she moves her foot. 'Cup of tea?' I ask, ignoring her question.

Maggie follows me into the kitchen, taking position at the edge of my counter top, blocking my exit. 'Why did you change the locks?'

'Just to be safe, Maggie,' I say, my back to her, filling up the kettle at the sink. 'I didn't know who David had given keys to, and since it's just me and Johnny now, I wanted to be sure.'

'Well, you'll have to give me a spare.'

'Why is that, Maggie?' I ask, turning back.

'I'm family.'

'We'll always be here, we can always let you in.'

'What happens if I need to get in and you're not here?'

'Why, Maggie?' I ask, smiling innocently. So you can snoop around our things? Pry into our business?

'In case I've forgotten anything, or . . . ' She stops, thinking. 'Or something happens to you.'

'We'll be fine,' I say, 'but thank you for the offer.' I hand her the tea. Earl Grey in a mug, tea bag still in, paper tag hanging over the side. We don't have any lemon. She takes it from me as if I have handed her one of Johnny's dirty nappies.

I walk back into the living room, placing my own mug on the coffee table and handing Johnny his beaker. Maggie follows us, holding the offending mug at a distance.

'Look, Annie,' she says, 'I don't know how to say this, but I don't think you are fine. Look at you.'

I look down. I am still wearing my pyjamas,

but to be fair, it is only just past nine.

'We're having a lazy day.'

'I hear you have quite a few lazy days.'

'Hear from who?' My skin starts to prickle.

'I didn't want to do this, Annie, but I've hired someone to keep track. To follow you. To check on you and Johnny.'

'Hired who? Like a private investigator?'

'He's very nice, extremely discreet. You haven't noticed at all,' she adds, as if this is a plus point. 'He says some days you don't leave the house except to go to the play park and the supermarket.'

'I've got a two-year-old son, Maggie. Where do you expect us to go? The art gallery?'

'Don't be facetious, Annie. I'm worried about Johnny. I don't think you're looking after him.'

At the mention of his name, Johnny glances up at us both, a lorry in one hand and a piece of bridge in the other. His chubby cheeks are healthy, his T-shirt and shorts clean and his nappy empty.

'What exactly is wrong with him?' I ask.

'Look at his knees, they're covered in bruises.'

'Once again, Maggie, he's a two-year-old boy. He runs about. He jumps, he kicks, he falls over. That's normal.'

'Is it? My David never had bruised knees.'

'Your David wouldn't have known an outdoor activity if a football had smacked him in the face.'

She gasps, one hand clutched to her chest. 'How dare you speak ill of the dead?' she exclaims.

'Oh, for crying out loud.' I can feel my hands starting to shake, and pick up my mug to calm myself. 'Maggie, we are fine. Johnny is fine. I would appreciate it if you would ask your private investigator to stop following us, and for you to leave us alone.'

She stands up, pulling her beige cardigan around her. 'I will not. I will give my file to the social services, and I will file for custody of David Junior.'

I slowly place my mug of tea back on the table and stand up next to her. I am trying very hard to stay calm. Even though I am hardly blessed with height, I tower over her tiny frame. 'Get out of my house, and leave us alone. You have no right to have us followed and no right to claim custody of Johnny.'

Maggie whirls round to face me. 'You are a terrible mother,' she shouts. 'I will make sure David Junior is taken away from you and you never see him again.' She picks up her handbag and pulls open the front door.

'Get out of my house, you crazy old bitch.' I can't control my anger now.

Maggie turns to me, her handbag in front of her as a barrier. 'My David was a winner in every way. You are always destined to be at the bottom, taking after your whore of a mother.'

'What do you know about my mother?' I am winded for a second, the breath knocked out of me.

'Do you honestly think this is the first time I've used a private detective?' she hisses, her chin jutting out. 'When we first met you, we checked your background, but it all came too late, you were already engaged. It would have been too much of a scandal to break it off, but we knew!' She waves a spindly finger in my direction. 'We knew about your druggy mother, how she died.'

'I'm nothing like my mother.'

'It's in your blood — and now it's in his!' She goes to move back towards Johnny, and I jump forward, putting my body and all my resolve in front of her. 'You have no idea what being a true mother is like.'

'And you do?' I growl. 'I know I love him. I know I would do anything to make him happy, to keep him safe. What else do you need to know, you fucking stupid woman?' I can feel my whole body shaking. I am tensed, muscles on alert, everything about me ready to protect my son.

She hesitates and backs away from me, half out of the door, unsure about what I might do. She goes to leave, then turns back, wrinkling her nose. 'You disgust me. You are not important. You wait and see what I can do, you little slut. I'll destroy you.'

'Just leave us alone,' I shout after her. 'Get out of our lives.'

I slam the door and lock it, watching from the window as she reverses at speed out of our driveway, nearly hitting an innocent Nissan Micra on the road. Brakes screech and horns blare at each other, and for a moment I am distracted, feeling a flicker of recognition, an awareness of déjà vu. I shake my head and watch as Maggie's BMW swerves out of view and she is gone.

I slump onto the sofa, my hands shaking and tears prickling in my eyes.

Johnny turns back to his cars, distracted for a moment by the shouting.

'Bye bye, Grandma Madgie,' he says. 'Bye bye.'

Bye bye, indeed.

34

Her girl found her. Arriving early for her daily ironing and cleaning session, she was surprised to find Maggie still in bed, motionless and staring up at the ceiling, unblinking.

Her girl is obviously of a delicate constitution and promptly vomited on the floor, cleaning it up in the time between calling the police and them arriving. Maggie had trained her well.

The police officer arriving first on the scene, my very own Detective Sergeant Coleman, recognised the name and called me straight away in a tone of voice I am getting used to. Not that I wasn't expecting the call; I just hadn't known when.

As I arrive at the house, the girl is still sobbing, sitting on a dining room chair, tissue in hand and a trace of pink puke on her white shirt. The police officer has that face on again, a mixture of barely mustered sympathy and badly concealed boredom as he asks his questions, notebook in hand, tiny handwriting scampering over the page. Johnny and I wait by the door, Johnny patiently holding my hand, quiet as a mouse as he has learnt at Grandma Maggie's house.

DS Coleman glances across and holds a finger up to me to show he has seen me and to ask me to wait, while the girl sobs on. I can hear them talking: ' . . . like a mother to me . . . always took care of me . . . ' Yeah, I think, as long as you didn't complain about being paid less than minimum wage and did her washing just as she liked it.

I move towards the door to the lounge, still wearing my shoes, a previously unforgivable crime, and look round before pulling the handle down. We haven't been in this room since David Senior died, and I slowly digest the space, taking in the bland, generic furniture. It's strangely sad, a featureless showroom, giving no clue to Maggie's personality.

The only thing in the room that implies some sort of feeling on Maggie's part is a framed photo of David Junior, positioned next to a candle, gently burning itself out. I pick up the photo and examine it, exploring myself for some sort of emotion. It is a corporate shot, a different one from the monstrosity at the funeral, and I recognise it as the one his company used for publicity when he became CEO. He looks smug. I feel the last vestiges of grief, a little remaining anger, but mostly the picture brings on a wave of relief.

DS Coleman clears his throat behind me and I turn, the photo still in my hand. Johnny moves closer to me, wary of seeing this strange man again; I grip him tightly, my arms wrapped around him.

'I'm sorry, Mrs Sullivan,' DS Coleman says. 'This must be a shock to you.'

'It's not been a great month,' I say.

He comes into the room, sitting on the sofa next to me, his hard black shoes leaving a trace of mud on Maggie's immaculate white carpet.

'The pathologist has taken the body away, but he says he thinks it was something similar to your husband. A catastrophic brain event.' So much so, I would learn later, that blood came out of her ears and tear ducts. Something blew up so efficiently in there, it turned her grey matter to mush. 'He did mention it's strange that all the family seemed to suffer from it; said it might be worth your little boy getting checked for something genetic.'

'Of course,' I say, knowing I will do nothing of the sort.

'Anyway,' he says, 'I'll let you know the outcome of the post-mortem and the body will be released soon after that. You know the drill,' he adds with a little laugh, then hides it with a cough. 'Sorry again, Mrs Sullivan.'

I smile weakly and he leaves.

Johnny taps my knee. 'Home now,' he says, with certainty.

I nod.

* * *

I wasn't surprised by how heavy the gun felt in my hand. I wasn't surprised that out of nowhere I knew how to unclip the safety, to pull back the firing pin and gently squeeze the trigger, both hands cradling the gun for support. I had opted for a gun, for a bit of simplicity. I had seen far too many Hollywood movies and wanted a taste of the action.

This time my subconscious seemed warmed

up to the event. It offered no resistance when I went in search of Maggie, finding her in a Chinese restaurant, a pair of chopsticks in her hand. I had never seen her eat what she called 'ethnic food', but here she was, plate of noodles, and prawn crackers in a basket, tucking in like there was no tomorrow. Which of course, there wasn't.

My arm offered no resistance when I lifted the gun, standing in front of her, barrel in line with her forehead.

The next bundle of dripping noodles was ready to be loaded into her mouth. She even had her napkin tucked into the neck of her blouse, like a common person, she would have said. Our subconscious is a funny thing.

'What are you doing here?' she said with disgust.

'Looking for you,' I said, and pulled the trigger.

The gun exploded with a loud bang, the recoil knocking my hand up and away, the bullet still somehow meeting its target and slamming into Maggie's head. Her skull exploded like a watermelon, shattering her face and scattering pieces of it onto the wall behind her in a cloud of red mist. She looked at me for a moment, the hand and chopsticks still hanging in mid-air, then everything collapsed and she fell into her chicken chow mein.

I was surprised about my lack of caution, my lack of hesitation. Maybe I'd thought something might hold me back; I might think twice or have doubts about what I was doing. What I knew would happen. But no, I didn't even flinch. Not even when I could taste the steel tang in my mouth and a piece of something biological hit my shoe.

I had been lied to; the people I loved had been hidden from me. My patience had run out and I was angry. I was really fucking angry. It burnt in my throat and bubbled in my stomach; my blood raced through my veins, keen to get going.

Killing someone gets easier once you have done it before. And I knew I was right to go ahead.

The room burst into life. Other diners screamed, and I could hear chairs being thrown and people running from the room. At the same time, I was aware of people running in. I turned and faced a row of burly Chinese men, heads shaved, all holding excessively large machine guns, all pointed at me.

How funny, I thought; in her dreams Maggie was the head of the Chinese mafia. It wasn't so funny when they all started to fire.

Revolver still in my hand, I jumped, executing an overhead spin, firing as I went and hitting the biggest guy. He went down with a thump, taking out the waitress at the same time. I landed perfectly, poised for the next round, then ducked and rolled under the closest table, pulling it over in a shower of cutlery and glass, using it as a shield as bullets thumped into the wooden tabletop. I was enjoying myself, relishing the ever-increasing crazy. I raised my hand and let off a few rounds, and in the silence as they all took cover, I ran, spinning and firing with precision and poise as I went. In the moment before the mirror shattered behind me, I caught a glimpse of my own reflection. Hair slicked back, black eyeliner, black jeans, black boots and a tight black top. Crikey, I look cool, I thought, as I leapt across the bar, optics and alcohol splintering over my head in the crossfire. I laughed as I shook the glass out of my hair. I was getting the hang of this; either that, or properly going mental. Whichever, I was having a lot of fun.

The gunfire stopped and I heard the approach of heavy pissed-off mafia underlings. I checked my revolver — out of bullets. That was entertaining, I thought, but enough was enough.

Wake up, I thought, and I was gone.

* * *

Outside Maggie's house, I load Johnny back into the car, then strap myself in. When I pull up in our drive — *my* drive — and let Johnny out of his car seat, he runs gleefully towards the house, arms waving in the air, almost tripping over his feet to get in as soon as possible. I have the same feeling as I reach over him and unlock the front door with a smile. The cool air greets me as we go inside, Johnny heading straight towards his toys, still in a messy pile from when we left that morning; me to the kitchen to get a drink for us both. A Diet Coke for me, drunk straight out of the can without a glass. Beaker of water for Johnny, left in front of him on the coffee table, no coaster in sight.

I sink onto the sofa, kicking my trainers off haphazardly on the rug. I cast my eye around the room, taking in what is now my home, my safe haven. Already I have taken down the photos and ornaments I hated, and replaced them with keepsakes of my own. A photo frame given to me by Becca on my fifteenth birthday, now adorned with a smiling photo of me and Johnny. A heavy blue glass paperweight, bought from a charity shop years ago with my first pay cheque. Memories I am proud of, to mark a future I can finally look forward to.

I watch Johnny arrange his trains in a line, contentedly chatting to them as he goes. Hello, Thomas, hello, Gordon, hello, James.

Goodbye, David, goodbye, Maggie.

Goodbye, Annie.

Hello, Annabelle, hello, Johnny.

35

She pulled at the stiff white collar of the cheap blouse irritating her neck. Her mother reached over and slapped her hand away.

'We're someplace nice, Annabelle,' she hissed. 'Try and act classy. And sit up straight.'

Her mother was dressed in a bright red nylon dress. Low-cut at the front, showing her skinny décolletage and empty boobs; better suited to a woman half her age.

Annabelle forced herself up in the uncomfortable chair, sitting straight and placing her hands on the table in front of her. She looked at her nails, bitten, uneven, dirty, and put them back on her lap, out of sight. She glanced around the room; it was quiet, only a few tables occupied. They were at the back, out of the way. One day, she resolved, I'm going to have perfect red shiny nails, and I'm going to sit right in the middle of the restaurant where everyone can see me.

* * *

Earlier that day, she had rushed home from the pub, her hard-earned twelve pounds clutched in her hand. When the final pot and pint glass had been dried and put away, she found herself surrounded by the owner and her workmates clutching a chocolate cupcake with a candle on top.

They sung a heartfelt 'Happy Birthday' and the owner of the pub held out the cake to her.

'Make a wish, sweet pea,' she'd said. 'Sweet sixteen.'

Annabelle closed her eyes. I wish tonight to go well, she'd thought, I wish to be free. And she blew.

* * *

The waitress came over to their table, pad and pen in hand.

Her mother looked up slowly from the menu. 'I'm afraid I'm going to be a pain,' she said, smiling and showing the red lipstick stuck to her teeth. 'I'm allergic to nuts, and I can't eat gluten or dairy. Oh, and I'm vegetarian. Is there anything here I can have?'

Annabelle looked down at her hands again, remembering the remains of a burger left by her mother in the kitchen late Saturday night.

The waitress leant over, tapping her pen on the menu. 'I could ask the chef to make some of the risotto up for you, mushrooms, butternut squash and avoiding the prawns.'

'Oh, prawns are fine, leave in the prawns,' her mother said.

The waitress scribbled on the pad, then looked to Annabelle.

'The pasta, please, thank you,' she said.

'It's her sixteenth birthday today,' her mother added.

Annabelle felt her cheeks redden. 'Lovely, happy birthday,' the waitress said, and walked quickly towards the kitchen.

Her mother leant over. 'A place like this, you should get a pudding on the house for your birthday. And I can get an allergic reaction from my dinner, and we're home free.' She smiled.

'Pizza would have been fine, Mum,' Annabelle said. She hadn't wanted to go out for dinner, but her mother had insisted, a rare gesture of pretend normality. Annabelle was desperate to finish; Becca was waiting for her just as soon as she could get away.

'Don't be so ungrateful,' her mother said. 'How often do we have an excuse to come to these fancy-pants restaurants?'

'I know, thank you,' Annabelle said, her insides already screwed up in a knot. 'Let's just have a nice quiet dinner.'

'Quiet?' her mum said. 'You know I don't do quiet. Why do quiet,' she cackled, 'when you can do free?'

* * *

'Was it that awful?' Becca said later, lying on her bed and tossing her newly permed blonde ringlets back from her face.

'Worse,' Annabelle said. 'She made such a fuss I was afraid we'd get thrown out of the restaurant. Here, give me some of that.'

Becca took a big swig of the toxic-looking red liquid and passed the bottle across to Annabelle sitting cigarette in hand by the open window.

'Was MD 20/20 the best you could get?' Annabelle said, screwing her nose up at the sickly-sweet alcohol.

'You try nicking from the offie next time. And besides, couldn't you just have stolen a bottle from your mum?'

'Nah, she'd notice.'

Annabelle and Becca were in Becca's room, joss sticks burning to mask the smell of Annabelle's smoking, Radiohead playing quietly on the CD player. Becca's mum had turned a blind eye to the late-night visit, muttering, 'Just this once' under her breath as she closed her bedroom door.

Annabelle opened the large bag next to her for the umpteenth time, mentally running through everything packed inside.

'Where are you going to go?' Becca asked. 'I could ask Mum if you could stay here.'

Annabelle smiled and reached out for her friend's hand. 'I know, thank you, but I need to get away. I can't stand being near her any more, even in the same town.' She took a final drag of the cigarette and stubbed it out on the window-sill. 'I need to go somewhere where nobody knows me — or her. A fresh start.'

'You'll keep in touch, won't you?' Becca looked close to tears. 'I'll miss you.'

Annabelle leant over and gave her a hug, smelling the familiar smell of hairspray and cheap teenage perfume. She almost couldn't bear to say goodbye, but the nugget of excitement was growing, churning in her stomach.

'I'll miss you too,' she said, closing her eyes, her voice breaking.

She looked again at the bag, then scrabbled through the contents, tipping the items out onto Becca's bed. Her stomach dropped and she covered her face with her hands.

'Shit,' she said, 'I've forgotten my sodding money.' She could see it, clear in her mind's eye, underneath her bed in the Tupperware box. 'I'm going to have to go back.'

* * *

On the way home through the darkness, she ran through what she was going to say to her mother if she was there. I'm leaving, I'm not coming back, I'll be in touch. *She sprang from one patch of light to another, the street lights guiding her way.*

As she approached the house, she felt a burn of anxiety, and it took her a few goes to get the key in the lock with her shaking hand. She opened the door slowly, and looked around. Everything seemed quiet; her mother wasn't often home at this time on a Saturday night.

'Mum?' she called, just in case, and receiving no reply, she moved slowly into the kitchen.

Her mother was sitting at the table, a half-finished bottle of vodka and a packet of cigarettes in front of her. Her head was bowed and she was struggling to stay awake. She raised her head as Annabelle came in.

'You're home,' she slurred. 'Where have you been?'

'At Becca's,' Annabelle replied, cursing under her breath and sitting slowly on the chair

opposite her mother. 'I told you, remember?'

Her mother waved her comment away. 'What were you doing with Becca?' she asked. 'Were you drinking?' She picked up the vodka bottle and took a swig. She didn't even wince as she swallowed the full mouthful.

'No, just hanging out in her bedroom,' Annabelle said, ignoring her mother's hypocrisy, the lies coming out of her mouth with practised ease.

Her mother laughed, a globule of spit landing on the table in front of Annabelle. 'You left so quickly earlier, we didn't even have time for cake.'

'That's okay.'

'It's not fucking okay. Here.' Her mother scrabbled around on the chair next to her and picked up a Tupperware box, putting it on the table. One five-pound note and a few coins rattled in the bottom. Annabelle's stomach dropped.

'Where's the rest of it?'

'The rest? Oh yeah, there was quite a bit, wasn't there?' her mother said.

'And the . . . the bits and pieces?' Annabelle didn't know how else to describe them. Her treasures, the memories of the good things in her life. The times that kept her going.

'The junk? That fuzzy thing and the receipts and stuff? In the bin. What did you want those for?'

Annabelle rushed to the bin and opened the lid, but they were gone. Buried under a mound of food leftovers and burger wrappers. She turned back to her mother.

'What were you doing digging around under my bed?'

'What the hell were you doing building up your little stash and not offering any of it to me?' her mother shouted. 'You're not cheap, you know, all that food, all that rent you never contribute to. This is my money! I've brought you up for sixteen years and you've never offered me a penny.'

'Where's the money?' Annabelle shouted back, tears rolling down her cheeks. Her escape plan, now in her mother's hands.

Her mother laughed, showing a row of stained, uneven pegs. 'All gone, paid for Mummy's vitamins, and Mummy's magic talcum powder. And this little bottle of something special,' she finished, gesturing towards the vodka. She took out the five-pound note and put it on the table. 'Go to the twenty-four-hour shop and buy us a cake — we'll celebrate your birthday.'

Annabelle felt the anger build, rolling her hands into fists. 'I hate you! I owe you nothing! Nothing at all! For my entire life you've been no more than a drugged-up alcoholic — ' She stopped as she felt the stinging slap round her face. Her mother stood in front of her, her hand still raised. Then she calmly reached down to the table, took a cigarette from the packet and put it in her mouth.

'I gave you life — I made you,' she said, not looking at Annabelle. She lit the cigarette and blew a plume of smoke across the kitchen. 'Without me, you're nothing. Worthless.' She held out the five-pound note and Annabelle stared at it. 'Take it.' Her mother waved it in her face. 'It's yours, after all.'

Stunned, Annabelle took the fiver and ran out of the house, slamming the door behind her. As she walked, thoughts whirled around in her head. She couldn't leave now, not without money. She could borrow some from Becca. But Becca was as skint as Annabelle. She could just go anyway, but what would she live off?

She bought a cake and carried it back, slapping it on the table in front of her mother. In the time she had been gone, her mother had managed to find a few candles, their ends already blackened from use; now she stuck them directly into the icing of the cake and lit them with her lighter.

'Happy birthday, my darling daughter,' she said sarcastically, letting out a cloud of cigarette smoke over the cake, blowing out the candles in the process. She laughed. 'Oh well, let's just eat the damn thing.'

Knife in hand, she cut a large slab of cake and placed it in front of Annabelle on the table. She did the same for herself, then took a large bite, chocolate icing all round her mouth. 'Absolutely fucking delicious,' she mumbled, and then stopped.

She placed the cigarette in the ashtray and put the cake back on the table slowly. She was struggling to take a breath. 'What the fuck did you buy?' she wheezed.

'What do you mean?' Annabelle asked, looking at her own untouched slice.

'What did you buy?' Her mother took another strained breath in and tried to stand up, clawing at her neck. 'I can't . . . ' she whispered.

Annabelle felt a calm wash over her. Her mother attempted to stand again, knocking her chair over and falling to the floor. Annabelle stood up and took a step backwards. Her mother groped towards her, and then towards the mobile phone that had fallen next to her. Annabelle carefully pushed it away with her foot, out of her grasp.

She saw the look of sudden realisation on her mother's face as she strained to get some air, her skin taking on a deathly pallor. Her eyes bulged and her mouth opened in wordless desperation. Her arm reached out to Annabelle, then she fell unconscious.

Annabelle looked at her mother's prone body, twisted and bent, her face puffy, her legs collapsed unnaturally under her, her lips blue. She turned and picked up the box for the cake. Chocolate peanut butter cup. Allergy advice: contains nuts.

She stood in the kitchen a while longer, then leant over to take her mother's pulse. Nothing. She reached down and picked up the mobile phone. The digital display marked the time: 4:13 a.m.

She was free.

36

'Where do you want this to go?' Becca holds up yet another black leather belt, this one brand new, still with its tag on.

I glance over from my cross-legged position on the floor. 'Charity,' I reply without hesitation, and she throws it perfectly into the bin bag on the other side of the room. 'How are we doing?' I ask, surveying the mess.

Becca looks around as I do, taking in the empty wardrobes, the line of bulging bin bags, carefully labelled and stacked in the corner. The bed in the centre of the room has been stripped of its white cotton sheets and I can hear them going round in the washing machine downstairs, set to ninety degrees.

'Pretty well, I think,' Becca says, running the back of her hand across her face, pushing her hair out of her eyes for the umpteenth time today. 'And I nearly forgot: Mum said would you like to come round for Sunday lunch this week?'

'We would love to,' I reply. I can't help the grin appearing on my face. Sunday lunch at Helen's is nothing like the weekends of old with Maggie. It's messy and noisy, with conversations abandoned in the middle then picked up again later. It's warm, and fun: everything I have always wished for.

'Good,' Becca says and looks at her watch. 'On that subject, time for some lunch?'

At the sound of the word 'lunch', both small children look up from their play area in the hallway outside the bedrooms. They're surrounded by Johnny's toys, and I managed to find some brightly coloured blocks to keep Rosie amused. Despite the age difference between them they have been playing nicely alongside each other, a mismatch of stacked blocks and towers of Duplo creating a tiny cityscape on the carpet.

'What do you say, Johnny?' I ask. 'Time for some lunch? Pizza?'

'Pizza,' Johnny nods, 'an' chips.'

'Please?' I laugh.

Johnny looks solemn. 'Please.'

We decamp downstairs, me carrying a few bin liners as we go and leaving them by the front door as Johnny descends the stairs on his bottom, followed closely by Becca carrying Rosie on her hip. I turn on the oven and unwrap the pizzas, lining them up on the counter ready to go.

I turn to Becca, who is standing in the doorway, watching the kids get distracted by the boxes of toys downstairs.

'Thank you for doing this,' I say. 'It would have been so depressing without you here. Today feels . . . something else, I don't know.'

'Cathartic?' she offers.

'Yes, like some sort of therapy. Clearing out the old.'

The chips go in the oven, followed by the pizzas on their trays. We lay the table in companionable silence, and Becca sets up a portable high chair for Rosie, placing it next to Johnny's at the table. Knives and forks, wet wipes, ketchup and tiny-people spoons are laid out in a square. For a family of sorts — a new family.

* * *

That morning, I woke up before Johnny. I lay in bed for a moment, the sun making an appearance behind the curtains blowing slightly in the summer breeze. I could hear cars moving out of the close, people talking; pigeons sat on the satellite dish cooing noisily.

I got up, cool in just my T-shirt and shorts, and opened the door quietly. I paused in the hallway for a moment, listening with Johnny's door slightly ajar until I heard it, the faint in and out of his breathing, repetitive and reassuring. Still asleep — it was early.

I stood for a moment in the hallway and regarded the closed door in front of me: the master bedroom where David used to sleep. Before now the door had remained resolutely closed, his life confined and shut away into one room, but now I pushed the handle down slowly, allowing the stale air to escape into the corridor. Warm, fusty, but still unmistakably David. Slowing my breathing, I made my way round the bed and pushed open a window, feeling the cool air on my face, listening to the early sounds of lawn mowers. Instantly I felt better.

I slowly pulled open the wardrobe, seeing rows and rows of stern suits. The line of white and pale-blue shirts I had painstakingly ironed and positioned; the ties, the cufflinks, the old copies of the *FT* left on his bedside table.

Becca and Rosie turned up expecting a relaxing morning of play park and ice creams. Ever since the funeral, Mondays had been our day, a new routine of friendship and chat, resurrected from years of silence without hesitation or any sort of grudge. But things had evolved from the drunken, blurry nights of old, to Play-Doh and tea and sandpits. There was nothing boring about our new routine and our new lives, just comfort and consistency.

Over the weeks, we had talked. Endless chatter and laughter, making up for those lost years. I apologised again; she seemed to forgive me. I met Matt, and Becca showed me photos of their wedding. He seemed nice: calm, easy-going, loving, everything David hadn't been. She confided a horrible period of post-natal depression and I shared pieces of my life with David. A lot remained unsaid. I wanted it to stay that way.

As I outlined my plan, she nodded without a word, and we unfurled lines of bin bags. We stripped suits and shirts from their hangers and stuffed them in without respect or care, throwing old hair products and moisturiser and razor-blades in another, ready for the bin. We took to the room as a surgeon takes to a tumour, systematically cutting away any part of David that remained, without emotion or thought.

At one point Becca turned to me, a pair of purple cufflinks in her hand: *that* pair, the pair I was sure were a gift from some woman or other.

I wondered how many other presents from his affairs had made their way into our house. 'Do you miss him?' she asked gently.

I paused, tying up one bin bag and opening another. 'I don't miss him as such. Not the reality of him, our day-to-day life. I suppose I do miss the nice parts of him, when we could pretend we were a normal loving couple.' I sat on the naked bed, pillows stacked waiting for their new clothes. 'But that was never really normal, it was always about waiting and being scared for the next time he would turn and be the different David, the real David. I guess I'm just sad about what could have been. Watching Johnny grow up together, getting old, having a normal married life.' I shook my head. 'But that was never real, and would never have been, not with David.'

'What would you have done, do you think, if he hadn't died?'

'I don't know.' I replied. 'I don't know.'

* * *

Pizza cooked and cooled, the chips distributed to happy children, we all sit round the table and eat. We laugh at Johnny's demands for more ketchup, and Becca tolerates Rosie's lunchtime diet of chips, chips and only chips, mushed into her face. She shakes her head and ruffles Rosie's hair. 'I'll force a banana down her later,' she mutters.

After lunch we drag the endless stream of bin liners out of the door and into my car, or straight into the wheelie bin with a thump. After we persuade two exhausted children to sleep, we wipe down every surface with anti-bac and window cleaner, and finally, on reflection, I take down the black-and-white prints of bleak trees and wind-bleached landscapes and put them in the car with the rest of the stuff for charity. All finished, we sit back in the room, windows still open and cool glasses of Diet Coke in our hands.

I already know what pictures I want on the wall: lots of photos. Johnny as a baby, Johnny aged four months, head up and smiling at tummy time, Johnny aged six months with pureed butternut squash round his month. Unashamedly the centre of my world now, unashamedly spoilt.

I glance at Becca and take a deep breath. 'So there's this guy.'

Her head snaps round. 'Really? What guy? Who?'

It's Adam, of course. We've met up at the park a few times, deliberately now, co-ordinating schedules by text, and Georgia and Johnny have enjoyed a few play dates arguing over toys while Adam and I drink tea. We talk about our day, the challenges of small children and shared concerns. He makes me laugh; I feel good around him. Normal.

So we have become friends. And while friends is good, the fluttering in my stomach and the constant checking for messages on my phone makes me wonder whether it could be anything more.

'He's a neighbour,' I say to Becca. I take a deep breath. 'I was thinking about asking him around for dinner.'

'Do it!' she says, with a big smile. 'What's he like? Have you got a photo?'

'He's nice. But don't you think it might be too soon? I mean, since David died?'

Becca puts a hand on my arm. 'Only you know that. If it feels too soon, then give it a bit longer. You've gone through a tough time. And besides, you don't want to rush things. Before too long you'll be married, normal and boring, peeing with the door open and arguing over whose turn it is to take the bins out. Just look at me and Matt.'

I laugh and finish off my Coke, looking out of the window. The sky is a perfect bright blue, with gentle white clouds scudding across. I'll give it a few more weeks, I tell myself, then give Adam a call. I'm not afraid of normal and boring. A bit of normal and boring is just what I'm looking for right now.

Newspaper

A loud banging on metal. Annie opened her eyes and found herself lying on a bed, staring up at the ceiling. A white ceiling. She heard the banging again, a fist against her door.

'Sullivan!' it shouted. 'You have a visitor.'

She sat up, swinging her legs down to the cold floor. She saw a pair of white slippers and slid her feet into them. She looked down at what she was wearing: the white top and grey tracksuit trousers again.

She stood up and walked towards the door, trying the handle and pulling it open. A large polar bear of a woman stood on the other side, her hands on her ample hips, a scowl on her face.

'I haven't got all day, Annabelle,' she said, and gestured down the corridor with a sarcastic wave of her hand.

Annie started walking. Her legs felt wobbly, like she hadn't used them in some time, and she ran one hand down the wall to keep her balance. Identical doors lined the corridor, the same metal doors with the tiny glass window. Too high to look in to find out what lay behind.

Her head was fuzzy; she couldn't work out what was going on. Only patches of memory poked through. David's leering face, Johnny's smile. A white car, red flowers. Poker chips and a blue train. Confusion shadowed her every move, blurring her thoughts.

They stopped at the end of the corridor, and the woman pushed past Annie to slide a key in the lock. It opened with a heavy clunk and she pushed the door open. Annie was cold, a deep chill down to her bones, and she hugged her arms around her. She saw a sign for a toilet and pointed.

'I need to pee,' she said, and the woman sighed.

'Go on then, I'll wait here.'

Annie pushed into the toilet and sat down in one of the stalls. It was bland and grey and boring; indistinguishable from every other public loo. The toilet roll came out in little squares from a dispenser, the flush was a button on the lid. She pulled her tracksuit trousers up and went to wash her hands, jumping when she saw the person in the mirror.

This wasn't her; it couldn't be her, could it? Slowly she moved closer to the image. She touched her protruding cheekbones, running her fingers around the dark circles under her eyes. Her hair lay dank and dirty, tied back roughly in a scruffy ponytail. She looked downwards, taking in the jutting collarbone, the empty bra, poking at her bony ribcage and concave stomach. She frowned at her face in the mirror, then turned as the toilet door opened and the woman stuck her head around.

'Come on, they won't wait all day.'

It was Becca. But not the Becca she was used to in real life. This one looked older: more worried, more tired.

The room was white, and packed with plastic chairs and tables reminiscent of their school days. When Annie went to sit down, she realised the tables were bolted to the floor. Becca was the only person there, and the woman moved back, watching them both from the other side of the room.

Becca had a small disposable cup of grey tea in front of her. 'Do you want one?' she asked gently. 'Are you allowed?'

Annie shrugged. This dream was making her tired and sluggish. She just didn't care; she didn't seem to have the energy.

'How are you?'

She shrugged again. 'Fine, I guess.'

'Are you eating? You look like you've got even thinner.'

'I don't know,' Annie said, and thought back. When was the last time she had had a meal? She couldn't remember, not in this dream anyway. But she didn't feel hungry; she didn't really feel anything.

Becca babbled on, talking about Rosie, about Matt, about her life. She kept her gaze on Annie's face, never wavering. She was giving Annie a headache.

'Did I bring you here?' Annie asked, cutting across her chatter.

Becca paused. 'No, I asked to come and see you.'

'So is this my subconscious?' Becca stopped and stared at her. Annie carried on. 'I mean, is this my dream or yours?'

Becca frowned, and looked at the woman

watching them from across the room. The woman shook her head slowly.

'I saw Adam the other day,' Becca said. 'He'd like to come and see you.'

'You saw Adam? Why would you see Adam?' Annie sat up in her chair.

'He got in touch, after . . . ' She paused. 'Would you like him to come and visit?'

'I only just saw him the other day, at the park. Why would he want to come here?' Annie asked.

'To see you,' Becca said.

'Five minutes,' the woman shouted across the room, and Becca glanced in her direction again, then looked back at Annie and took her hands in hers.

'Annie, look at me,' she said, and Annie glanced up. 'We had the appeal yesterday.' Becca took a deep breath and Annie could see tears in her eyes. 'We tried. Both Adam and I, we did all we could, but I'm sorry, Annie, he's gone.'

'Who's gone?' Annie said.

A tear ran down Becca's cheek and she angrily brushed it away. 'Johnny. I'm so sorry, Annie.'

Annie sat up and pulled her hands away. 'What do you mean, he's gone? He's at home, he's fine, he's in bed.'

The sides of Becca's mouth went down and her chin crumpled. 'Do you remember what your doctors discussed with you, Annie? Do you remember what they said?' She took a newspaper out of her bag and put it in front of her. 'Look at it, Annie. Read it.' She was talking slowly and deliberately, a red blush creeping up her neck as she pointed at the page. 'How is this gone from your head?' she said, rubbing her face in frustration. 'Why do you not remember?'

'I don't know what you're talking about!' Annie shouted, putting her hand on the front page of the paper and ripping it off, balling it up.

The woman moved across from the other side of the room, her body language ready for action, but Annie had jumped up from the chair and was gone, running back down the corridor, back to her room, the white room, lying down on the white bed, looking up at the white ceiling. She couldn't make sense of what Becca was saying; she didn't understand. Her brain felt slow and muddled.

But she knew one person who would know what was going on, and she knew how to find him.

The ballroom

Annie stood in a massive room. The high ceilings were arched and elaborately decorated with blues and purples and silver stars. Huge vaulted curves towered above her, each one individual, each one designed to the highest quality.

Her panic had gone, faded out as quickly as the ballroom had appeared. The blur in her head cleared, replaced by a sense of calm, of belonging.

'Do you like it? I put it together, I hope you don't mind.'

'Jack, what's going on?' Annie turned to face him, knowing who would be behind her. 'I'm having a recurring nightmare and I can't control it.'

'Do you like it?' he asked again, ignoring her and pointing around the room. The walls were covered in artwork of some kind, colours jumping out at her, intense and rich. Floral scenes, animals, portraits, patterns, different in period and technique.

She took a deep breath. 'It's incredible.'

Jack was dressed in a black dinner jacket and bow tie. The white shirt looked crisp and bright and the silk lapels of the jacket glowed in the light. He smiled, and held out his hands.

'Would you like to dance, madam?'

She realised a band had started playing, a light and bouncy tune, something she recognised from a dark recess of her mind but couldn't place. She looked down at a wooden dance floor, varnished and sparkling. She caught a glimpse of her feet, encased in the highest silver heels, fitting her perfectly, and took in her dress, an intricate creation of shimmering silver covered in sequins, fitted on top, billowing out with layers of silk.

She placed her hand in his and he pulled her to him in an elaborate spin. She executed it perfectly, and fell into place next to him, her back arched, one hand in his, the other round his slight waist. They started to move in perfect synchronisation and she laughed, her previous worries temporarily forgotten. Their movements were smooth and in time with the music, swaying together and moving gracefully round the dance floor, feet matching perfectly, perfect speed, perfect timing.

'Amazing,' she whispered as they danced.

He looked down, his eyes meeting hers, their feet never missing a step.

The song came to an end, and Jack went to start the next one, but Annie led him away, to the tables laid out round the room. Each table was covered with a crisp white tablecloth, a bouquet of white lilies with big green waxy leaves in the centre. She took a seat next to him, her eyes never leaving his face.

'Jack, please tell me. I'm having this dream — it's a white room, and I'm a prisoner there.'

He looked away from her, back out to the throng of dancers. As ignorant as the other dreamers were, they certainly looked like they were having fun. People of all shapes and sizes, dressed in their best finery from all eras — stiff corsets and top hats, silk ruffles, tiny cocktail dresses, a bit of velvet here, a sequin there — all dancing together without a worry in the world.

Annie took his hand. 'Jack? Please?'

He looked back at her, his eyes worried. 'Oh Annie, how can you not know?' he said.

'Please tell me. I'm scared, Jack,' she pleaded, trying to keep her voice measured.

Jack ran a hand through his hair. 'When I first found you, I didn't understand. I couldn't see how it was possible. But then I took it for the gift it was, and I got to know you.' He shook his head. 'I still don't understand now.'

He cleared his throat, and looked out into the crowd of dancers, now engaged in a quick foxtrot to something upbeat.

'And then you started talking about David, and wanting him dead, and I just thought . . . ' He stopped, and shook his head. 'I don't know what I thought.'

Annie looked at him, more confused than ever. 'I don't understand,' she said.

He sighed. 'Annie, it's so hard to explain, and I hope you won't be angry with me.'

'Why would I be angry with you? You've changed my life so much, so much for the better.' She tried to catch his eye, but he wouldn't face her.

'For not telling you the truth from the very beginning. But I couldn't, I didn't know how. I hope you'll be able to see that.'

Around them the scene changed. The dancers

slipped away, the walls closed in and the ballroom was replaced by the comfortable living room that she'd been to before, the browns and the beige, the spider plant and the complicated-looking television.

'This is the house I grew up in,' Jack said. He was sitting on the edge of one of the sofas, looking odd in his black formal dinner jacket and bow tie. Annie stood up with a swoosh of grey silk, and moved to the mantelpiece, picking up the photo of the older couple.

'Are these your parents?'

Jack nodded. She studied the photo. 'They look happy.'

'They were. We were. I had a very happy childhood. I was lucky. It could have easily worked out differently.'

Annie put the photo down and turned back to him. 'What do you mean?'

He gestured towards the other photo frames, the ones face down. 'Look at the photos, Annie.'

Annie picked one up and looked straight into the bright blue eyes of a little boy she recognised. A face she knew better than any other, and loved more than anything in the world.

She turned it round slowly so it faced Jack.

'This is Johnny,' she said.

Jack nodded. 'There's a lot I need to tell you.'

Smudged and worn

The living room faded out, and the ballroom reappeared. Time stopped. The dancers slowed, the room paused in time, frozen in a second. And then it began to move again, a merry-go-round starting up, accelerating until everything was full speed once more.

'But your name is Jack,' she stuttered.

'My name is David John Sullivan. Or at least it was.'

Annie jerked backwards, her head spinning. 'It was?' She grasped the table and stared at him, taking in his blue eyes, the features of his face. It was hard to make out the small boy from the adult, but now that she knew, she could see his eyes were hers, and they had the same eyebrows. But there were also traces of David: his jaw and his mouth. Now that she knew, he was unmistakable; he was hers. Her little boy.

'My name now is John Bennett, or Jack for short. I was adopted when I was four.' He was talking very slowly, watching her face closely to see how she was taking it. 'I was adopted by a wonderful couple, and I had the best childhood. But I always wondered what happened to my parents.'

He stopped and looked down, thinking for a moment.

'Go on,' Annie said tentatively.

'My parents, my adopted parents, gave me a letter.'

‘A letter?’ Annie was afraid to ask. ‘What did it say?’

He turned away and looked back to the dance floor. ‘I can show you.’ He smiled. ‘You won’t be able to read it, but I can tell you what it says.’

She nodded, barely daring to speak. Jack pulled something out of his pocket and put it in front of her. The letter sat neatly centred on the place setting, the silver cutlery and delicate crockery at odds with the small, tatty white envelope. Worn to nothing in places, the sides held together with yellowing sticky tape.

On the front, she could see the squiggle of a word, but couldn’t make sense of the writing. She picked it up and turned it over in her hand, then gently pulled the letter from the envelope and opened it out. She looked at the smudged, worn black handwriting. It was shaky and messy. But the loops and whirls were unmistakably hers.

‘What does it say?’ she asked quietly, and closed her eyes as Jack began to read.

Dear Johnny,
By now, I guess you are about four. Your little face I remember so well has probably changed — I imagine you are taller, your hands and feet bigger, talking properly, but still with the same bright blue eyes, your same smile, your same laugh. I had a photo of you a while ago, and somehow it got lost, but I can still see you as clear as day when I close my eyes. I can hear your giggle, and sometimes, in my dreams, I smell your unmistakable baby smell.

I don't imagine you remember me. In a way, I hope you don't, because it will mean you don't remember the bad times and the sadness when you missed your mummy. I hope you have a new mummy and daddy, much, much better than the ones you were born with.

I hope you grow up to be the sort of man I want you to be. Someone who cares and looks after the people around him. Who puts himself last, who is gentle and kind. Who can love unreservedly without worry about pain or loss. Let me tell you now: material things don't matter, nor money or power. I hope you are humble but strong, and fight for what you know is right in our complicated world.

Most of all, I hope you are happy, and cared for, and loved. I miss you every day, Johnny. I miss you with an ache in my throat and my chest that never goes away. All I care about is that you are warm and joyful and safe. Please know that I loved you above all else, and I never wanted for this to happen, for us to be apart. My only wish is that one day we can see each other again.

Until that day, all my love,
Mummy xx

Jack stopped, his voice catching, and put the letter back into the envelope. Annie opened her eyes and took a deep breath, wiping away the tears rolling down her cheeks with a soft linen napkin from the table, her hands shaking.

'I still don't understand,' she said. 'Why would I write that? Why were you adopted?'

She looked at Jack, and he was crying, his hands covering his mouth. 'Why don't you remember?' he said, but Annie wasn't listening. She had gone. She had gone home.

37

When I wake, my body feels heavy. I'm shattered, and every part of me aches. I open my eyes and take in the room, the same bedroom I've slept in for the last few years, the same house, the same me. Now that I'm home and awake, I feel calmer. The dreams have gone.

I think back to everything I have seen. It makes my head hurt trying to make sense of it all, imagining Jack is my son all grown up, and that we could create a dream world that would impact real life. It feels ridiculous to believe the dreams are real, yet my husband has gone. Maggie has gone. That much is true. We have the chance to have a second life, Johnny and I — without David, without fear, without someone telling me what to do and how to live every day. A second chance to get it right.

In the pitch black I move out from under my warm duvet into the cold of the house, knowing my way around without ever needing to turn on a light. I gently open the door into Johnny's room, slowly stepping inside, being careful not to wake him.

I can see just enough to make out the contours of his face, the gentle swell of his plump cheeks, his eyes flickering behind his delicate eyelids. His breathing is regular and steady, Rabbit clutched in his arms. My beautiful, perfect little boy. I reach down and smooth his hair, fluffy and delicate, his cheeks warm and soft.

He opens his eyes sleepily and looks at me. He smiles, still half in dream world.

'Night night, Mummy,' he mutters, falling instantly back to sleep.

'Night night, Jack,' I say, and laugh at myself, shaking my head.

I go back to my bedroom, and pull the duvet over me. It feels late, and I can't hear any noise from outside, no cars moving in the street. I glance at the clock. The digits shine in the darkness, but I can't make out the time. I rub my eyes, and lean over and pick up the clock, hitting it harder than I intend when I still can't understand what it says. I turn a light on and blink. With fumbling fingers I pull out the batteries, then push them in again, turning the clock over to see the same thing: lines and shapes, just lines and shapes.

My hands are shaking and I am breathing heavily as I open my bedside drawer and pull out a paperback, untouched and neglected since David's death. I open it to a page, then frantically flick to another, staring at the black-and-white type, over and over again. Letters blurry, words unintelligible. Another page. I can't read. I can't make it out.

In my panic, I pull the pages out one by one and hurl them across the room. I lie in my bed face down and howl, beating my pillow powerlessly with my fists.

The paper flutters to the floor. Lines and shapes, just lines and shapes.

Epilogue

Wake up.

Annie lay back on her pillow and stared at the ceiling, her heart racing. The white cube, the featureless walls, the same smell of disinfectant. The same bars on the windows.

She could hear the march down the corridor as the lights were switched off one by one. She could hear their progress towards her as they plunged the place into darkness and the screaming started, some people scared of the dark, others just scared.

She was back here again, this endless nightmare, this dream she couldn't control. She screwed up her eyes and dug her nails into the palms of her hands. Anything to stop the whirring in her head and the jittering in her stomach. Something had gone horribly wrong, but she just couldn't remember. Nothing made sense.

She rolled over on the hard mattress and heard a rustle of paper. Something in the pocket of her tracksuit trousers. She pulled it out: it was the front page of the newspaper, scrunched up and shoved out of view when she ran from Becca. She sat up on the bed and smoothed it out in front of her, squinting in the low light to make out the letters.

She saw the garish red banner at the top, then a screaming headline. The moon shone through the window, lighting up random phrases as she moved the piece of paper, her mouth open. ' . . . husband stabbed in frenzied attack . . . well-respected CEO . . . claims of self-defence dismissed . . . mother-in-law, pillar of the community, mowed down in street . . . ' Then the flashes started. The memories. The knife, the blood.

* * *

'I'm sorry — ' she started, then stopped as the back of David's hand smacked across her face. It made her head spin round, her teeth clatter together. She gripped the counter top to stop herself falling, her legs wobbly and unstable, heart racing.

In seconds he was next to her, grabbing the top of her arm, pulling her round roughly so she was facing away from him. Pushing her head with one hand, he pinned her down, bent over the kitchen counter, holding her tight on the back of her neck.

'You're all out to fuck with me,' he shouted, all his strength on her neck, her face pressed roughly into the chopping board, her arms trapped behind her. 'I am in control, me! Only me!'

Ignoring his screaming son, he grappled one-handed with his belt, pulling his trousers and boxers down, then doing the same with Annie's skirt and knickers. He didn't care how rough he was; he didn't care what got broken or who he hurt.

Annie tried to get away, but she was trapped, and he pushed into her, holding her tight, her face next to the chopped carrots, the peeler, the knife. Her hands flapped uselessly behind her as he thrust again, blind with anger, blind with power and his need to punish.

She was making a gagging noise, struggling to breathe, her hair over her face, but he didn't care, just pushed her down harder, his son's crying escalating to a scream.

He was so occupied with his attack, so led by fury, that he didn't notice her hand moving, bit by bit, each time he withdrew and bashed again inside her. Closer and closer until the handle of the newly sharpened blade was just inches away from her fingers. She could touch it, and then, in one move, she gripped it in her right hand and flayed round, determined to make contact with something, anything, to make it stop, so she could breathe, so she could live.

The blade hit the fleshy part of David's upper arm, cutting through his shirt and nicking his skin. In his surprise, he moved back, enough for Annie to come round again, this time slashing the edge of his neck. The blood was sudden and bright, arcing across the kitchen cabinets. She reached again and again; she felt the resistance of bone, the softness of flesh, the sticky splash of his blood.

David's hands went to his neck, his mouth open, his eyes wide. He tried to move away from her, but the trousers round his ankles caught him, and he fell, hitting his head heavily on the cabinets behind.

Annie stood above him, the knife still in her hand, breathing heavily, poised, ready to attack again if he moved. But he was still, completely motionless, his eyes open and looking at the ceiling, a bright red pool widening across his shirt and the kitchen tiles. A wet gurgle came from his lips, and a line of blood ran from his mouth down the side of his chin.

Annie looked to her son. He had stopped crying, and sat in his high chair in silence. A line of blood splatter ran across the tray, and he reached out with a pudgy digit, putting a perfect tiny fingerprint in the droplet.

With shaking hands, Annie reached for her mobile, leaving three concentric blurry thumb-prints on the nine of the keypad.

'Please send an ambulance,' she said. 'I think I've killed my husband.'

She looked across at Johnny, his blue eyes watching her, and her mobile slipped out of her grasp. What the hell had she done? Nobody would believe her; nobody would take her word over the reputation of a successful CEO. Annie hadn't told a soul about David; she had no photos, no evidence of his abuse. She grabbed her car keys, pulled Johnny from his high chair, and ran.

She remembered pulling out of their driveway, her foot to the floor. She remembered seeing Maggie's white BMW waiting to turn into their road. She felt the anger, the blind rage and the tension in her body as she gripped the steering wheel. In that moment she knew she was going to get caught, she knew she was going to be arrested. She saw Johnny being brought up by *that* woman, his life no better than when David was alive. She had to protect him; she had to stop that happening.

Instinct took over. She saw Maggie's face in the driver's seat, looking at her in a brief moment of recognition, before her car slammed into the BMW's driver's-side door. She remembered the grind of metal, a pain in her leg, Johnny crying. Blue flashing lights, people shouting, men talking, rough hands pulling. She remembered. She remembered.

* * *

The newspaper fluttered to the floor, the words clear and precise. The full force of the wave of loss, of despair, screwed her up into a ball, her knees tucked into her chest as the grief, the pain, the sorrow hit her like an avalanche. She felt his absence with every cell in her body; he was a part of her, and now he was gone.

Everything was gone. Her life, where she was free and where calm breakfasts with Johnny could be followed by trips to the park with Adam. There was no future for her with Adam, not now. No prospect of a first date or an exciting kiss under the stars. Just nothing. Her reconciliation with Becca hadn't happened, not that way anyway. Nothing was real, nothing was true any more.

She stayed curled up in despair for hours, until her body was empty and there was nothing left. Until she was clear and knew what she had to do.

She sat up on the bed and opened the drawer of the bedside table, pulling out a sheet of paper and a pen. The letter was quick to write; she knew what it needed to say. Becca had said Johnny was gone, but Jack would get this and know she missed him. He would know that all she ever wanted was for him to be warm and joyful and safe, and loved above all else.

She put the lid back on the pen, then folded the letter into four and sealed it in a matching white envelope. She knew where she had to be. At home, their home, with the trains and cars and lunches of beans on toast. She wanted to be with Johnny.

On the wall outside, the clock ticked. The long hand pointing up, the short hand to the right. Four a.m., it read, crystal clear. The hour of souls.

Annie lay back on the bed, on the white pillow and the white sheets, and fell asleep.

Acknowledgements

This book would never have seen the light of day without Ed Wilson, agent extraordinaire, and legend in his own time. Thank you so much; I couldn't have wished for a better guide in the world of publishing.

To Harriet Bourton and Bethan Jones at Orion, it is a privilege and an honour to work with you both. Without a doubt, your vision, honesty and feedback has made the significantly better book we see today.

Thank you to Divinia Hayes, Debbie Mitchell, Ryan Mortimer, Lindsey Wallis and especially Teresa Andrews, who had the misfortune of reading one of the first versions of this book and made encouraging noises anyway.

Everyone needs their own personal squad of cheerleaders, and I am fortunate to have many people in my life who tolerated my book talk and celebrated every step of the journey. In particular, Jo Lawrence, Eloise Ponting, Tom and Mel de Lange, Karen Barker, Gemma Coleman, Rachel Derby, Marie Bennett, Tor Riley, Jonts and Susan Scarr, Mhairi Crawford, Sue and James Burford, Anne Roberts, Seetal Gandhi, Meenal Gandhi and Nikki Wallace — thank you.

To my parents, Janet and Richard de Lange, for your unwavering belief in me, even when I quit my nice steady career to go and type in a library.

And finally, to Chris Scarr, who is thankfully nothing like David, and Benjamin, who may be a little bit like Johnny. None of this would have been possible without you.

To you all, thank you.